THE

TIN

KICKER

AN AIR CRASH DETECTIVE'S HUNT FOR THE TRUTH

A GRIPPING, NERVE-JANGLING THRILLER THAT
EXPLORES EVER AIR TRAVELLER'S WORST NIGHTMARE

IAN FRASER

The Tin Kicker

An Air Crash Detective's Hunt for the Truth.
A Gripping, Nerve-Jangling Thriller that Explores Every
Air Traveller's Worst Nightmare.

Ian Fraser

ianfraserpublishing@gmail.com

Cover design by Ian Fraser

ISBN: 9798665020303

Prologue

The explosion occurred in the lower section of the fuselage, just aft of the wing struts. Ballooning out in an expanding sphere, the blast wave tore through the airframe, ripping away supporting struts and bulkheads like a hurricane through a paper village. Aluminium skin panels blistered and stretched to the very limit of molecular cohesion, but somehow did not rupture.

Unfortunately, the airliner had been mortally wounded within.

The backbone of the plane was shattered by the blast, carbon fibre violently splintered and severed. Floor beams were contorted, distended outwards, leaving a gaping cavern in the plane's vulnerable underbelly.

With nothing to hold it together internally, the fuselage began to warp and buckle. Hull plates rippled like a ship's sails in a raging gale, before being torn apart. Fracture lines snaked up each side of the aircraft's hull.

The man was jolted in his seat as the shock wave surged through the cabin interior. It was instantly followed by the ugly sound of metal being ripped asunder. Instinctively he gripped the armrests of his chair. His right hand closed around that of the young woman in the adjacent seat.

She was aroused from her slumber by the pressure on her hand. Her confused mind could not comprehend the rising wind that soon became a raging gale of ice-cold air, tearing at her clothes and body, sucking the air from her lungs. The seatbelt cut deeply into her midriff. Items small and large – anything not bolted down – pummelled the back of her head.

His eyes briefly met hers. A bond was formed between them as they squeezed each other's hands. They knew they would die, knew these were their last few moments, but at least the two strangers would not die alone.

Then her skull was shattered by some loose debris, her cranium exploding in a shower of blood and bone.

The man knew it would be his turn next.

He would not have long to wait.

The forward section of the fuselage pivoted upwards like flicking a jack-knife closed. As it did, the centre fuel tank erupted. A fireball surged forward, devouring the high-pressure atmosphere as it sped towards the nose of the aircraft.

The man looked down, his hand still clutching that of the limp corpse next to him. He stared with bemusement at the bloodied stumps where his legs had been three seconds earlier.

Then the fire reached him and, like those still alive around him, became a screaming, incandescent torch.

The expanding wall of flame reached the cockpit and was momentarily halted before it exploded through the windshield, taking the charred remains of the flight crew with it.

The two halves of the aircraft, still held together by wiring and fibre-optic cabling, began to spiral towards the ground, six miles below.

The forward section finally blew apart, ripping the aft section away and sending it in a parabolic arc toward the terrain of the Welsh hills.

Amid a blanket of burning aviation fuel, the dispersed remains of the nose section hit the wide slope of the hillside. The starboard wing tank, which had remarkably held together during the break-up and descent, now erupted in an expanding ball of fire.

Five seconds later, the aft section struck a hilltop four and a half miles south-west. It had survived the six-mile descent relatively intact, but was instantly ripped apart by the force of the impact.

Lighter pieces of debris were sent flying through the air to land harmlessly in the surrounding fields. Larger sections rolled down the hill and came to rest against a sturdy row of trees.

In a few short hours, the small Welsh town of Llancadoc would become very famous indeed.

One

Alex Jamieson squeezed the bridge of his nose with thumb and forefinger as he pressed the receiver hard against his ear.

'Where did it come down?' he asked, forcing the tiredness from his voice.

'Somewhere in mid Wales,' the man's voice said, sounding harsh and booming in his ear. 'Don't know exactly where, or the exact type, but it was a big one. CNN mentioned that it could be a D500.'

A Dramar Aerospace D500: a heavy passenger transport with capacity to haul nearly four hundred people. It would be the biggest air crash over British soil for years.

'You still there, Alex?'

'Get everyone in. I mean everyone. I don't care if they're in bed, on holiday, or in Holy Communion with the Pope. This is the big one, Stu. We've got to hit the ground running.'

'I'll get on it,' Stuart Davenport, Alex's deputy, replied.

'Good. Prep the go-team when they start to turn up. We're going to need transport to the site, accommodation, an operational base, logistical support…' He tried to think of everything at once, but Davenport came to his rescue.

'I know the drill, Alex. Procedures, you know? Just get your ass over here. I can handle things until you arrive.'

The phone nearly slipped from his grasp as he struggled into a clean shirt. Davenport was never one to mince his words, but was the best man to have around in a crisis.

'Okay Stu. I'll be there in under an hour.'

Dropping the phone back into the receiver, he shrugged the recalcitrant shirt over his shoulders. "This is the big one." He mulled his own words over as he finished dressing. He was ready. The entire Air Accidents Investigation Branch was ready. This was something they had all planned for, trained for, but still he felt uneasy. If he messed this up, it would spell the end to his career.

Alex buried the negative thoughts. This was not the time for self-doubt. His team needed him. He gathered his belongings and slammed the door behind him.

Samantha gently closed the door. The scent of his cologne still pervaded the small apartment: the living room; the kitchen; the hallway; but most strongly the bedroom. Ah, the bedroom. She squeezed her thighs together, feeling those little aftershocks of pleasure the action elicited. She smiled at the half-finished bottle of wine and glasses on the elegant bedside table and the soft cotton sheets strewn over the bed and floor.

It had been a good evening. The lovemaking was one of the best experiences to date. A no-holds-barred passion fest of biting, scratching, screaming, thrashing pleasure. New relationships for her were always like this to begin with. The raw, animalistic passion would consume her, obsess her, and that yearning needed satisfying. It was only later that things would settle down, the lovemaking less urgent, less imperative. For now, though, she would enjoy the sheer zealous fury of shared pleasure.

But Jesus, she would ache tomorrow.

As the Air Accidents Investigation Branch's newest recruit, Samantha Shore could not allow herself too many moments of unfettered pleasure such as this. Too much to do, still so much to learn.

Her mind drifted reluctantly from thoughts of her evening to more pressing matters. The report she had written for Alex Jamieson, her guide and mentor, was finished but still needed checking. She mused over the thought that her degree in aeronautical engineering had been relatively easy by comparison. Engineering was basically just mathematics and physics in a practical environment. Simple. Air crash investigation, on the other hand, was a different beast entirely. Unlike engineering, it did not seem to be a world of absolutes. Two and two may make four, but not necessarily. There were always other factors involved, facts that were concealed in the jumble of evidence.

It was this apparent lack of certainty that worried her the most. Air crash detectives had to hypothesize. They had to take a few pieces of scrap metal and say, 'what if?' They then had to put these theories into a workable scenario.

This required a degree of imagination. Something that she had never felt she possessed.

It was not as if Alex was an unapproachable character. On the contrary, he was a very charming and likeable man who always had time for her, never berating her for errors of judgement, never chastising her for simply not knowing an answer. They worked well together. She had even briefly entertained the notion of a relationship with him, before consigning the thought back where it belonged. She wanted to succeed. She wanted to be the best. But she wanted to achieve it on her own merits, without resorting to the obvious, underhanded shortcuts.

The electronic trill of her mobile immediately swept away the cobwebs. She spent a few frantic moments scrabbling through the bedsheets until she located the insistent device and managed to answer with some semblance of composure.

'Hello?'

'Hi, it's Jamieson,' the disembodied voice replied.

'Alex? A little late for a social call, isn't it?'

9

'A Pacific Atlantic D500 has come down in Wales. How soon can you get back to Farnborough?'

Her eyes went wide. This was huge. 'I can be there in an hour. Is that okay?'

'Great. Be prepared to be away for a while. This is a big one. Got to go. Bye.'

That was it. No details. No real explanation. Samantha went into the bedroom and grabbed her pre-packed suitcase.

When Alex arrived at the Aerospace Centre in Farnborough the security guards at the Queen's Gate waved him through. He parked in his usual spot and hurried past the ornate fountain that dominated the façade of the Defence Evaluation Research Agency main building. The AAIB offices were beginning to fill with people summoned to the site, or who had just been watching television or flicking through their phones when the news broke, eager to be a part of the events that were now unfolding. Some might even be useful.

It had been agreed some months previously with Sir Roger Coombes, the AAIB's Chief Inspector of Accidents, that Alex would lead the next major investigation. He had shown himself to be a first-rate investigator, and also displayed the necessary organizational skills to coordinate his people effectively.

His first order of business would be to arrange his staff into separate groups, each having its own set of duties. This system was supposed to prevent everybody from getting under each other's feet, but was usually only partly successful.

Samantha Shore arrived in time to see Alex screaming down the phone line at an officious RAF duty sergeant, demanding he make a helicopter available immediately.

She joined the group that looked busiest, organizing accommodations for the investigation team when they reached the crash site. This was probably the least glamorous, but almost certainly the most important task of the first day. People not only needed somewhere to sleep, but the go-team required a base of operations. A reasonably-sized local hotel normally fit the bill nicely.

Rooms in Llancadoc were filling up quickly as journalists from around the globe made bookings, but Samantha managed to get the entire go-team of twenty into two hotels in the village: the Priory and the King's Arms. It was fortunate that they were approaching the end of the tourist season. Running the investigation from a distance would have been ten times more difficult.

Alex finally finished his colourful conversation with the RAF officer and turned to address the group.

'Okay everyone, I've just finished talking to one of our colleagues from the RAF and a helicopter is on its way. We're going to go in two groups of ten people each. The first team will fly out tonight. The second group will go tomorrow morning. We're going to need transport from the drop zone to Llancadoc.'

Stuart Davenport spoke up. 'I've been in touch with the Sennybridge Army Field Training Centre and they've agreed to give us any help we might need.'

'How far is that from the village?'

'About ten miles.'

'Good. What about accommodation?'

'We're booked into two hotels in Llancadoc.' Samantha said. 'I'm sorry, I couldn't get everyone into one hotel,' she added a little guiltily.

'It's a nuisance but we can work around it. Can they accommodate all our equipment?'

'No chance at the King's Arms, and the Priory's conference suite has already been booked by CNN, but they do have a lounge area we could use.'

'Well done. Right, what about equipment?'

This time it was Andy Styles' turn to speak. 'All boxed up, accounted for and ready to go.'

'Do we have the D500 schematics available?'

Bernie Cheadle looked up from his computer screen. 'I'm copying the files now.'

'Good. Email a copy to everyone in the go-team before we leave. Everyone make sure you have a tablet with you.'

This series of checks continued for the next ten minutes. At the end of it, when he was satisfied that most eventualities had been catered for, Alex decided that his people, especially the relative newcomers, needed some sort of pep talk.

'Some of you were with me five years ago. It wasn't pleasant, but this is likely to be a lot worse. You've all been well trained. Focus on your jobs. We can't help these people. They're gone. But we *can* prevent it from happening again. Remember that.'

He looked around the room and noted that the ones who had paid the closest attention were the ones who had had seen it before. They had some idea of what to expect and acknowledged that they had a job to do. The others had a cockiness about them, a feeling of preparedness which he knew to be just illusory, because five years ago he had been the same. The distant rumble of rotor blades scything through the night air meant that it was time for him to round up. 'The American investigators will be here tomorrow, so let's show them how to do this properly.'

The National Transportation Safety Board, their American counterparts, would wish to conduct their own investigation. As this was a US registered aircraft; that was their legal right.

'That's all for now. Let's go kick some tin.'

TWO

Donatella Martinelli waited several moments before replacing the telephone receiver in its cradle. The appalling images all came flooding back, unwelcome and invasive, like a cancer in remission that had just returned with renewed vigour. Her long, slender fingers rested on the receiver as she fought to regain her composure.

It was the end. Her life was finished. The money. The power. The life of privilege. All were now gone.

The blood had drained from her face. She was thankful she was alone. She did not wish anyone to see her like this: feeble as an infant and just as defenceless.

The only time she had felt anything similar was following the death of her father, Dramar Aerospace's founder and CEO. This was when she had realized that the fate of the entire corporation rested upon her shoulders. A wrong move at this point, a tiny error of judgement, could have brought the entire edifice crashing down around her. At the age of twenty-six, this had been too much of a burden for the spoilt and naïve child that she had then been. Donatella had initially wanted to run away, to escape the responsibility that had been thrust upon her. Instead, she had elected to stay and face the future with dignity.

Her only option had been to employ an astute entrepreneur to run the company for her, which was when she had met the charismatic Douglas Harrington. He had assumed control of Dramar, and, she'd had to admit, done far better than her own father in reviving the company's fortunes. Once again she could sink into the background and enjoy the money that the company started to earn. Ten years on she realized, belatedly, just how great her mistake had been.

Her world was crumbling around her, and this time running may be her only option. How could things have become so desperate so quickly? She tried to rationalize the situation, to make some sense of the chaos, but kept coming to the same inescapable conclusion: Dramar Aerospace was finished.

'Dramar is finished,' she whispered aloud, the words grating against her own ears as she said them, tears welling in her eyes. There had to be another way, she thought. Some way to save the company and at the same time save herself. She could not do this alone, she knew. She would have to, once again, turn to someone else to help her.

Whom among her fellow company directors could she trust? They were all in this together, and all stood to lose not only the corporation, but also their liberty if the truth became public.

As it undoubtedly would.

There were too many people involved now. None would think twice about betraying their colleagues to save their own hides. She realized with a rising feeling of nausea that there was no way that Dramar Aerospace could now be saved, if it was indeed "the anomaly" that was to blame for tonight's accident.

She would not act rashly. Running now without adequate preparation could prove disastrous. Donatella needed an ally within the corporation, and reluctantly kept coming back to the same name. She closed her eyes, and mentally braced herself for the pact with the devil. It would not be pleasant, but she could not go on alone if her escape were to be successful.

She would speak with him after tonight's emergency board meeting.

Samir moved swiftly along al-Jalaa, wary of any pair of eyes that met his along the way. Turning into one of Gaza City's secluded side streets, he was immediately confronted by a throng of people. They surged through Yarmouk Market in the early morning sunlight, before the oppressive Mediterranean heat became unbearable. He slowly wove his way through the crowds, mostly women, in search of the market vendor. He acted as normally as possible, stopping at various stalls to inspect the goods on offer, even though his heart was pounding.

Samir had learnt from the experiences of some of his luckless compatriots that covert assignations such as this were fraught with danger. This could be yet another ambush prepared by the Israeli Defence Force. His only comfort was the mass of people within the market. His people. The IDF, for all their barbarism, were generally unwilling to declare war on women; a fact the Palestinians exploited at every opportunity.

He hoped it would not come to that today.

After twenty minutes of wandering through the market he came to the stall he was seeking. The old woman gave him a toothless grin, her dark skin wrinkled and worn from a lifetime of working in the scorching sun of the Middle East. The fruit stall was one of the least well stocked he had seen that day. The sad, over-ripe produce showed signs it had spent too long baking in the Mediterranean heat.

'What can I offer you, sir? Oranges, lemons, grapes, melons?' she asked, waving the flies away from her precious harvest.

Samir eyed the woman carefully, searching for any sign that she might be a Zionist spy or collaborator.

'I require lemons for a lemonade.'

That was the code-phrase, and Samir stared at the old woman intently, waiting for some reaction; perhaps a sideways glance at an unseen enemy. The woman continued to grin stupidly, but eventually replied in the prearranged manner.

'I do not think the lemons are ripe enough, but the oranges are perfect.'

'Oranges would be acceptable.'

The woman tossed half a dozen oranges into a bag and held out her hand for payment. Samir handed her a ten-shekel note, which was rudely snatched away. The vendor scrabbled around in her apron pocket for the change and passed over a handful of coins, along with a scrap of paper which Samir had been expecting.

'*Shukran*,' he thanked the woman curtly before turning to leave, resisting the urge to look back.

It was not until he was well clear of the market and safe from prying eyes that he read the note:

> *Samir Abdallah – Unit Commander, Strike Force 17*
>
> *Phase one of operation complete. Begin phase two. Meet with representative of Unified National Command at 11 a.m. today, Municipal Park. Fourth bench from Omar al-Mokhtar entrance. Usual precautions.*
>
> *A/M.A. U.N.C.*

Samir retrieved a cigarette lighter from his jacket and burned the note, ashes drifting lazily to the floor.

The Tin Kicker

Lewis Kramer squinted into the late afternoon sunlight, his chiselled, movie stars' face creasing as he did so. But he was too old now to break into Hollywood. Besides, he was a news man, and always would be. 'If we set up over there away from the gate, I reckon it would make a much better shot, don't you think?'

The cameraman looked dubious. He hated it when the 'talent' started to encroach upon his territory. 'Lighting's not great.'

'I think Mr. Kramer could be right,' cut in Madison Flynn, the segment's producer. 'Showing all those security guards at the gate kinda' defeats the object.'

She was new on the Stateside News program, and still somewhat in awe of the almost legendary Lewis Kramer. This was the man who had taken a cable news show that had been languishing in the ratings doldrums and turned it into an incredible, if unexpected, success story. CNN and NBC had both made bids for his services, but for now he was honouring his contract. For how long would this last, only Kramer himself knew.

Tonight's exposé was pretty weak, even Flynn could tell that. Security in America's nuclear power stations was good, and it would take a small army to penetrate the defences of one of these facilities. The gofer they had sent to try to infiltrate the complex had been quickly identified and detained.

This was but a minor setback to Lewis Kramer. His verbal attack on atomic energy security had been damning. Flynn could see it would take a full division of tanks even to get close to the site's more sensitive areas,

19

and surface-to-air missiles made an aerial assault impossible, but Kramer's delivery had been so effective that even she had been convinced. Almost. Now they just needed the tagline. Kramer would say a few words condemning America's cavalier attitude towards the protection of its nuclear power plants, and how shocking it was that the Archer Administration cared so little for the welfare of American citizens.

The Post would condemn the show outright – it always did. The Times would do a little research of its own *before* condemning the show. The Enquirer would do some completely fictitious piece on how it had walked into an atomic plant unhindered and been in a position to wipe out half of the United States. Fortunately for Stateside News, a lot more people read the Enquirer than the Post or the Times.

Flynn felt a vibration against her hip as her cell phone discreetly demanded her attention. 'Madison Flynn,' she said formally, brushing a lock of unnaturally blond hair from her face. 'Yes. Yes. What? Jesus H!'

The exclamation attracted Kramer's attention. He was not a man who easily tolerated being kept in the dark. He waited with as much patience as he could muster, shifting his weight from one foot to the other and listening intently.

The one-sided conversation continued. 'When did it happen? Uh-huh. Any survivors?' A longer pause. 'We're just finishing up… We should be back in a couple of hours. Yeah, I'll talk to Lewis about it. Whose airline was it?'

Kramer could wait no longer. He rudely snatched the phone from Flynn, earning himself a fleeting look of venom, which she quickly concealed.

'This is Lewis Kramer.'

'Mr. Kramer, it's Skip Thornton, newsdesk. A Pacific Atlantic D500 has gone down in Britain. We don't have a lot of details yet, but first reports suggest it exploded in mid-air.'

'How many passengers were aboard?'

'No information on that yet. The AP flash only came through a few minutes ago.'

Kramer vaguely recalled a conversation he'd had with a Dramar employee several months previously. Damn. Why had he not followed it up? 'Get myself and a crew onto the next available flight to London.'

'I've already started making arrangements, sir. We've contacted our people over there and they're on their way.'

'Good.' This boy showed some promise. Better than the airhead they'd saddled him with as a segment producer. 'Cancel everything for the next week or two. This is the big one, and I may have an angle.'

'We were kind of hoping you would, Mr. Kramer. Get back to DC as soon as possible. We'll sort out all the arrangements and have some more information by then.'

'I should hope so.' Kramer terminated the call. 'Very well, Miss Flynn. Let's finish up here quickly.'

She loathed being addressed as a 'Miss'. The mistake she had made was reacting the first time he had said it.

The cameraman moved away from the security entrance of the site and Kramer began summing up like a seasoned prosecuting attorney.

'The question we must ask ourselves is…'

Unsurprisingly, they got it in one take.

Three

The flight was uneventful but not exactly what could be described as comfortable. Noise from the engine and rotor blades made conversation virtually impossible and the incessant rattling shook the passengers until they felt the fillings in their teeth would be jarred loose. The air crash detectives were more than a little relieved when the helicopter touched down at the Sennybridge Army Field Training Centre, more digestibly known as Sennybridge Camp. No fewer than twelve Land Rovers had been made available to the AAIB team. Stuart Davenport had neglected to inform the military facility of the modest size of the group that would be arriving on the first night.

Four Land Rovers set off for Llancadoc carrying the ten passengers from Farnborough. The night was dark, low clouds concealing the moon and stars. The comparative lack of street lighting meant little ambient light was being reflected back to the ground. A fine drizzle hung in the air, displaced in swirling eddies by the convoy of army vehicles surging westwards.

Alex tried to discern the layout of the local topography, but it was hopeless under these conditions. Instead, he discussed the plan with Samantha and Stu Davenport. The army driver remained quiet all the way to Llancadoc, but listened intently to the conversation.

'This weather could be a problem,' Alex said, peering out of the window at the worsening visibility.

'The forecast said the rain should clear by morning,' Samantha said.

'Yeah, but the weather in Wales can go from shite to catastrophic shite in no time,' Davenport replied. 'If the flight recorders—'

'That's my biggest worry,' Alex interrupted. 'If they were damaged on impact, this moisture isn't going to do them any good at all. I suppose we should count ourselves lucky the plane didn't come down fifty miles further on. If it had, we'd be spending the next six months fishing bits of airplane out of the Irish Sea.'

'There's a cheery thought. Still, it's not going to be easy.'

'Okay, let's go over what we know so far.' There was no point dwelling on things that were outside of their control. 'Air Traffic Control in Swanwick lost radar contact around ten-thirty. One strong contact turned into two weaker ones, plus various smaller contacts, which points to an aerial break-up of some kind. The crew hadn't mentioned any problems previously, and no mayday was received. A Virgin plane around thirty miles behind reported seeing an explosion, which was almost certainly our D500. So, if the plane broke in two then we are likely to have two major debris fields to work on. Any theories?'

Davenport had thought about little else since the call had come through, almost three hours beforehand. 'If the Virgin pilots saw the explosion thirty miles away, then that's got to be the fuel tanks. The big question is: why did they ignite?'

No one had an answer. They had plenty of ideas, but nothing that wasn't wild speculation, so Samantha added a few concrete details.

'The plane was operated by Pacific Atlantic Airways,' she continued, 'and was bought from the Dramar Aerospace Corporation five months ago, part of the third batch to be delivered. The launch customer was British Occidental Airways, and they received the first three aircraft in February.' She flicked through the notes on her phone. 'The second consignment went to Quamar Airways in March. There have been a few teething troubles with the D500, but nothing particularly out of the ordinary. The biggest problem seems to have been with the Fuel Management System, but on the face of it I don't see how that could cause the aircraft to blow up.'

'Stranger things have happened,' Davenport said, more to himself than to anyone else as he mulled the problem over. 'You know, it *could* be a problem with the Fuel Management System. Perhaps one tank was emptied too quickly and the fumes ignited, like TWA 800.'

Alex held up a hand. 'But TWA 800 took off with an empty centre fuel tank, this D500 didn't. CAA regs won't allow it now.'

'That's assuming Pacific Atlantic weren't bending the rules,' Samantha added.

'They'd be pretty stupid if they did. Still, it wouldn't be the first time. What else have you got for us, Sam?'

'The maintenance records don't show anything out of the ordinary, but I haven't had time to go through them in any detail. Been too busy acting as the AAIB's travel agent.'

'Sir,' the driver spoke up for the first time since leaving Sennybridge. 'We're just coming into Llancadoc now.'

Alex peered out of the rain soaked windscreen to see the lights of the small town. He noted with some surprise that there was little activity, despite the enormity of the night's events. It would take a few more hours for the world's media to descend on the remote little town. They arrived at the Priory Hotel before they even realized they were at the centre. The white façade of the three-story building was bathed in light from strategically placed spotlights. The small car park at the front could barely accommodate the four Land Rovers and Alex wondered what would happen once the CNN crew arrived.

He now had a few minutes to himself in the privacy of his single hotel room. The only other single that had been available had gone to Samantha, for obvious reasons. Although more than a few would have been happy to share. Instead, the rest had to share twin rooms. His seniority carried a great deal of responsibility and few perks, although this was one of them.

Leadership is a lonely existence, he had come to realize, and he could empathize with others who carried the burden of responsibility: the responsibility to do the job correctly and efficiently, responsibility for the welfare of the people under his authority, and a responsibility to the truth. He counted himself lucky. He had a good team working with him.

This would be his last moment of privacy for hours, perhaps days. He savoured it with relish and resented the knock on the door when it came. Alex Jamieson, Investigator-in-Charge, took a last glance at the bed, the pillows puffed up invitingly, the scent of fresh cotton in the air. He was weary, and very soon adrenaline would be taking over.

The room would not be slept in a lot this week.

Three of the four Land Rovers left the hotel an hour after arriving. Les Thompson, the AAIB's specialist in flight recorder analysis and Ken Stanley – metallurgy and composites – stayed behind to coordinate the proceedings. Neither man was keen to participate in the initial survey of the crash site. Their talents would be utilized later.

Llancadoc fell behind them and the convoy was immediately engulfed by darkness. The driver of the lead vehicle informed Alex that they would be travelling north for about three miles before going cross-country.

Fires that had raged earlier in the night had by now been extinguished. A series of giant halogen lamps had been erected around the site, bathing the debris field in their stark beams. A temporary command post was established on the field's southern edge, between the wreckage and the road. Police officers, who had been drafted in from all over southern Wales, patrolled the perimeter fence that had been hastily erected.

The illuminated area was a scene of total devastation, and Alex could feel the weight of their task pressing down on him. Until this moment, his mind had been too busy to fully appreciate the enormity of the undertaking. No aspect of his surroundings had the air of familiarity. Not a single piece of wreckage was larger than the engine of a family car. All of it was torn, twisted, mangled, scorched.

'Air Accidents Investigation Branch?' A deep, gravelly voice drew Alex's attention away from the wreckage.

'Yes?'

'They told me you were coming. I'm Chief Constable Hugh Merrick. I'm coordinating the operation.'

'Alex Jamieson, Investigator-in-Charge,' Alex smiled, proffering his hand, which was shaken firmly. Merrick was a tall man, and broad, filling his immaculate uniform until the seams stretched. Alex gestured in the direction of the crash site. 'How bad is it out there?'

'Bad. My officers are finding it very tough. Very tough indeed. None of us have ever seen anything like it. Just the sheer...' He dabbed his forehead with a handkerchief. 'The sheer totality of the destruction. The poor kid who was first on the scene has been taken to hospital, suffering from shock. He was practically catatonic.' The senior police officer shook his head and leaned forward. 'They give us guidelines for disaster management, but how can anyone prepare for something like *this*?' He removed his peaked cap and ran his fingers through straggly, thinning hair.

Alex was surprised that this man was taking him into his confidence at this early stage, but realized that the police officer, like himself, required an individual of similar rank to share tonight's experiences. They were both men in senior positions who were expected to show strength and resilience. It was an almost impossible task, and Alex could certainly empathize with Merrick.

'I know. Half of my people are relatively green. The problem for us is that we don't get enough serious crashes in this country for our investigators to become desensitized to it.'

Merrick shot him an accusatory glance, but kept his mouth in check, acknowledging that he was already emotionally drained and hypersensitive. No sane person, he knew, would ever wish for something like this to happen. He simply asked, 'Can anyone ever get used to this?'

Alex shrugged. 'The Americans seem to manage it, but they do a lot more business than we do.'

Merrick grunted an acknowledgement. 'We have marked out the positions of crash victims with red stakes. A team should be arriving within the hour to begin removing them. I suggest you keep your people away from those areas. I've seen a fair number of dead bodies in my time, but some of those out there...' He didn't finish the sentence. He didn't have to, the haunted look he wore saying more than words ever could. 'Get yourselves some coffee before you start. You'll need it. Now, do you require anything from us? Torches, tools?'

'No thanks,' replied Alex. 'I think we brought most of it with us. Have you located the other site yet?'

Merrick's face paled visibly. 'Other site? There was another aircraft involved?'

'No, we don't think so. According to Air Traffic Control, the plane broke in two at high altitude. No one told you?'

'No,' Merrick fumed quietly, pausing as his weary brain processed this new piece of information. 'Have you any idea where this second site might be?'

'None.'

'I'll get some helicopters in the air to begin the search.' Without another word, he headed back to the makeshift communications area.

The go-team had been waiting patiently some distance away, pensive but anxious to get started. He called them over and they all helped themselves to coffee. It was now time to give them their final instructions.

'Okay everyone, this is just a preliminary survey of site A. We're not expecting to find anything of real value straightaway. We will work in pairs – no one is to go off on their own. If you find it's getting too much for you, then come straight back here. Try and stay away from the red poles in the ground. They mark the positions of crash victims. We all know our jobs, and we're bloody good at what we do, so let's go.'

The party of eight from the Air Accidents Investigation Branch moved towards the illuminated area.

The pre-dawn sunlight was beginning to diminish the glow from the lamps as Samantha moved gingerly through the debris. Alex was a few feet away, his attention focused on the ground.

The grassed field was littered with paper, now reduced to a sodden mulch after the night's rain. The fragments of metal around her appeared to be from the aircraft's outer skin. Some still showed peeling paintwork from the Pacific Atlantic jet.

The two investigators were now moving closer to the centre of the debris field, where more substantial remains rested. These heavier items had partially embedded themselves into the soft turf of the hillside. Samantha came upon a section of composite material around six feet long, possibly one of the floor beams. These ran across the fuselage and supported the pressurized passenger cabin. She squatted down to inspect the object more closely.

The surface had been scorched by fire. Samantha rubbed at a small area with her gloved finger and some of the soot came away. The exposed material displayed some evidence of blistering, which was not surprising considering the intense heat to which it had been subjected.

There were no signs of the pitting that was indicative of the detonation of an Improvised Explosive Device. Samantha was not too disappointed, though. She hadn't really expected the piece to yield any answers, yet there was a certain rivalry between the investigators to find the 'diamond in the dust', something which would provide a definitive answer to the mystery of this crash.

She could still make one discovery, though. If the underside was also burnt, it would prove this section had been subjected to heat from a fire whilst still in the air. It wouldn't really be much of a revelation. They already knew that the aircraft had suffered a mid-air explosion, but it might establish that this section had been subjected to a heat source prior to the impact. Once the section had been identified, they could begin to map the extent of the aerial inferno. That would, at least, be something.

She gauged the weight of the piece. It was heavy. Very heavy. The young investigator found the best leverage point and began to prize the piece from the ground. Slowly it began to budge and once the suction of the soft, moist soil released its purchase with a loud squelch it became easier, and she was able to manoeuvre it over.

What she saw beneath chilled her blood. Buried below the object lay the partial remains of a human being. A young woman. One side of her head had been torn away, exposing soft cranial tissue. The remainder of the face was contorted into a hideous grin, the maniacal but lifeless remaining eye staring back at her. Hair that had once been long, dark, and lustrous was entangled like spiders' legs into the congealed blood that covered the face. The lower torso had also been ripped away revealing some of the shattered ribcage and vertebrae. Most of the internal organs had been sucked away by explosive decompression.

'Alex?'

She felt him appear at her side, rather than saw him.

'Accident victim,' he said unnecessarily. 'Don't look at it Sam, and don't think of it as a human being. Treat it with respect, but not reverence.'

She nodded and wiped a tear from her cheek. There would be many, many tears shed this awful day.

The two of them turned and trudged off sombrely, silently coming to terms with what they had just seen, and preparing themselves for the horrors still to come. Samantha's hands were thrust deep into the pockets of her bulky Hi-Viz jacket as she and Alex headed across the field to kick some more tin.

Four

The most dangerous stage of the transfer had been the crossing of the English Channel, although even this risk was minimal. The British authorities were at the present moment in too much of a state of turmoil to consider seriously monitoring all air and seaports. Even if they had been watching, who would suspect a well-dressed American businesswoman travelling on the Eurostar to Paris?

The boarding of the United flight from Charles De Gaulle was uneventful to the point of being boring, however Artemis did not lower her guard. She had seen operations go terribly wrong at this stage precisely because others had allowed themselves to relax at the very time that they needed to be at their most vigilant. There was always the possibility that the security services had been forewarned of her journey, or that some overzealous customs official might inadvertently stumble upon a flaw in her cover.

The dark business suit matched her naturally tanned complexion. The cream blouse was unbuttoned at the top, but not too much. The skirt ended above the knee, but not too far. And the shoes had raised heels, but not too high. Blending in with one's surroundings truly was an art form, and she had perfected it after many months of patient tuition in another lifetime, so many years before. To deliberately attempt to try to conceal her natural beauty would act like a beacon to a trained field agent, as would nervousness or furtive sideways glances at her surroundings. At the same time, she had to be careful to avoid any extrovert behaviour, which would also draw the attention of the intelligence services. It was a very fine balance. Caution. Always caution. It could save your life, and had more times than even she realized.

When she arrived in New York, John F. Kennedy Airport was in turmoil. News of the crash had spread quickly and, as she had hoped, the Americans were in a state of pandemonium, wishing to vent their anger on someone, though they knew not whom.

She waited at the baggage claim carousel, ignoring the lecherous glances from middle-aged men while their wives were distracted by the more mundane sights of the terminal building. She retrieved her suitcase when it appeared. Only light luggage had been taken: clothes, cosmetics, toiletries, gifts of French perfume and Belgian chocolates – which would be discarded at the earliest opportunity – and a laptop computer. Nothing that would be in the least bit incongruous for an American woman returning home should a customs officer choose to search her belongings, as they often did to attractive women travelling alone.

Having gone through the ordeal of JFK, she hailed a taxi to Rego Park, then another to Brooklyn Heights, then a third to the apartment on the Upper East Side.

The drab, four-story building had changed little in the past hundred years or so, it's yellow-brick walls stained by the airborne filth of the city.

One of the two elevators was out of commission but the other seemed to be working. The ancient carriage stank of urine, and she was glad when she could escape its confines into the dreary hallway. It smelled little better, the bare light bulbs casting harsh beams across the narrow passage.

When she entered the apartment, the stench of human excrement was replaced by the smell of stale cigarette smoke and cheap, musky perfume. Low wattage bulbs added to the gloom and claustrophobic atmosphere of the place. A pile of syringes littered the coffee table in the living room. Cindy, to whom she sub-let this urban prison, was still, it seemed, perpetuating her course of self-destruction. If the foolish little whore wanted to kill herself then that was her business. But if by doing so she drew the NYPD's attention to this place, it would cause an unwelcome complication to Artemis' activities. Perhaps it was time to terminate her contract, and in this line of business the word terminate had only one meaning.

There was no evidence of any male visitors, which had been a stipulation of the agreement. If she wished to entertain her 'guests', then she would have to do it elsewhere. The young prostitute's clients were normally content with a few minutes of feigned passion in the backs of their own cars anyway, or against a stinking dumpster amongst the rats and filth of the city.

Artemis checked her private room to see whether anything had been disturbed. It had not. If it had, then there would be no question as to Cindy's fate. She would have to make the decision when she saw her in the morning. For now, sleep was the priority. She needed to be well rested for her meeting tomorrow.

She carefully removed her clothing, jewellery, and make-up, and knelt by the bed, beginning a long prayer for redemption.

Five

'Mr. President, there is a problem,' the Personal Aide whispered into the ear of Bob Archer, President of the United States, Harvard law professor, former Olympic rowing silver medallist and reluctant host to the Israeli Ambassador.

'Excuse me, Gerald,' Archer said with a diplomatic smile to the diplomat. 'It seems the country really can't be left alone for five minutes.'

Gerald Solomon stood graciously and raised his glass as the President left the Red Room of the White House.

Archer was led along the west colonnade to the Oval Office, Secret Service agents muttering discreetly into microphones as he passed. Waiting within the office of the president were George Kenton, his Chief of Staff and Harry Macfarlane, the National Security Adviser.

'Okay, what's happened?' Archer asked.

Kenton spoke up. 'Mr. President, a Pacific Atlantic plane has gone down in Britain. We don't know a lot at the moment but it looks like heavy casualties.'

'How heavy?'

'In excess of three hundred,' Macfarlane said.

'Shit!' came the Presidential reply. He paused for a few moments as he collected his thoughts. What effect would this have on him? Like most politicians, his first concern was of how this might affect his own position. Would it be politically damaging to him? 'Where was the plane travelling to and from?'

'London to Washington. We don't know—'

'I'm not interested in what you don't know,' Archer cut Kenton off. 'What *exactly* happened?'

Kenton drew a deep breath before continuing. 'A Pacific Atlantic Airlines Dramar Aerospace D500 left Heathrow at around ten p.m. local time and it seems it broke up in mid-air at about thirty thousand feet.'

'No survivors, then. Any indications as to the cause?'

'None yet,' Kenton said awkwardly. He was well aware that the lack of information was not going down well with his boss.

'London to Washington,' Archer mused. 'So there were a lot of Americans aboard.'

'It would seem likely, Mr. President.'

Three hundred people. At least half of whom would be US citizens. With an approval rating of only forty-two per cent he couldn't afford another public relations disaster. The press seemed to have spies everywhere, and were even more resourceful than the KGB had been during the Cold War. He had to find a way to turn the situation around. 'Okay, so how do we handle it?'

'Well sir,' said Macfarlane, 'it all depends on the cause of the crash. If it was an equipment failure of some kind then that could finish Dramar, which would put a hundred and forty thousand out of work, not to mention several dozen sub-contractors, and several *hundred* support services; restaurants, cleaning agencies, stationery suppliers. You name it. Plus there's the litigation to think of. That could be a quarter of a billion if negligence by the manufacturer can be proved. Maybe more. There are no legal limits under those circumstances. Not good politically.

'However, if it was deliberate then that *could* work in our favour. It would be a useful way of uniting the American people behind you, and there would be a legal cap on litigation.'

'So our best stance at this time would be to assume it was an act of terrorism.'

'With no evidence to the contrary it would seem to be the best course, at least in the short term.' The National Security Adviser, being a typically abrupt and forthright Texan, appreciated the President's straightforward approach to matters of security.

Archer lifted the telephone receiver. 'Get me Director Stone.' The receiver had already been replaced in its cradle before the White House secretary had a chance to reply. 'Do we have any jurisdiction in a criminal investigation?' he asked Kenton.

'Strictly speaking it would be an entirely British operation, sir, but they will give full cooperation all the way down the line, I can guarantee it.' He said this with absolute confidence. Complete cooperation was a dividend of the 'special relationship' that existed between the United States and Great Britain.

'We ought to get Dan Cole over here,' Macfarlane added.

'Who?' asked the President, vaguely remembering the name, but unable to link it to a face or position.

'Head of the NTSB. Good guy. Knows his shit and he's not afraid to say what he really thinks.'

He now remembered the head of the National Transportation Safety Board from some state function a few months previously. 'Get him here now.'

The phone rang as Macfarlane left to make the call. The President answered it hastily. 'Jack, you heard the news?'

'Sure did, Mr. President. Shit's gonna hit the fan over this one.' FBI Director Jack Stone had known Bob Archer for years, and often tended to forget that his long-time friend was now his Commander-in-Chief. A tough-talking New Yorker whose business *and* pleasure was busting organized crime syndicates, Stone was an intuitive, intelligent and resourceful investigator who cared little for Washington's social pleasantries.

'No argument here. How do you want to handle it?' The President heard the director exhale heavily before replying.

'Big investigation – and expensive. Even if a crime has been committed, the plane has gone down over British territory, which means we have no jurisdiction in the case.'

'Open the investigation. You have full Executive Approval for all extra expenditure. Get the wheels in motion. Then I need you over here within the hour. Got it?'

'Got it. Thank you, Mr. President.'

The line went dead and Archer turned to Kenton who had switched on the TV and was studying CNN's breaking news coverage of the disaster. 'Do they know anything we don't?'

The chief of staff gave him a knowing look. 'They *always* know more than we do.'

They switched their attention to the TV commentary.

'The aircraft was travelling from London Heathrow to Washington Dulles International when it disintegrated in mid-air over Wales in the United Kingdom. A Pacific Atlantic spokesperson has confirmed that three hundred and eleven people were aboard the stricken airliner. All are believed to have died. The cause of the crash hasn't been established but terrorism has not been ruled out'. The anchorwoman paused momentarily as she received instructions from the news program's director.

Good, thought Archer. *The seeds of suspicion have already been sown.* Now it would just require him to deliver a half-decent address to the nation, and three hundred million people would be baying for blood. It didn't really matter who was responsible: ISIS, North Korea, Iran; the list with a grudge against the United States was seemingly endless. The electorate could decide, and he would worry about the small matter of *the truth* later.

Four miles away at the DAC Skysoft site on Canal Street, overlooking the northern shore of the Potomac, Douglas Harrington paced his office like a caged animal. His eyes kept flicking up to the TV on the wall, images of darkness and fire filling the screen, a rolling banner moving along the bottom mocking him.

This was it. It had happened. The thing that he had most feared had become a reality. Harrington cursed the air.

Unlike the ornate surroundings of the Oval Office that the President enjoyed, his was an austere environment. Ornamentation was kept to a minimum, save for the large glass cabinet containing effigies of Dramar Aerospace's creations, which were there more for the benefit of visitors to this room than for his own amusement. The beautifully detailed models were a constant reminder to him of the great heritage of the venerable company.

The inelegant DM09 dominated the upper part of the display, representing Drake and Martinelli Aviation's early triumphs in the world of aeronautics. His eyes moved slowly downwards, each level covering a decade of the company's history. The DM20, Dramar's first attempt at producing a jet airliner, which had been moderately successful. The '25, the '30, and the D33, the disastrous rival to the 737, which had come so close to bankrupting the company.

It had struck him the moment he had first entered this office to take control of the Dramar Aerospace Corporation that the organization had never come close to leading the way in commercial aviation, always reacting to the competition. He had resolved at this point to reverse that situation. The Dramar Aerospace Corporation was a sleeping giant, one that he was determined to awaken. The D220 and the D440 were just the start, providing the world with new classes of aircraft, filling niches in the market that had never really been exploited to their full potential.

The next stage had been the D460, which was now going head-to-head with the 737 and Airbus A320 on the short to medium range market.

His eyes moved down to the last, but by far the largest model in the collection: his beloved D500. This was to be it. This was the aircraft that would smash the Boeing and Airbus monopoly on the high capacity passenger transport market. An innovative and aesthetically pleasing design; this would be the key to the company's future success. Failure for the project would be too disastrous to contemplate.

Now, a single incident thousands of miles distant threatened this new dawn for the corporation that Harrington had mapped out.

Many years before it had not taken much to destroy the reputation of the DC10, and with it the future prospects of the McDonnell Douglas Corporation, which had eventually been swallowed by the Boeing empire. A simple flaw in the design.

One simple flaw.

The buzz from the desk intercom awoke him from his reverie.

'Mr. Harrington, the board members are arriving now.' The sharp tones of his personal secretary cut through the malaise that had descended upon the room.

This was a meeting that he had hoped would never happen. The accident would obviously be a public relations disaster, although if dealt with carefully, the damage to the company *could* be controlled. He was sure of it. He would have to show the world a concerned yet determined face, resolute in his desire to discover the cause of the crash, and ensure that such a thing could never happen again. Etcetera.

He entered the ostentatious boardroom, a total contrast to his own office, and closed the double doors behind him. The subdued tones of the members of the board – ten men and two women – ceased abruptly, and they all waited expectantly for him to speak some words of wisdom, almost like a Messiah preaching to his disciples, he thought wryly. They looked nervous. No, they were terrified, he realized. They could already see the entire edifice of the Dramar Aerospace Corporation crashing down upon them. He would have to be tactful *and* discreet.

'Good evening, ladies and gentlemen,' he said with a warm smile in that velvet tongue of his, making eye contact with each in turn, ensuring none were omitted from his sage-like gaze. 'You have all, I trust, been made aware of this evening's events across the Atlantic?'

A dozen heads nodded in confirmation.

'This is a situation we had all hoped would never happen, but we all knew eventually would. The question is: how do we deal with it? The next few days, and possibly weeks, until the cause of the disaster can be established, will be a difficult time, but if handled appropriately the corporation will continue to flourish.'

There was still no visible reaction, but he could sense that some of the tension seemed to have been lifted from the room.

'We have planned for this eventuality, and there is no point in fearing the worst. That would be counter-productive and, quite frankly, a waste of time and energy.'

'Was it the anomaly?'

Every eye in the room turned to Thomas Purcell, seated at the far corner of the table.

'It's possible,' Harrington replied slowly, 'but most unlikely. Our projections have established that it would take at least two years of normal operations before we suffered a hull loss. The D500 in question had been in service for only four months, which means we have to explore other avenues of investigation.'

Purcell shifted in his seat uneasily. He, along with his colleagues, remained unconvinced. However, they had placed their trust in this man a long time ago and they now found themselves on a road with no turns.

Harrington continued, sensing the mood in the room was deteriorating. 'The problem initially is: what do we do in the interim? All official statements will come from me. You must not allow yourselves to be cornered by the media. If you are, make a prepared statement, ignoring their questions. If at all possible, say nothing. The only person who answers questions from the press is me, as I have the most experience in this area.' This was an arrogant statement but the look of relief on some of the faces before him showed that they had been hoping that this would be the case.

Donatella Martinelli spoke up. 'What if the press get wind of the anomaly?'

'How could they?' Harrington replied confidently, spreading his arms wide in an expansive, but feigned gesture of openness. 'We have already agreed that this particular anomaly was not responsible for this evening's crash.'

'But could it not be discovered during the investigation?'

'There is a very, very remote possibility, but it is so well concealed that they really would have to be looking for it specifically. After all, if it was that obvious *we* would have spotted it long before delivery, wouldn't we?'

'I suppose—'

'Good. Now we must move on to the likely causes of the accident.' Harrington rearranged the papers on the table in front of him. 'Considering the nature of the incident I see that there are only five possible scenarios that would lead to an accident of this kind: terrorist bomb, mid-air collision with another aircraft, fuel tank rupture, inboard fire, and explosive decompression leading to a catastrophic structural failure. The answer could be any one of these or a combination. As yet it is too early even for wild speculation, however we must be prepared for all possibilities if we are to respond promptly and effectively to any of the initial findings or allegations.'

The emergency meeting went on for another hour as Harrington continued to brief the Dramar board members. When it finally came to an end they filed out of the room slowly as their chief executive shook each one's hand in turn, and offered a few soothing words of reassurance.

Eventually he found himself alone in the room. He had managed to bolster the spirits of most of them, but one or two might prove to be a problem.

They would need watching.

Donatella Martinelli emerged from the front entrance. Darkness had by now fallen but soft amber lighting illuminated the immaculately kept gardens that surrounded the DAC Skysoft building. A line of limousines crowded the private roadway that adjoined the building and disappeared into the trees, to eventually emerge onto Canal Street. She remained in the doorway and waited for a few moments. It was beginning to get colder in Washington now as summer faded and the onset of winter began to make its approach felt. She drew the cashmere cardigan closer around her shoulders and kept her stilettoed feet tightly together, the autumnal breeze scything through the sheer silk business suit. She tried to suppress a shiver, but her slim body convulsed involuntarily regardless. Finally, after three intolerable minutes of waiting, the man she wished to speak with emerged from the building.

She detested Thomas Purcell, but despite this she found herself now needing his assistance. She tapped him lightly on the arm as he walked past.

'Walk with me, Thomas.'

He nodded curtly and followed her down the manicured path, rose bushes flanking them on either side.

'What's your opinion, then?' she asked, seeing her breath condense ahead of her.

Purcell stared straight ahead as they strolled among the foliage and flora that lined the path, the rhythmic clicking of her heels on the gravel path focusing his thoughts. 'Harrington's in the shit, and if he is, then so are we.'

'I agree. What do you think we should do about it?'

They walked on in silence for a full minute before he replied, just the sound of footsteps and the far off rumble of traffic punctuating the stillness of the evening. 'At this stage any action on our part would be premature, but that doesn't mean we should spend our time resting on our laurels, though. We need to formulate contingency plans.'

'Quietly. If Harrington or the others find out it could cause… complications.' She glanced around, instinctively watching for spies.

'What did you have in mind?'

She smiled. 'Nothing that I wish to discuss at this time. Give me a week to think things through. I will make some discreet enquiries, and I suggest you do the same. If we can come to some form of agreement then we should be able to do business.'

'That sounds reasonable enough,' he said.

They stopped, facing one another, and he lifted a hand to lightly brush her cheek.

Ordinarily she would have instantly pulled away from such a blatant invasion of her person, but she had to stand and endure the roaming of the hand as it moved slowly around her long, slender neck.

Purcell finally spoke, aware of her discomfort and relishing the moment. 'Don't try and play the game alone, Donatella. If you do an end-run around me, I'll find you, and that's a promise. I'll take this pretty neck and snap it like a dry twig. Goodnight, Miss Martinelli.' He turned and walked briskly in the direction of his limousine.

She breathed a sigh of relief once he was gone, and again shivered involuntarily, but this time it was not due to the cold. Her loathing for Purcell had just re-intensified. She would have to tread carefully for the next few weeks.

Donatella briskly returned to her own limousine and did not bother waiting for the chauffeur to open the door. Washington had suddenly turned a lot colder.

Six

Since the earliest days of the Intifada in the late nineteen eighties, the Israeli Defence Force had taken to burning the houses of offenders' families in an attempt to discourage youths from joining the strike forces. This had done little to intimidate the young activists, but it had driven them further underground, forcing them to abandon their mothers and fathers, brothers and sisters. They lived a nomadic existence, some hiding in the hills surrounding Gaza City at night, others being accommodated by households that wished to support the Uprising, but stopped short of engaging in the violence themselves.

Samir was one of these dispossessed souls, the *Shabiba*, and moved from house to house each night, never allowing himself to establish any patterns, always staying one step ahead of the IDF.

Since his early morning meeting at the market he had wandered the streets of Gaza. There had been no point in taking the risk of going to a safe house, just to rest his own feet for a few hours, so he had kept moving until the appointed hour.

Samir entered the Municipal Park a few minutes early. The trees and shrubs were limp, their leaves yellowed after spending too long in the fierce sunlight, and receiving too little water. The earth in which the flower beds subsisted was dry and cracked, the foliage looking unhealthy and yellow. A similar area in Beersheba or Tel Aviv would be awash with luscious shades of green, demonstrating the economic divide that existed within Israel.

The fourth bench was empty so Samir walked on and began a circuit of the park, keeping a careful eye on the time and surreptitiously observing any others as they strolled through the gardens.

He returned to the rendezvous point after ten minutes but the seat was still vacant. Something was wrong, and he felt he had to leave this place quickly.

'Going so soon, Samir Abdallah?'

He stopped dead in his tracks and his eyes sought the source of the voice, the words spoken in native Arabic. An old man emerged from the shadows thrown by a group of sycamore trees.

'One can never be too careful these days,' Samir replied guardedly.

'I agree. It is sad that two friends cannot meet without going to such extremes.' The man spoke in soft, sing-song tones, and with a vigour that belied his age.

'I do not know you,' Samir said guardedly.

'This is true. Come, let us walk so we can enjoy these lovely gardens.'

They strolled slowly through the park which clearly gave the old man a lot of pleasure.

'My associates and I have been following your activities. Some of them are uncomfortable with the level of violence you are willing to employ, though I hasten to add that I am not among them.'

'What I have done has been for the good of our people. We *are* fighting for our freedom.'

'I know, I know. It is all for the greater good. We shall never gain independence by non-cooperation alone. Peaceful protest will only ever be partially successful. It is time to begin preparations for Phase Two.'

'When will the operation commence?'

'In less than four weeks. Are your people prepared to move so quickly?'

'We are ready,' Samir said with a smile. 'The word needs to be spread.'

'Security is vital,' the old man cautioned. 'Our people must not know of the methods we are employing. They would not understand.'

'None of my people in Palestine know of the greater plan, and they will follow me.'

'Good. Be prepared to move on the 19th October. Any delay would destroy the operation, and is unacceptable.'

'We will be ready.' Samir looked around. The park was becoming busier now. 'We have been here too long.'

'I agree. Good luck, Samir Abdallah, and may Allah watch over you.'

Lewis Kramer sank into the business class seat of the 777, Madison Flynn dropping lightly into the adjacent chair. The cameraman and sound engineer were making themselves comfortable some distance behind in economy class, and availing themselves of the hospitality liquor that was supplied by the airline.

Looking around the cabin, Kramer could see quite a few familiar faces; TV reporters, newspaper journalists, even some of the top brass from the media industry who would not normally attend newsworthy incidents. His initial instinct had been correct. It was going to be a *very* big story with some far-reaching ramifications. But how far? That was the question.

When he had returned to his office at the Stateside News studio the first thing he had done was to inspect his diary. He flicked through the pages covering June and July, and located the entry he was seeking.

The telephone conversation had been with a Dramar employee named Clarence Grant, who claimed to be one of the company's senior designers. He recalled that the man had information relating to a design flaw on the D500 airliner. He had not been willing to discuss the nature of this flaw on an unprotected line, but had stated that it was serious enough to endanger the lives of passengers, and hinted at a Dramar Aerospace cover-up. This, the anxious man had hoped, would be enough to secure him a hefty payout from Stateside News. Unfortunately, he had made his naïveté far too obvious. It might make a moderately interesting story for a newspaper hack to follow up, however television required visual images, something to keep the eye amused while the ear digested the information in the commentary. This story, although interesting, did not fulfil the criteria for good television news, and thus was not something that Stateside News would be prepared to pay exorbitant amounts for.

But the situation had just radically changed. This had now become the biggest story of the year, and the show would happily pay three times the amount that Grant had been demanding.

Kramer dialled the number in the book and Grant answered after just two rings.

'Hello?' He sounded even more timid now than the first time the reporter had spoken to him.

'Hi, Clarence. It's Lewis Kramer from Stateside News.'

'Oh… er… Hi. What can I do for you, Mr. Kramer?'

'I take it you've heard the news.'

Grant hesitated before replying. 'Yes, it's terrible.'

'I agree. A genuine human tragedy. But now it means that we may be able to do business. Do you still have information that you wish to trade?'

There was a notable pause before the designer replied. 'So now that three hundred people have died, my story is suddenly newsworthy?' he asked edgily, with a bravado that seemed a little incongruous to his personality.

Shit. The little twerp's already sold. 'Well current affairs are an organic commodity. Following today's events, the nature of the story has evolved. The station is now in a position to offer you double what you originally asked for. No, what the hell, we'll pay you triple. To have someone like you working with us on this, it'll be worth it.' If it was possible the man seemed even more flustered than before.

'Well I... I've already entered into an agreement.'

'Yes, but a verbal agreement is not legally binding. It *is* just a verbal agreement, isn't it?' Kramer probed confidently.

'No, I have a written contract.'

Christ, that was fast. 'May I ask who the contract is with?'

Grant was becoming more confident now, feeling that he was in control of the situation. 'I'm sorry, I am not at liberty to divulge her name, but I can tell you that she is from one of your rival TV stations.'

'Which one?' Kramer realized that he was now the one who was becoming tense and agitated.

'I'm sorry, I can't say. You'll find out in good time. Bye, Mr. Kramer.' With that, the line had gone dead.

Kramer had not realized that the plane was now in motion as it taxied slowly towards the runway. Who the hell was he having to compete with? The crash had only occurred four hours previously. Grant must have made the agreement some time prior to this evening's events.

He glanced around the cabin interior. Flynn was playing mindlessly with her phone. Many of his colleagues and rivals were engaged in hushed, extremely intense conversations. They would become noisier as the alcohol began to flow. He happened to make eye contact with his WCN counterpart.

'Hey Kramer, what's your angle gonna be?'

'The *right* angle,' he replied with an enigmatic smile. The man realized instantly that he would get nothing of value from the CTVN representative and scanned the area for a more forthcoming individual.

Kramer's network of contacts within the industry was extensive, so it should not take him long to discover the identity of this mysterious woman. She might even be on this flight.

He put thoughts of Grant aside for the time being, and concentrated on the more urgent issue of his initial broadcast from the crash site. He was oblivious to the sensation of being compressed into his seat as the aircraft accelerated down the runway.

Kramer closed his eyes and to all observers he was just catching up with some well-earned sleep, but in reality his keen mind was contemplating the days ahead, formulating a variety of approaches to the addresses he would be delivering to his viewers. But however hard he tried, he could not force the issue of Grant from his mind for long. The story had been his for the taking, and now he may have lost it.

Who had beaten him to it?

Seven

The early morning sunlight that had greeted the air crash detectives was soon replaced by low, oppressive clouds. A fine drizzle hung in the air, the surrounding hilltops remaining shrouded in a cloying, impenetrable mist.

Daylight had also revealed the full extent of the disaster – and just how close the town had come to bearing the brunt of the conflagration, the two primary debris fields lying just a few hundred yards either side of the town's centre. Aerial reconnaissance of the surrounding area had soon located the second of the major crash sites, just half a mile from the western edge of the town.

When news of the tail section's discovery finally reached him, Alex Jamieson immediately commandeered a helicopter to take himself and a small team to survey this new find. From the air, Alex was able to form an instant impression of what had happened. A small, irregularly shaped crater had been blasted into the hilltop, and the wreckage had deposited itself down one side, wiping out dozens of trees and bushes in the process. The bulk of the debris lay at the foot of the hill, resting against a bank of fir trees. The fuselage had broken into a number of cylindrical segments, indicating that the tail section had been spinning at a brisk rate when it impacted with the hill.

Alex was surprised to note that there was no apparent fire damage to this section of the aircraft. *So it was only the forward section that was on fire,* he thought detachedly. So many questions and as yet, no real answers.

The helicopter moved away from the site and landed at the nearest stretch of clear, level ground a quarter of a mile away, and the group of six hurriedly disembarked, thankful to be free of the confines of the noisy and uncomfortable vehicle.

Small fragments of wreckage peppered the field as they trudged awkwardly through the mud, their boots quickly becoming caked in the viscous mire, dirt spattering their Hi-Viz orange jackets.

When the team reached the main area of the wreckage site, Alex could not believe their good fortune. A metaled road ran just a few scant yards from the components of aircraft that were their quarry, with a dirt track running along the foot of the hillside that would provide easy access to the site.

The road had been sealed off by the police, the local constabulary having already learned lessons in disaster management from the previously discovered site.

Red stakes were dotted around the area, and Alex did not have to be told that these indicated the positions of crash victims, as at the other site. Under normal circumstances the corpses would be removed before the air crash detectives arrived at the scene of an incident, however the sheer scale of this disaster had made that impossible. The unfortunate soldiers from Sennybridge Camp would arrive presently to begin this unpleasant task. The remains were to be stored temporarily at the army base before being transported to the Human Identification Centre at the University of Dundee.

Nearest to the road lay the vertical stabilizer – the tail fin, lying on its side having been violently torn from the fuselage, but remaining remarkably undamaged. The Pacific Atlantic logo stood out distinctly and would make a poignant image for the newspapers tomorrow morning, but would not do Pacific Atlantic Airways' share prices a lot of good.

This was the area of the aircraft that initially was of the greatest interest to the investigators, as the flight recorders were located in this portion of the airliner. The Cockpit Voice Recorder and Flight Data Recorder were the air crash detectives' greatest allies in the quest for answers to the cause of a major incident such as this.

Les Thompson, the AAIB's flight recorder specialist, had been informed of the discovery of the tail section and was on his way from the Priory Hotel. He would want to be present when the black boxes were located and would be clucking around them like a mother hen, ensuring that they were handled correctly and ascertaining the level of damage they had sustained.

As his team moved over this area of wreckage Alex walked down to the far end of the debris field to survey the area of the initial break-up. This section was around twenty feet long and had been badly crumpled. Through the shattered windows Alex could see passengers still strapped into their seats, images of terror frozen onto their bloodied faces. He looked away, wishing his morbid curiosity hadn't compelled him to investigate this aspect of the disaster. His trained mind switched to the job at hand.

The metal skin in the area of the break-up had been ripped unevenly from top to bottom; or bottom to top. There was no way to determine which at this stage. No rivets or rivet holes were visible along the tear, the stresses of the break-up simply tearing the metal apart. If the skin had torn along rivet lines then this might have been an early indication of metal fatigue causing the crash.

He carefully ran a finger along the jagged metal. For the moment this crash was a complete mystery, which was something he found irritating. He was naturally a man with a neat and tidy mind. He enjoyed puzzles, but loathed chaos. All he had seen since arriving in Wales was confusion. Nothing as yet had begun to gel into a coherent picture. The cause of the accident and chronology of events were still unclear. But they *would* find the answer, of that he was certain.

Scorch marks and blistered paintwork in this area of the fuselage indicated that it had been subjected to a heat source, although the fire damage appeared to be superficial.

Something began to stir at the back of his mind as his consciousness tried to make a connection.

He stepped back in order to give himself a better overview of the section of debris.

If the centre fuel tank had ruptured causing the break-up of the fuselage there should be much more evidence of fire damage.

Alex paused for a moment as he began to assimilate this. The explosion appeared to be the *result* of the separation of the two halves of the airframe, and *not* the cause as they had originally speculated.

He glanced over at his colleagues who were still working away carefully at the wreckage in the area of the tail fin. There was no point in informing them of his apparent discovery yet. They were focused on locating the flight recorders and their task would not benefit from the excitement that would be generated by this.

Alex felt quite pleased with himself, even though he knew this feeling was probably terribly premature.

The fuel tank was not the cause of the crash, which was one item they could now cross off their list. That only left about a thousand to go. Still, it was a start.

However, this did little to answer the fundamental question: if it wasn't the centre tank, then what did cause this crash?

Eight

A rtemis pushed open the swing door of the pizza restaurant on Callowhill Street with confidence and scanned the eating area, her nose held high, breasts thrust out, skirt ending well above the knee, heels towering. Today she was a journalist, a woman of unflagging bravado and superiority. A careerist and go-getter, because that was how her character *should* appear.

It was only just gone noon, so the hordes of businessmen and women from the Philadelphia business sector had only just begun arriving.

In a relatively secluded cubicle on the far side of the restaurant sat a small, thin-set man staring intently into a half-empty glass of clear liquid; probably mineral water – he looked the type. A few moments before as she had walked up to the premises, she had noted that he'd been studying the doorway with a similar level of intensity. Now he was obviously doing everything in his power to *avoid* making eye contact.

The Tin Kicker

'Clarence Grant?' she asked. Artemis did, of course know exactly who he was. She would not have lived this long by being careless enough to omit details like that.

He looked up with feigned surprise, which was painfully obvious. 'Hi. Yeah. You must be Diana Kearn.'

She rewarded him with a broad smile. 'Hi. It's good to meet you at long last. How've you been keeping since we last spoke?'

'Fine,' he said. 'Please, take a seat.' He stood and saw her safely into the opposite chair, acting the perfect gentleman, however she noted his furtive glance downwards as she slid into the seat, the hem of her skirt riding up well over her thighs. The restaurant was air-conditioned to a comfortable level, but even so he was sweating. Grant looked around at the assorted company, revelling in the attention that his guest had generated. Several of the other diners gave him dubious glances, surmising that this sad little man was either incredibly rich, or (more probably) that he was employing the services of an escort agency. He didn't care. They could never *know* the truth and he found that, despite his nerves, he was enjoying playing this game.

They ordered pizzas, garlic bread, and a bottle of Californian red while exchanging pleasantries, before moving on to the purpose of their meeting.

Artemis leaned forward, aware that she was exposing a significant amount of cleavage. The blouse was ridiculously tight, buttonholes straining, her nipples creating tiny dark mountains through the white fabric. Men were such superficial beings, and this hapless creature was shallower and more transparent than most, making her task even simpler.

'So Clarence, what have you got for me?'

From his briefcase, Grant withdrew a thick, brown manila folder. 'The complete technical schematics of the D500; the *original* schematics that Harrington and the others don't want anyone else to see.'

'What about the evidence of a cover-up?'

'It's all there. Well...' he paused and a look of uncertainty clouded his features. 'I couldn't get it all, obviously, but I reckon there's enough here to indict. There's certainly enough for your story, I would say.'

Artemis slowly looked through the plans to the aircraft, ensuring she wore a slightly bewildered look. Journalists are not supposed to be technically minded.

'Where's the central fuselage section?' she asked innocently.

'Structural schematics – fourteen point two.' Grant was relishing this, his sense of male superiority being well satiated. He glanced triumphantly around the room, but the other diners had already become disinterested in the odd couple. Never mind. He'd already achieved his satisfaction.

'Information on the carbon fibre production processes?'

'That's in there, too. Appendix K.'

She dutifully turned to the appropriate set of pages. 'This is good stuff, Clarence. We'll be able to hang the lot of 'em with this. What about internal communications: memos, emails and such like?'

'They're in the envelope at the back.' Grant waited impatiently for his guest's cursory examination of the folder to end. He wanted her attention to be focused upon *him*. After a few interminable minutes he decided to venture the question. 'So, what do you think? Can you use it?'

Artemis carefully returned all of the documents to the folder and slid it into her shoulder bag before looking up at him. 'Well Clarence, this stuff is just great. We can build a good story around it.'

She was interrupted as the food and wine arrived, the waiter filling the two glasses.

Artemis continued. 'As I was saying Clarence, this is everything we could have hoped for, and with the events of last night…' she looked down thoughtfully into her glass, twirling the stem slowly between her thumb and forefinger and studying the blood-red liquid. 'We'll make the bastards pay.'

Grant stared intently at her face, and for the first time noticed that those beautiful almond eyes held real pain. She was not just a hard-nosed reporter looking for a story, but a human being demanding justice on behalf of those three hundred people.

However, the people she wanted justice for had not died the previous night. Those unfortunate souls were just collateral damage; casualties of war, and this *was* a war. A war against oppression. A war against subjugation. A war of retribution.

'You've done a good service here Clarence, and services merit rewards.' She reached into her handbag and withdrew a brown paper parcel, which she slid across to his side of the table. 'One hundred thousand in cash. If you wish to count it, I suggest you go to the men's room,' she said with a twinkle in her eye.

Jesus, a hundred thousand! 'Why…?'

'The station recognizes a good contact when it finds one, and we may wish to enlist your services again sometime. Not to mention a token of our appreciation for the risk you ran procuring this information for us. This isn't over yet. It's just beginning. You're a good guy, Clarence. You've done this for the right reasons. Never forget that. Last night's *accident* was no accident. We both know that, and soon, so will everyone else. It could have been prevented, and we can make sure it never happens again. Those responsible will pay for this criminal act.'

'I guess so,' he said sheepishly.

Artemis raised her glass. 'Here's to the future, Clarence.' Their glasses made contact with a satisfying chink and they both sipped at the alcohol whilst staring into each other's eyes, Grant's feelings somewhat at variance to his companions'. 'Now, you are going to have to be careful. Other news firms are going to be pestering you because of your position in the company. Don't say anything to anyone.'

'I know. I had one last night.'

'Who?' Artemis asked uneasily.

'A guy named Kramer at CTVN. He turned me down before I contacted you. I didn't tell him anything, just said I'd already sold the story. He wasn't happy, but I handled him well enough.'

'Good for you, but try to avoid speaking with him. He's a canny old dog, and he'll end up getting you to say things without even realizing it.'

'I'll remember that.'

Artemis noticed that he was pawing at the parcel of cash anxiously. She smiled at him warmly. 'You know, I think you should take that trip to the men's room before you wear the wrapping away,' she said, her eyes darting down at the parcel he held in his sweaty hand.

'I hope you don't mind.'

'Not at all,' she grinned.

In the privacy of the washroom he tore open the package and stared stupidly at a thousand hundred-dollar bills. He pulled one from the centre of the pack and held it up to the light from the frosted window.

When he returned to the eating area the opposite seat was empty and a hundred-dollar bill lay beneath the glass that his absent guest had been drinking from.

Clarence Grant finished his meal self-consciously and left the restaurant, ignoring the smirks from the other diners.

Nine

D ust hung in the air. It covered the carpets; covered the furniture; covered the walls. Timbers lay at odd angles and Stuart Davenport had to tread carefully to avoid the fallen masonry as he stepped through the empty doorway, the front door having been blasted across the street by the force of the impact. He looked upwards through what was left of the roof of the residential property at the clearing sky, the rain clouds of earlier rising to allow shafts of sunlight to begin illuminating the town. A lone starling, perched precariously on one of the splintered roofing beams, took flight at his intrusion.

Davenport moved forward cautiously, flanked by fire fighters who were not at all happy to be escorting a civilian through such a dangerously unstable structure, their eyes darting left and right, up and down as they sought hidden dangers.

One of the airliner's four engines – they did not yet know which – had come crashing through this house the previous night and had done a pretty comprehensive job of destroying the property. It was sheer good fortune that the old couple who had lived here had been in bed at the time of the impact, for if they had not retired for the evening before the propulsion unit had hit, they would not have survived to tell their tale.

The reason for his presence here lay embedded in the floor directly in front of him. The power plant had survived the impact remarkably intact. The casing, although understandably battered, had held together, a testament to the quality of construction by the venerable engine manufacturer.

About half of the unit lay submerged in the ground so this could only be a cursory examination. He crouched down and shone a flashlight into the front of the nacelle. Peering inside he could see that many of the fan blades had been chipped at their outermost edges, which was damage consistent with the impact of the unit with the ground as they windmilled without power. It was not unheard of for a blade to snap and puncture the skin of an airliner, although this did not appear to be the case with this engine. He stood and withdrew a camera from his knapsack. The main purpose of the visit was to obtain a photographic record of the engine in its final resting position. In a few weeks' time back at Farnborough one of these images could give the investigators the answer to the mystery, or at least allow them to disprove a theory. His was only one pair of eyes and it would be easy for him to overlook some vital piece of evidence, especially considering his present working environment. A fresh set of creaking noises from the weary timbers gave evidence to this, eliciting nervous looks from the firefighters.

Davenport snapped away with the Nikon camera, photographing the engine from every possible angle. He was so thoroughly engrossed in this task that he failed to notice himself leaning against an upright beam, which promptly gave way, releasing a rain of debris upon the group. Initially he had thought it overly cautious for the fire crew to insist that he don full protective garb, though as the tiles, bricks and various other debris ricocheted off his hard hat he felt supremely grateful for their caution. After a few seconds, which felt like a lot longer, the cascade of rubble subsided.

The senior firefighter moved forward. 'Right, that's it. Everyone out! Now!'

Davenport was not about to offer any argument. Besides, he already had what he wanted.

Once outside the house, he could see a fresh cloud of dust pouring from the window frames. 'That was a bit close, wasn't it?'

The senior firefighter at the scene grinned back at him. 'You should've been here when we got the old folks out. Now that *was* a bit scary.'

Stuart Davenport realized that he was really not cut out for an adventurous lifestyle, and felt a new respect for these heroes. 'So, how do we get the engine out?'

'We don't – yet,' came the simple reply.

'But we need that engine.' Davenport was still flustered from his recent escape, and cordiality often did not come naturally to him.

'Now listen, no one goes into that house again. I'm not risking another one of my crew in that place. Your bloody engine isn't, believe it or not, my chief concern at the moment.' He stalked off before Davenport could offer any further argument.

He looked up to see an NBC news crew had filmed the exchange. That was the last thing he needed right now and was about to storm over and do something he would later regret when he heard someone calling his name. He looked round to see a young police constable – they all seemed very young – running over to him.

'Mr. Davenport?'

'Yeah?'

The man was out of breath and sweating with exertion, but obviously too excited to care. 'They've found another wreckage site. Well it's not exactly wreckage. It's luggage, sir. Suitcases.' He was clearly puzzled, and half-expecting a reprimand as this news sounded crazy. Why luggage and nothing else?

'Let me guess – four or five miles east?'

Now the young police officer was really baffled. 'Yes. How did you know?'

'I didn't, but I'm not surprised.'

When an aircraft disintegrates in mid-air, lighter items such as suitcases, seat cushions and blankets tend to fall straight downwards in windless conditions, the resistance of the air halting their forward motion, whereas heavier items are carried forward by their own mass and momentum.

'I need a car to get me out there.'

'I'm parked at the end of the road. I could take you.'

'Great, let's go.'

With blue lights flashing and siren blazing the police car sped along the A40 before taking the turning near Pentrebach. A couple of dirt tracks later they reached the debris field.

What Davenport saw surprised him. He had been expecting these personal belongings, which he presumed were from the cargo hold closest to the point of the break-up, to be badly burned from the explosion of the fuel tank. Instead, they seemed to be in pristine condition. Many had burst open on impact with the ground; others had obviously opened during descent, the relatively high pressure within snapping them open.

'Get this area sealed off immediately,' he shouted to the group of police milling about aimlessly nearby. 'This takes priority over everything else.' Once the ghoul hunters arrived, personal items like these would rapidly begin to disappear.

As the police officers set about their business, Davenport's mind began to cover the possibilities. The fuel tank *had* exploded, that fact was not in question – unless it was not the *centre* fuel tank which had erupted, but one of the wing tanks. Could a wing tank explosion cause a plane to break in two? For sure, it could. An airliner is, after all, just a flimsy, pressurized aluminium tube. He realized that since he had first mooted the idea that the centre tank could be to blame, he had subconsciously adopted it as the only possibility. He silently chastised himself for the assumption. If the centre tank had exploded initially, then the luggage in the affected area would now be as black as pitch, but it wasn't. What if the aircraft broke up for some other reason, expelling the luggage before the tank erupted? That would make much more sense. Damn. That meant his number one theory had just flown out the window.

Davenport plucked his mobile phone from his belt and called Alex Jamieson's number. 'Alex, it's Stu.'

'Hi Stu. Any luck?'

'Yes, and no. We've found a luggage dump, but it looks like the exploding fuel tank theory may be wrong.'

'I know. The tail section shows virtually no sign of charring. Certainly nothing that would be consistent with a centre tank rupture. How did you find out?'

Davenport glanced around. 'I'm in a field piled high with suitcases, and not so much as a fag burn on any of 'em. What about you, any progress?'

'Well, we've got the flight recorders.'

'How are they?'

'Pretty good. Les has them and is on his way back to Farnborough. Nothing else to speak of.'

'Okay,' Davenport said, 'I'll stay up here for a while and then head back to site A.'

'Fine.'

With that the call was terminated.

Later that evening, the entire AAIB investigation team assembled in the function room of the Priory Hotel. The suite was little larger than a reasonably-sized living room, and with the makeshift desks and computer equipment lining the walls and filling the centre of the floor, fitting the whole team in was a squeeze, to say the least. Electrical cables snaked across the floor, making Alex nervous. Electrocuting eighteen investigators would not look too good on his CV.

'Okay everyone,' he began, scrolling through the notes on his tablet, 'this isn't exactly the perfect set-up so we'll keep it as brief as possible. Let's concentrate on what we know, rather than what we don't know. At approximately ten-thirty last night Pacific Atlantic Flight 4401 disappeared from radar screens at Swanwick Air Traffic Control. The aircraft split in two and ended up at sites A and B. Around the same time a Virgin Atlantic flight,' Alex checked his notes, 'Flight VIR9 L644, reported an aerial explosion some distance ahead of them. Eyewitness reports from the ground support this. Because of the severity of the explosion we're pretty sure there was a fuel tank rupture, although it seems that this was a *result* of the break-up, and *not* the cause as we had originally speculated.' He looked over at Andrew Styles. 'Andy, you've got something you wanted to say about the fuel tanks, haven't you?'

Styles cleared his throat. He was naturally a nervous type and was never happy to address a group. He began in the monotone that everyone in the room was accustomed to.

'We've been going over the wreckage at site A. There's not much left of either wing, however we have been able to ascertain that it was the starboard tank that exploded on impact with the ground. Some fragments of the motor assemblies from the slat extenders survived the blast, and these are unique to each wing. Also, we have now located all four engines, and the two from the starboard side are in the area of site A. The other two are miles away, suggesting they disengaged at the time of, or soon after the break-up.'

'Just one query on this point,' Davenport spoke up. 'When I saw the engine that had crashed into a house in the town, I couldn't see any sign of burning, so perhaps there was a secondary explosion.' There was a notable pause as the other members of the group digested this and tried to understand Davenport's reasoning. 'It's just a thought.'

Alex nodded. 'Okay, so let's get this straight, Stu. The sequence of events so far are,' he had discarded the tablet and was feverishly scribbling notes in his trusty notebook as he spoke, 'something causes the aircraft to break in two, but we don't know what yet. This in turn ignites the centre fuel tank, which then ignites the port wing tank. Is that what you're saying?'

'That about sums it up. But the point is, the port engines must have disengaged *after* the port tank explosion.'

Ken Stanley, the metallurgy expert spoke up. 'Our analysis of the wreckage at site A would support that theory. Thanks to Ms. Shore's earlier endeavours, we knew from an early stage that the forward section had been subjected to intense heat before it hit the ground. Temperatures that would be consistent with exposure to a Jet A ignition.'

'I think we need to concentrate on establishing two things,' Alex said. 'First of all, prove or disprove Stu's theory about the tanks, and find the initial cause of the break-up. Any suggestions?'

'Find as much of the port wing as we can,' said Styles. 'We can't go much further until we know for sure the sequence of disintegration, and that wing could tell us a lot.'

'Good idea,' Alex agreed, scrawling notes as he spoke. He waited a few moments but no one had anything further to add to this particular line of discussion. 'We've done well today, but it was only ever going to be a broad overview of the situation. I suggest tomorrow we split into two – no, three groups, which I'm going to imaginatively call groups A, B, and C. Group A will concentrate on the port wing investigation. Group B will look for anything that could cause a structural failure in the fuselage, and group C will coordinate everything from here, and liaise with Farnborough. I'll work out in a minute who goes where. Has anybody got anything else to add?'

Davenport had a point to make. 'The place is crawling with press and TV people, and by this afternoon they were becoming a real problem. Is there any chance we can get them kept out of the way?'

'In a word – no, but I take your point and I'll have a word with the police chief and see if he can get anything done about it. Anything else?'

'How is Les doing with the flight recorders?' asked Bernie Cheadle.

'I spoke to him earlier this evening but he said he didn't want to start on them until he'd had a good night's sleep, which is good advice for the rest of us.'

'What about arrangements for getting the wreckage moved back to Farnborough?' Andrew Styles asked.

'It's a little early to worry about that, but I understand there is a plan to move a lot of the smaller items to Sennybridge Camp, ten miles down the road.'

A few more questions were fired his way before Alex dismissed the group, allowing himself a few minutes to work on the logistics for tomorrow's activities. Looking at his watch, he realized that he had been awake for almost thirty-six hours, as had most of his team.

Davenport would lead group A on the port wing investigation. After all, it had been his idea. Andy Styles could lead group B. That just left group C. Samantha had shown immense skill at motivating others, and was organized and methodical. That settled it. He had his three team leaders. Now he just had to assign people to those teams, which he did over the next few minutes.

Everything was now in place for tomorrow. He closed his weary eyes and rubbed them carefully, gently trying to force the tiredness from them.

'I might've guessed you'd be asleep in here.'

Alex looked up to see Leon Baptiste, senior investigator with America's National Transportation Safety Board, grinning back at him from the open doorway. His dark skin was lost in the shadows, the only distinct features being his bright eyes and flashing white teeth. 'Who the hell let you in here?' Alex asked harshly, trying desperately to conceal the look of joy he felt at seeing his old friend.

'I bribed the manager. Looks like you could use our help though, buddy.'

'Well, somehow we've managed to struggle on without you so far. You just got in?'

'Yeah. Hell of a journey. How can a country the size of my back yard be so goddamned hard to get around?'

'You exaggerate. A little.'

'Maybe. You seem to have landed yourself the big one, Alex. How's the investigation going?'

'Better than you might have expected. You know, Leon, I never thought I would ever say this, but I'm *almost* pleased to see you.'

Alex Jamieson had first met Leon Baptiste fifteen years earlier, following the crash of a Chinese airliner in Japan when Alex was just another gifted British Airways pilot. It was during the lengthy inquiry that followed that Baptiste managed to convince Alex that a career in air crash investigation was far more rewarding than being a "glorified bus driver", as he had so graphically described it, and Alex's future was settled.

Baptiste dropped into the chair opposite and pulled a sizeable flask of Jack Daniel's from his pocket, along with two small tumblers. 'So, you wanna show me what you've got so far?'

Lewis Kramer stood at the crest of the hill and looked out across the expanse of the Welsh countryside. At the bottom lay the remains of the tail section, and to the east the sun would soon be rising. This was the last opportunity they would have to film the debris from this vantage point until the sun passed over into the western sky in the afternoon. He would have to get this report right first time.

The cameraman and sound engineer stood twenty feet to one side, ready to play their part. Madison Flynn began the countdown. 'Five, four, three…'

'I'm standing on a hillside in Wales where a large section of Pacific Atlantic Flight 4401 hit the ground. At around five-thirty Tuesday evening Eastern Standard Time, the tranquillity of this idyllic setting was shattered by the worst disaster in British aviation history. As I look down,' the cameraman began his prearranged panning manoeuvre which would encompass Kramer and a large portion of the wreckage, 'I can see a forest of dead trees, lain waste by the violence of the impact, and at the base of the hill lie the remains of the aircraft itself. The level of destruction is incomprehensible, and a chilling reminder of the frailty of us human beings.

'Facts are still very elusive, however some details have emerged in the thirty-six hours since this tragedy occurred. The Dramar Aerospace Corporation D500 with three hundred and eleven men, women and children aboard, broke in two at around thirty thousand feet, following a massive explosion.'

At this point the graphics department back in Washington DC would replace the images from Wales with a computer generated animation showing the sequence of events which were believed to have taken place, while Kramer continued the commentary.

'The forward half of the plane, together with the wings and fuel tanks, was completely destroyed and the remains lay a few miles east of where I am standing. The tail section, as you can see, came to rest here. The inhabitants of the tiny Welsh village of Llancadoc must be the luckiest people alive. Despite the fact that wreckage rained down around the town, not a single person suffered serious injury. Last night I spoke to some of the local people.'

'Cut,' shouted Madison Flynn. 'That was great Lewis. Tony, did we get it?'

'We got it,' replied the cameraman.

'Okay, move around and get some atmosphere shots.' She scrambled over the ruined woodland to where Kramer was standing and they began to discuss the next stage of the news report.

'We've just got to hope one of those air crash guys will speak to us,' she said, shaking her head. 'Any ideas?'

'Not yet, but I'll come up with something.'

Kramer was unhappy. There was nothing wrong with the report *per se*, but it was essentially just like a hundred others that had been broadcast over the past day or so. It lacked the individuality and flair that his stories were famous for. He needed an angle that would set it apart from the others. He needed Clarence Grant.

Ten

Les Thompson arrived at the AAIB labs at six in the morning, his entire staff of one already there and eager to begin the examination of the flight recorders.

As neither of the two units had been subjected to excesses of heat or water, it had not been necessary to inspect them immediately, notwithstanding political pressure from Downing Street and the White House. The devices were designed to withstand temperatures of up to eleven hundred degrees Celsius for thirty minutes, or two hundred and fifty degrees for ten hours, and water pressure equivalent to twenty thousand feet. Neither the Flight Data Recorder nor the Cockpit Voice Recorder had been exposed to anything like these conditions and were apparently completely undamaged.

'Good morning,' Thompson said cheerily.

'Good morning, Les,' Faye Beresford replied with the customary familiarity. She had worked with

Thompson at the AAIB for twelve years and they had a good working relationship.

'It all has to be strictly by the book today, Faye. There are a lot of eyes on us right now.'

'Goes without saying. Just make sure the coffee keeps coming; I barely had a wink last night.'

'Me neither,' Thompson admitted. 'Right, first order of business would be an exam of the CVR. We'll move on to the FDR later.'

He withdrew the Cockpit Voice Recorder from its storage compartment and set it gently on the bench. The unit was in pristine condition and one would never have realized that it had just been dropped from thirty thousand feet. He began the task by removing the screws in the casing with the care and precision of a surgeon.

'How was Mr. Beresford this morning?' he asked detachedly as he worked.

'Snoring contentedly. I must confess I was a little envious.'

Thompson smiled as he turned the Voice Recorder around to work on the other side. 'Yes, it's been a while since I had to be up at four-thirty in the morning.'

The last screw came away and was dropped into the receptacle with the others. He gently lifted the casing away to reveal its more delicate contents.

This model of Cockpit Voice Recorder used magnetic tape to record the sounds of the flight deck on a thirty-minute continuous loop on four tracks – three 'hot mikes' attached to the headsets of the pilot, co-pilot and jump seat occupant if there was one, and a Cockpit Area

Microphone. This last track was important for registering all the ambient noises on the flight deck not audible on the hot mikes.

'Could you hold the unit steady for me, Faye?'

Beresford clasped her fingers around the box as Thompson detached the recording heads and removed the spools. The Voice Recorder itself was now completely useless and was stored away. The tape could now be replayed, and they would be the first two people to hear the final words of the flight crew. Initially they would listen to all four tracks simultaneously to get an overall picture of events from the beginning of the tape, which covered the take-off procedure, to the moment power was cut off to the Voice Recorder – the break-up of the airliner thirty minutes later.

Thompson and Beresford were both veterans in this field. However, hearing the mundane conversations of the recently deceased crew of an aircraft always brought into focus the importance of their work, and the last few words spoken were disturbing evidence of the fact that real people – real individuals with families and friends – had just died prematurely. This was not a task that induced levity.

The take-off and climb were completely normal, with no indication of any problems. All four tracks had registered the brief exchange between the captain and Swanwick Air Traffic Control. The pilot and first officer resumed their conversation, rating their prospects in a forthcoming fishing trip up the Occoquan River. It was terribly sad to listen to these voices, full of life and vitality, knowing that very soon these sounds would be abruptly terminated.

There was still no sign of any trouble and Beresford found herself involuntarily hoping that all would end well, despite the knowledge that this could not possibly be the case.

At twenty-nine minutes and fifty-one seconds it began.

A rumble could be heard, followed by an alarm. Two more alarms had begun to sound before there was any audible reaction from the crew.

'What the hell?' said the first voice with a note of rising unease.

'Nose down! Nose down!' shouted the second.

'Forward! Forward!'

'It's too late!'

The last two seconds of the tape were a mixture of crashes, bangs, and indefinable noises before it came to the end.

Thompson stopped the replay and sat back in his chair, several moments elapsing before he spoke. This job never became any easier.

'Well, it sounds like an instantaneous catastrophic failure of some kind. I didn't hear any obvious indications as to the cause. Did you?'

Beresford's gaze remained fixed on the tape player. 'We need to isolate those alarms. I'm not that familiar with Dramar equipment.'

'Neither am I. Something to look at later.' He made a note of this. 'What did you make of the "nose down" phrase?'

'It sounded like a command to me,' she mused, 'rather than a reaction. I think I heard a stall warning towards the end, so perhaps they thought they needed to push the sticks forward and get some lift.'

Thompson nodded silently.

The next stage was to listen to all four tracks separately, and make a written transcription of events. This was something of an art form in itself, and one that Faye Beresford had proven in the past to be particularly adept at. Thompson left her to this task and moved on to the Flight Data Recorder.

Most of the modern recorders store information digitally, however Pacific Atlantic had opted for one of the old style units using magnetic Kapton tape as a cost-cutting exercise. The new generation of Digital Flight Data Recorders were twice the price of their analogue predecessors, which, when outfitting an entire fleet of aircraft, would constitute a significant increase in expenditure. Although the manufacturer produced these units, Pacific Atlantic had gambled that they would not suffer a hull loss that would prove to be so severe that the Data Recorder was completely destroyed. Tape is a far more delicate recording medium than a digital disk. On this occasion they had been lucky, but the niggardly attitude of the carrier would be mentioned in the AAIB's report when it was published.

The initial procedure for the retrieval of data from the Data Recorder was much the same as for the Voice Recorder, and Thompson set about removing the orange casing.

The Flight Data Recorder initially recorded data into one of two memory stores, each capable of holding about one second of information. When the first store was full the data was checked by the second store, which always took much less than a second to accomplish. Once this data had been formatted it was passed to the permanent memory tape, which had a twenty-five hour recording duration. The second store was now ready to record the next second of data, which would then be checked by the first store, and the procedure would repeat *ad infinitum*. This 'checkstroke' operation was designed to ensure that as little information as possible was lost when power to the recorder was cut off. It was a good system for the analogue Data Recorders, however it still meant that up to one point two seconds of data could be lost from the two 'volatile' memory stores, something that would not happen to a digital Flight Data Recorder.

Once the casing was removed, Thompson waited until Beresford was free to help, not wishing to undertake the delicate operation unaided. Impatience could cause damage to the delicate Kapton, and once the data was lost it could never be recovered.

Beresford stayed with him until the tape was safely installed into the AAIB's computer and the decryption process had begun.

Because of the disjointed nature of the recording procedure, each second of information contained some 'preamble' data from the previous second, which was edited out by the computer. What was left was an unbroken data flow, which could be more easily analysed.

At a later date this information would form the basis of a computer generated representation of the latter stages of the flight, but for the moment the parameters recorded would have to be correlated to the Voice Recorder transcript. When a circuit breaker was heard on the Cockpit Area Microphone track, the Data Recording could be consulted to ascertain which system was being used, and every discrete event recorded by the Data Recorder on a certain parameter had to be cross-referenced with the other sixty-two. This was a protracted process, but the results often provided a vital insight into what had happened on the flight deck and to the aircraft's systems.

Thompson began looking at various parameters individually, but could do little of value until the cockpit area microphone was put through the dynamic signal analyser. This was a device that could isolate and examine the various ambient noises within the cabin.

The Cockpit Voice Recorder often gave an immediate answer to the mystery of an air crash, however this would not prove to be the case today. Cross-referencing of the data acquired by the two units would take several weeks to accomplish.

The AAIB, the police, and the media would have a long wait before the flight recorders could provide any solution to the mystery.

Eleven

A ndrew Styles had decided to split his team into two groups – one for each crash site. Group B, his group, had been given a broad brief: to look for any evidence of a structural failure. This could mean virtually anything, and Styles had been awake until three in the morning planning today's operation. The two-pronged approach seemed to be the most efficient way to use his people.

Ken Stanley had taken two investigators with him to site B to study the separation point of the tail section.

Styles had a much more difficult task: sifting through the charred remains of the wreckage of the forward section at site A. The previous day had mainly been spent mapping the area, isolating various recognizable pieces of the aircraft, making Styles' and his three associates' task a little easier, but not a lot. Realistically, he felt the best they could do was continue identifying pieces from the schematics supplied by Dramar Aerospace and catalogue them. The exercise was daunting. He had never before seen at first hand devastation on this scale.

'Andy,' yelled Damian Beaumont, 'come and have a look at this.'

Styles jogged over to where Beaumont was crouching. The junior investigator was examining a section of carbon fibre about four feet long.

'Look at this pitting and tell me what you think.'

Styles leaned closer and was able to see what his colleague had indicated. The indentations, which he suspected to be gas-washing craters, were close to the point where the shaft had broken. 'I don't know,' he said at length. 'It could be imperfections in the manufacturing process, or a result of exposure to the heat,' Styles spoke absently as his mind raced.

'They could be,' pressed Beaumont, 'or they could be the result of an explosive.'

Styles remained silent, going over all the possibilities he could think of before voicing them aloud. There were a hundred and one things that could have caused these marks, and he was loath to accept that it was what Beaumont obviously believed it to be. 'Have you touched the piece?'

'No, not yet.'

'Then let's turn it over. Gloves.'

The two investigators both donned latex gloves to avoid any contamination and gently turned the object over.

'Oh, my God,' breathed Styles. 'Don't jump to any conclusions,' he added a little belatedly.

The underside of the carbon fibre section was still blackened from its exposure to fire, but not as badly as the top. A black substance stood out from the darkness of the charring; a black, liquorice-like substance, glistening in the sunlight.

Beaumont sat back. 'Now tell me that's not plastic explosive residue.'

Styles was not sure how to reply, and regretted his earlier exclamation. 'It's certainly a possibility. I'll call the chief. We need an explosives expert to look at this.'

The operations room at the Priory Hotel was a much more orderly setting than it had been the previous evening. Alex Jamieson had been in conversation with Leon Baptiste and the other two representatives from the NTSB who had arrived in the UK the previous night. That conversation was quickly curtailed as his phone began to vibrate frantically for attention.

'Alex. It's Andy Styles. We've... found something.'

The Investigator-in-Charge could tell immediately from Styles' tone that this was important and held a finger up to silence his three colleagues. 'What is it?'

Styles hesitated before answering, but decided that the totally professional approach would be best. 'Damian Beaumont has discovered what we believe could be evidence of an explosive device. It's a piece of carbon fibre, V-shaped in cross-section and just over a meter in length, possibly a fragment of one of the main stringers.'

These ran the length of the airframe at its highest and lowest points, keeping the structure rigid. Smaller stringers ran along the sides of the aircraft, fulfilling a similar function, but individually possessed nothing like the support of the main stringers.

'It's displaying some small indentations on one side, and a black, viscous substance on the other. We require advice on how to proceed, but suggest that an explosives expert examine the piece.'

Alex felt empathy for his colleague. This might well be the 'diamond in the dust', and Styles did not wish to be accused, at a later date, of acting in any way that might be viewed as unprofessional, or to the detriment of the investigation. Alex knew Andrew Styles to be a thoroughly professional investigator, and would defend him to the hilt, if in the unlikely event that accusations were made.

'I understand, Andy. You are to remain with the piece until advised differently, and a ten-meter cordon must be established around it immediately. No one is to go near it. No one. Is that understood?'

'Completely.'

Alex could sense the relief in the man's voice. 'Well done, both of you.' He ended the call and began to ponder the new problem that had just arisen: he didn't *have* an explosives expert with him in Wales. An oversight on his part, which he silently berated himself for.

'Well?' asked Baptiste impatiently.

'One of my people has found some plastic explosive residue. At least he thinks he has. Trouble is, I haven't got an explosives specialist here.'

Baptiste leaned back in his chair and a broad, Caribbean grin crossed his features. 'Yes you do.'

Alex felt he was walking into a trap, but uttered the next sentence regardless. 'Leon, you don't know *jack shit* about explosives.'

'True, but Miguel here does.' The US investigator gestured towards his colleague. 'May I suggest a little Anglo-American cooperation?'

Alex gave in. 'All right, you've got me this time.' How had Baptiste known? Probably just good old Yankee paranoia, but he welcomed his good fortune anyway, even if it did mean that his American counterpart would be unbearable company for the remainder of his stay. Still, just two days into the investigation and they probably had their answer.

Alex would never realize the level of respect that Baptiste felt for him and his team, but neither were under any illusion that the real work was yet to come.

They had their first diamond in the dust.

There would be another.

News can be spread in the most bizarre and unlikely of ways, although the truth, or some version of it, can normally be extrapolated from a mass of rumour, conjecture, and misinformation.

This had proven to be the case in Llancadoc today.

Damian Beaumont, the young and terribly eager investigator, who had been a member of Andrew Styles' team at site A, had momentarily allowed his enthusiasm to get the better of him. The police officer whom he had spoken to had simply asked what all the commotion was about. Beaumont's mistake had been to tell him.

The next person whom the law enforcement officer had spoken to was a certain American gentleman named Lewis Kramer.

The reporter now had his scoop, and what a scoop it was. Many had suspected that a bomb had been responsible for the crash, however until this morning no evidence of explosive had been found. The information had not been officially verified yet, but that did not matter. A brief telephone conversation with one of the investigators at the Priory Hotel had told him what he needed to know. The young woman had denied all knowledge of the discovery of an Improvised Explosive Device, however Kramer had been playing this game for too many years to be fooled by an amateur. The AAIB were just being overly cautious, which was to be expected.

The report went out at lunchtime in Llancadoc, and caught the breakfast news in Washington DC.

An hour later Damian Beaumont was given a severe dressing down, and a curt lecture on professional discretion.

Twelve

After seven days of intensive field investigations, Alex Jamieson, Investigator-in-Charge, had been reduced to hitching a lift back to Farnborough. The 'lift' was, admittedly, an RAF C-130J Hercules, but he felt it was a less than glamorous return.

Little had changed since he had left the Defence Evaluation and Research Agency on that dark Tuesday night. His desk was still a jumble of papers, the corridors were still dark and musty, and the coffee from the machine was as bland and uninteresting as always.

The one thing that had changed, though, was the main hangar. This impressively-sized grey-green structure in a quiet corner of the airfield at Farnborough was usually occupied by several piles of wreckage from various light aircraft that had met with disaster somewhere within the British Isles. These testaments to the fallibility of human flight would be neatly cordoned off by black and yellow striped ropes suspended from three-foot high poles. An incident involving a light aircraft was normally attributed to engine failure, bad maintenance, poor weather conditions, CFIT – controlled flight into terrain – still a disturbingly common cause of accidents the world over, or, most commonly, crew error, which had now been given the more accurate term 'human factors'. The AAIB dealt with around fifty such cases a year, and in most instances the cause of the accident was quite obvious, though there were always some that threw up the occasional surprise. The team were also responsible for British registered aircraft that were involved in incidents abroad, and would assist the local authorities with their investigations. After all, the AAIB *had* tutored many of these people themselves at the Cranfield Aeronautical Institute in Bedfordshire, rightfully regarded as the best air accident investigation training facility in the world.

These incidents would be investigated as thoroughly as ever, however the remains of those smaller aircraft had now been relegated to the four corners of the chamber.

Dominating the area was the wreckage brought back from Wales, laid out on the floor in the vague shape of an airliner. Each item carried a tag indicating its part number, a brief description of the component, and the location of its discovery. Lighting within the hangar was poor, the skylights and windows lining the walls doing little to banish the gloom, so halogen lamps mounted on tripods lit the areas that investigators were working on.

Alex could see a dozen or so people moving slowly amongst the debris, some with tablets or clipboards cataloguing the latest pieces to arrive, others shining flashlights into inaccessible areas. He slowly walked down the side of what had once been the forward half of the fuselage, exchanging greetings with those who saw him. Under these circumstances it was easy to understand why a pilot would refer to his or her airliner as a million spare parts flying in close formation.

He stopped when he saw Stuart Davenport tucked inside a section of mangled panelling, as he carefully wielded an endoscope inside the piece. Atop the long narrow metal tube was an eyepiece, and he adjusted the focus with his right hand as the flexible section of tubing wove its way through the internal area of the piece, which was impenetrable to the unaided human eye.

'Hi, Stu. Found anything interesting?'

Davenport did not look up as he replied. 'More questions than answers. There's something odd about this. ANDY!' he yelled into the empty hole in front of him. 'Get out here; the chief wants a word.' Andrew Styles emerged from the hole, and removed the protective mask and helmet, which were covered in dirt and ash.

'Hi, Alex. Good to have you back.' Styles and Davenport extricated themselves from the wreckage with some difficulty, their white protective overalls caked in grime.

From the nearby equipment trolley Davenport removed a ring binder and began searching for the set of photographs he wished his superior to see.

Styles began the explanation. 'We've come across an anomaly. It's now clear that the lower main stringer bore the brunt of the blast, so that's where we've been concentrating our investigation. The lower main stringer is held in place by these supports, designated KX-7s in the schematics.' He pointed to one of the photos that Davenport had by now located, and Alex could see the inverted 'V' shape of the piece that attached the stringer to the airframe. 'They should, according to the Dramar schematics, be placed at fifty centimetre intervals along most of the fuselage, and thirty centimetre intervals in the mid-section, but they're not.'

'How far is the spacing?'

'Every meter throughout, by the looks of it, but we haven't finished our study yet.'

Alex flicked through the photographs and the spacing of the KX-7s did indeed appear to be a lot more than the specified fifty centimetres. 'I suppose the question now is: which is wrong, the plans or the aircraft?'

'That's the sixty-four thousand dollar question,' Davenport said.

'Is there *any* chance that you've made a mistake?'

'There's always a chance, but I don't think so. I'll go through the schematics again to see if we've missed anything, but I'm pretty sure we'll come to the same conclusions.'

'That's good enough for me. I'll get in touch with Dramar and try to sort this out.' He turned to leave.

'Better make it soon,' Davenport shouted after him. 'If these plans *are* duds, it'll really slow us down.'

Alex's next port of call was the flight recorder analysis lab. Les Thompson and Faye Beresford were busy at their respective workstations, but Thompson looked up when he saw the Investigator-in-Charge enter the room.

'What have you found so far?' Alex asked.

'Not much, I'm afraid. At least nothing interesting. Records from the Data Recorder cover the final flight and the outward journey from the States, but there seems to be nothing untoward.'

Alex had not really expected the flight recorders to shed much light on the crash, but he had been hoping for something. It was not enough to simply know that an explosive device had been responsible, they had to ascertain the actual method and sequence of destruction from the available evidence.

'There *was* one slightly unusual thing, though.'

'What's that?'

'The Flight Data Recorder was of an old analogue design.'

'On a brand new wide-body jet?' That was unusual. 'Still, that was Pacific Atlantic's prerogative. Nobody can force them to buy the best technology.'

'No, but I decided to contact Pacific Atlantic myself and ask why. They were advised by Dramar Aerospace to opt for the more inexpensive model.'

'Why would Dramar recommend *that*?'

'Your guess is as good as mine.' Thompson shrugged his shoulders. He was as bemused by this as his superior. 'I just thought you might be interested to know that little titbit.'

'Thanks, Les. Good work. I'll look into it.' Alex left the lab and made his way to his office. First, there were the erroneous schematics or faulty installation of the KX-7 supports, and now some dubious advice given to the carrier by the manufacturer.

He needed some time alone to think this through.

Thirteen

The buzzer on the desk intercom demanded Douglas Harrington's attention.

'Yes, Mrs. Baird?'

'Mr. Koenig to see you, sir.'

'Send him in, send him in,' he replied blithely.

A short, overweight, and balding man in his late forties entered the room, his dour expression the antithesis of his chief executive's. He ambled over to the desk and dropped heavily into the opposite chair. Greg Koenig was DAC Skysystems' technical director, who oversaw all aspects of the design and fabrication of the company's creations. The engineer had an extensive knowledge of technical matters, however his time nowadays was mostly spent as a manager, rather than a 'hands on' designer.

'So Greg,' asked Harrington enthusiastically, 'how are things at Crystal Lake?'

Koenig did not share his superior's optimistic demeanour. 'Not too bad, but I think you could be celebrating a little prematurely. We're not out of the woods yet.'

'Of course we are. Oh, I grant you, there'll still be a few awkward questions, but we've got all the bases covered. Everyone knows it was a bomb. That's all people are interested in. We're the victims. If anything, the publicity is doing the D500 some good. I've made a plan. For the rest of this week I'll be doing a lot of publicity stuff, TV appearances and the like, and next week we invite the press out to the Ohio factory for a tour of the plant to show them how safe our aircraft really are. We'll take them up in a D500 and do some aerobatics – real gut-wrenching stuff. By the time they leave, they'll wonder why they ever doubted our D500.'

'Scare the crap out of 'em. That'll do the trick. Are you crazy? Allow the press into the fabrication and assembly areas? If they get one whiff of a cover-up, they'll eat us alive.'

'You show me one hack who knows anything about aircraft.'

Koenig considered the proposal for a few moments. Harrington was right, of course. The risk was negligible. 'I guess it wouldn't do any harm. They'd have to be carefully herded, though. We can't have some idiot going off on his own and asking the wrong people questions.'

'Of course not. I'll plan the tour myself. We'll get Jacqui Kosinski to show them round. They'll be so busy lookin' up her skirt, they won't even notice the aircraft.'

Koenig had to smile at this one. 'Okay, the tour is on. I do have a couple of other things we need to discuss, though.'

'Fire away.' Harrington was on a roll.

'I've had a communication from a guy at Britain's Air Accidents Investigation Branch.'

Harrington's mien immediately became a little more sombre. 'What did he want?'

'Clarification. The schematics we originally sent the AAIB a few months ago were for the revised design. They've noticed the discrepancies, and are asking questions.'

'Do they suspect anything?' asked Harrington.

'I don't think so. They seem to think that a genuine error has been made. They just want some plans that correspond to the wreckage.'

'Not an unreasonable request,' the chief executive smiled. 'Well that's just fine. We'll invite them over for a tour as well. You know, show them our production processes and the like.'

'Now wait just a Goddamn minute! Showing a bunch of dumb reporters round the place is one thing, but the AAIB are professionals. It's too much of a risk,' he said, shaking his head vigorously.

'Nonsense. Listen Greg, our production processes have altered since we discovered the fault. Right? There's nothing going on at Crystal Lake or Gunpowder Falls to suggest anything abnormal, is there?'

'No, but—'

'And the substitute plans we will supply them with will correspond to the wreckage they hold, will it not?'

'It'll look fine on paper, but still—'

'Well there you are, then. You said it yourself. This guy, what's his name?'

'Jamieson.'

'This Jamieson guy doesn't suspect anything. He thinks he got sent some out of date schematics. Nothing more. If we show him the way we are doing things now, he'll be none the wiser and will go away a happy little investigator.'

'I still think the risk is too great.' Koenig was aware that there was no way he would win this argument, but wanted to make his feelings clear.

'That settles it, then. Don't worry, Greg. Jamieson will be shepherded even more closely than the press will be. Looks like Jacqui will have a busy week,' Harrington chuckled. Koenig did not reciprocate.

'There was a related issue I wished to discuss with you: Lewis Kramer at CTVN.'

'What about him?' Harrington sighed. He was becoming irritated by the engineer's consistently negative attitude. Things were just not *that* bad now. A week ago, yes, the situation seemed dire. Things had changed.

'He knows too much about what is going on. His reports haven't said anything outright, but it's obvious he has information the others don't. You know what that means?' Koenig let the sentence hang and relaxed further into his chair. This was one argument that he would win, he could tell from Harrington's expression.

'We have a security leak. Any ideas who?'

Koenig produced a sheet of paper. 'I've drawn up a list of possible suspects. There are about eighty candidates. Forty or so are unlikely. Twenty-three are possible, and eighteen are definite maybes. I suggest we organize surveillance of this last group.'

Harrington nodded. 'I'll get it organized.' He unlocked a drawer in his desk and dropped the sheet of paper in.

The technical director was unsure of how to ask the next question, and was even more concerned as to what the answer might be. 'What do we do when we discover who was responsible?'

Harrington's expression remained impassive. 'We employ any response that is necessary,' he shrugged. 'We plug that leak.'

'Not much doubt about it,' Alex Jamieson was staring at the monitor of the scanning tunnelling electron microscope in the metallurgy lab. Ken Stanley stood by and watched as his boss – nearly twenty years his junior – adjusted the dial on the side of the apparatus. The tiny sliver of composite material moved one micron, and the image that Alex was observing moved jerkily across the screen. 'Gas washing craters. Odd shape, though.'

'That's because this is a composite,' explained Stanley. 'To some extent they follow the grain of the material, which gives them their slightly elongated shape. Metal has a denser molecular structure and the grain is less pronounced.'

Alex murmured an acknowledgement. He was fascinated by this aspect of the AAIB's work, and often wandered into the lab to talk to the metallurgy and composites guru, although his understanding of the subject was fairly limited. Fortunately, Stanley did not seem to mind explaining the basic principles to the younger man. On the contrary, he always became very animated when talking, happy to answer the senior investigator's enquiries.

'Is there any way to tell how much distance there was between the stringer and the bomb?' Alex asked, reluctantly pulling away from the screen to face the scientist.

Stanley considered this for a moment, a wry smile crossing his features. 'I was afraid you might ask me that. It all rather depends on how much material the shock wave had to pass through before it encountered the stringer. The dispersion of the cratering should give some indication. As a general rule, the more closely packed the craters, the closer to the point of origin, although as this is an organic matrix composite and not metal, it may have reacted differently. The yield of the explosion is also an important factor. It'll be the devil's own job to find out for sure. That's the problem with bombs in cargo holds. With luggage dispersed all over the shop, it's impossible to accurately recreate the effects of the explosion.'

'You mean you don't know,' Alex grinned, teasing the scientist.

'I mean we have more tests to run before I will commit myself to an answer,' Stanley replied with mock indignation. 'Tomorrow we will conduct some test detonations to see how the material reacts. I may be able to give you an educated guess in the afternoon. You're welcome to come and observe, if you wish.'

Alex wished he could stay and watch, but he had another appointment to keep. 'Sounds like fun,' he said, glancing at his watch. 'But I've got meetings to go to. Lucky me, eh?'

'I don't envy you.'

'Let me know if you find anything. I've got to dash. Be careful not to blow yourself up. I haven't got the time to do the extra paperwork.'

The investigator made the brisk walk to his office to gather his briefcase and jacket. As an afterthought, he checked his emails. Four were waiting for him. Three were inconsequential and could be dealt with later; the fourth was definitely not. It was from Douglas Harrington. *The* Douglas Harrington. Himself. Alex read the message and was intrigued. The invitation to visit Dramar Aerospace had been extended, and etiquette dictated that he had to accept. Besides, this was one place he had never seen up close, and would be interested to see how it differed from Boeing's plant in Seattle. The problem was finding the time. Technically, he should be working fifteen-hour days for at least the next two weeks, but if he appointed Stuart Davenport to fill his role for three days the following week, it would free him up to make the journey across the Atlantic. This was one problem that could be circumvented.

The next question was: who would accompany him? To go alone would not be according to protocol. After much deliberation, he was forced to admit that Samantha seemed to be the best and, realistically, the only choice. Alex simply could not spare anyone else.

The discrepancies in the design of the D500 needed to be cleared up. It was obviously a mistake of some kind, but nevertheless something didn't *feel* right. He could not put his finger on it; he just felt that something was not as it should be. Perhaps Leon Baptiste's paranoia had infected him. That was probably it, and after all, who had *not* been affected to some degree over the past couple of weeks?

Fourteen

Donatella Martinelli stepped lightly from the hire car onto the tarmac, the loose gravel crunching beneath her stilettoed feet. The Florida humidity was oppressive and she was thankful she'd worn the light silk business suit, although the scarlet ensemble now felt a little too conspicuous for her liking.

From today everything would be in place, after ten days of frantic preparations for her enforced departure – should it become necessary. Dealing with such rudimentary matters herself was something of a novelty, having spent her entire privileged life relying on others to handle her day-to-day needs. Born into her late father's wealth, she had never had cause to fend for herself, and the arrangements of the last couple of weeks had presented a steep learning curve.

Her substitute identity had been the first task to be tackled, and a new persona had been bought for a trifling two thousand dollars from a woman in New York, after she had carried out a few background checks. She did not wish to be saddled with a criminal record she knew nothing about, or ex-husbands she had never met.

The next stage had been to find a new place to live. Rio seemed to be the obvious choice, so it was immediately rejected. Switzerland was too cold, and as an Italian American, she would stand out too much.

She eventually settled on the Caribbean. The Cayman Islands would have been her first choice due to their favourable tax laws, however Dramar possessed offices on Grand Cayman, and she didn't want to run the risk of accidentally running into one of her former colleagues. After an hour of pawing over a map, she decided on the island of Guadeloupe, fifteen hundred miles from the Florida coast. Like the Cayman group, it would provide a pleasant climate and relaxed lifestyle, but anonymity was assured, which had to be her primary concern. She had purchased a large beach house near Petit-Canal, on the eastern part of the butterfly shaped island. The property offered breathtaking views of the western half of the island, and the Caribbean Sea, making this the perfect domicile during her exile.

The third objective was to arrange for her own personal fortune to be transferred to the Breibacher Bank, one of the numerous Cayman financial institutions. The discretion of these businesses was renowned, but even so, she had felt the need to 'launder' the money through several companies in several countries first. She would be able to access the capital through a second account held with a local bank on Guadeloupe.

The final stage was the reason for her presence in Florida today. The airfield outside Tampa was a magnet for small privateer air carriers, and dozens of Learjets and Gulfstreams crowded the taxiways, as well as numerous other makes and models. Not that these names would mean much to Donatella. Her involvement in aviation had only ever been as a business concern, and she possessed none of her late father's enthusiasm for aircraft. To her, a plane simply moved one from A to B in the shortest possible time. She did not care about power output or fuel efficiency, just as long as it was comfortable – and safe – something her own company could no longer guarantee.

The squat control tower was surrounded by a small city of business huts, but she eventually found the one she was looking for.

Over the telephone the previous day, Mitch Levitt had informed her that he was a veteran of the Iraq War with more than twenty years flying experience, and that Rapido Travel consisted of himself, his secretary, and one serviceable Learjet. Complete confidentiality was assured, and cash was preferred – American dollars only.

With her customary self-assuredness she threw open the door and strode in, but stopped short as she was confronted by a wall of cigarette smoke. Through the smog, she could see a woman – quite a large woman – perched on the edge of a cheap, prefabricated desk that was obviously straining under her considerable weight. A tattered couch rested against one wall, and a row of filing cabinets lined the other. The woman, presumably the secretary, wore a tight sweater, which did little to conceal her more than ample breasts that threatened to spill out from the sweetheart neckline, and a denim skirt that was far too short for someone of her size. The heels were even higher than her own, and she wondered how those tiny points supported the woman's bulk. She felt like turning around and leaving immediately, but thought better of the idea. This was just one of the ordeals she would have to endure, and she simply had to get used to it, for the time being.

'Hey, sweetheart. What can I do for you?'

'I have an appointment to see Mr. Levitt.'

'Let me consult *Mr.* Levitt's diary,' the secretary's voice dripped with sarcasm. 'Oh, yeah. Nina Ferroni. You wanna charter the Lear. He'll be back in a minute. Take a seat.' She gestured to the couch.

'I'd rather stand.' God alone knew what she might catch if she sat down.

'Suit yerself.'

In her entire life, Donatella Martinelli had never felt so out of place. This was not her environment. These were not her people. Shopping at Bloomingdale's or Versace's, and polite dinner parties, that was her life.

The flushing of a toilet somewhere beyond the desk announced the arrival of Mitchell Levitt. When he emerged he stopped to admire his new guest.

She felt his eyes moving over her body, making no attempt to conceal his lust.

'Hey, baby. You Nina?'

'You may address me as Ms. Ferroni,' she replied haughtily.

'Whatever. You wanna see the Lear?'

This was beginning to feel like a really bad idea, but the lecherous pervert could stare as much as he liked, as long as he did not try to touch her and could fly a plane.

Levitt swung the door open. 'After you, *Ms.* Ferroni.'

She walked ahead of him, feeling his eyes upon her, but closing her mind to it. Why had she worn the short skirt and heels?

The Learjet was old, but immaculately maintained. Once he had begun to speak of the business transaction, his demeanour changed, and she felt slightly less uncomfortable in his presence.

'Guadeloupe, eh?' he mused. 'French Antilles. Very nice.'

'Yes, and I need you to be able to go with no more than twelve hours' notice.'

Levitt sucked the air between cigarette-stained teeth. 'Twelve hours,' he muttered as he considered the proposal. 'Could be difficult. It may well mean cancelling another booking. Pricey.'

'How pricey?' she sighed.

'An extra ten grand. Can you afford that, Princess?'

'It will not be a problem.'

'I'll need half now, the other half on completion.'

Donatella had anticipated this, and withdrew the cash from her shoulder bag. He ogled the money more intensely than he had her own body a few minutes before.

'Do we have a deal, Mr. Levitt?'

'We do, Miss Ferroni.'

Fifteen

Nick Romani glanced up from the computer screen. She had been staring at him again, but her eyes darted away as they suddenly met his, her cheeks flushing slightly as she stared fixedly at the monitor of her own workstation in the open plan office. What was her name? Mindy? Millie? Misty? Something like that. He continued observing her, which was not exactly a hardship: slim, blond, and wearing the *de rigueur* short skirt that all the young female research assistants seemed to dress in. Tall or petite, blond or brunette; it made little difference. They were all pretty much the same to him. Just a constant stream of young American girls to seduce, and he had a feeling that this one would be the easiest yet.

She looked up again, but this time she smiled before her eyes returned to the computer. Definitely the easiest yet. He smiled to himself and shook his head, still bemused as to how easy these American girls were, how readily they opened their legs for him, dignity an alien concept to them.

His desk phone rang and he lifted the receiver. 'Nick Romani.'

'Hello. Can I speak to Diana Kearn?'

The girl looked up again and smiled, her gaze remaining on him for several seconds before she looked away, obviously confused as to why he had looked straight through her, his swarthy features completely impassive.

'I'm sorry, Diana isn't in the office at the moment. Can I get her to call you back?'

Several seconds of silence elapsed before the man answered. 'Okay, tell her it's Clarence Grant and...' Another pause. 'Ask her to call me at home tonight.'

'Sure thing. Does she have your number?'

'Yes, she does. Thanks.' The line went dead.

Romani gently replaced the receiver in its cradle and left the office, oblivious to the perplexed look from the girl as he walked straight past her without any acknowledgement.

He had to make a call. A very private call.

Artemis parked the car two blocks from Grant's house and walked briskly down the street, the cold autumn evening quickening her pace. Clouds scudded across the sky, the moon and stars appearing briefly before being obscured again, as ephemeral as phantoms in the mist. As she turned into his road the wind chill bit even harder at her face, and scythed through the thin dark overcoat that she had mistakenly thought would be sufficient to ward off the chill of the frigid October evening.

She moved more slowly now, counting down the house numbers along the quiet suburban road until she came to the one she sought. Just as she began to walk along the garden path to his door the moon reappeared from behind a bank of cloud, bathing the street in its stark blue glow. Across the road she could now see that one of the parked cars was occupied. Two men in dark suits were watching her. It was too late to turn around. She had already started up the pathway, and to backtrack now could prove to be disastrous. Under normal circumstances she would have walked the length of the street first, however the cold had numbed her natural sense of caution and forced the error of judgement. When she emerged from the house later, they would undoubtedly have a camera lens trained upon her. She would just have to go through with it for now and improvise a solution to the problem while she was inside.

She reached his door and rang the bell, curling her toes within her shoes to generate some warmth as she waited for him to answer, resisting the urge to glance back over her shoulder.

The door opened a couple of inches, a security chain preventing any further movement, and the sickly little man stood there with his mouth agape. He had obviously not expected a visit from anyone, least of all *her,* as he was dressed in just faded denims and a food-stained T-shirt.

'Diana?' he said in a dismayed tone. 'I thought you were going to call me.'

She smiled with feigned affection. 'Clarence, if you want to talk to me, then the least I can do is come and see you in person.' She glanced down at the shirt. 'Perhaps I should have called ahead first,' she grinned playfully. 'So, are you going to invite me in or leave me to freeze on the doorstep?'

'Of course, sorry.' The door closed momentarily as he fumbled with the chain and opened it fully. He stepped aside, visibly flustered. 'Come in, please.'

She entered the house and savoured its warmth while taking in her surroundings. The place was quite small by American standards, but immaculately kept. The pictures on the walls were all hung perfectly straight, frames matching the pastel decor, and ornaments were carefully positioned in display cabinets. However, the entire place had the unnatural feel of a show home, nothing of the interior reflecting the personality or tastes of the occupier, just a random selection of items gathered to contribute to a confused façade.

Grant took her coat and gestured for her to go through to the lounge, hanging the garment in the hallway, but taking the time to sniff the material and enjoy her perfume. When he returned he found her relaxed on the couch, the knee-length skirt having ridden up to reveal a healthy expanse of stockinged leg. After a brief moment of indecision he decided to be daring and sat down next to her.

'So, Clarence, what is it you wanted to talk to me about?' The men in the car must have been watching Grant's house, and could not have been specifically waiting for *her*.

'I'm a bit worried that things are taking so long. It's been two weeks since the crash, now. Don't you think the news could be getting a little stale.'

He had probably let something slip at Dramar, and it was they who were watching him. The little fool. 'I understand your concerns, but an investigative report such as this requires time to put together. We are still gathering information from other sources. Try to be patient, Clarence, and don't worry about the story becoming stale.' She gently clasped his clammy hand in hers. 'An exposé this important doesn't have a timescale. It's too big.'

Her hand was still cold, but the flesh felt soft and smooth against his skin. 'I'm sure you're right, but I'm still nervous. I can't be certain, but I think someone followed me home the other night.'

'Who? You haven't told anyone at work about our little agreement, have you?'

'Oh, no,' he said emphatically. 'Not a soul.'

She appeared to be in thought for a few moments. Only one other person knew of her visit tonight, and Khalid would never betray her. Never. 'It could just be Kramer or one of his cronies. Has he tried to contact you again?'

'No. You think it's him, then?'

'It's the most probable explanation.'

Grant shifted in his seat, preparing to make one of his bold statements. There's a team from the AAIB visiting the Skysystems site the day after tomorrow. The senior investigator is a man named Alex Jamieson. I think that perhaps I should try to speak with him. Let him know about the fault and what's been going on at Dramar Aerospace.'

'That would be a mistake.' He flinched visibly and she realized that she had spoken a little more sharply than she had intended. Artemis released his hand and began to run her fingers through his hair. 'If you do that, then you might end up incriminating yourself. If that happens they could try to use you as a scapegoat.' Was it her imagination or could she actually hear his heart pounding?

'I suppose you're right.'

He didn't sound convinced. This was a problem that needed dealing with quickly, but she could not do it now, not with a surveillance team outside. Tomorrow she was back in New York. It would have to be the day of the meeting. A greater risk, but unavoidable. 'It's a big gamble, Clarence, but you must do what your heart tells you.'

'Thanks,' he smiled at her appreciatively.

Grant had become a liability, and was, after all, no longer of use to her. 'I've got to go, now. Think about it, Clarence, and think about the possible consequences.'

They stood and he walked her to the door. Artemis retrieved her coat and turned to face him. 'If you think you *are* being followed, take a circuitous route to and from work, a different route each day. Don't establish any patterns.'

'I'll do that. Thanks for being so understanding.'

He opened the door and the chill of the night air rushed in. She glanced casually across the road and noted that the car was still there. She turned and kissed him on the cheek, lingering a moment longer than if she were just a friend. With any luck the men would think she was just some visiting hooker.

'Goodbye, Clarence. I'll see you again.'

Madison Flynn watched the woman turn the corner and disappear. The two men in the car fifty yards down the road made no attempt to follow her, presumably only interested in Grant himself.

Her instructions from Kramer had been specific: follow Clarence Grant, which she had been doing assiduously for the last six days, sleeping only while he was at work. She now had to make the decision whether to stick with the man from Dramar, or follow the woman.

As the porch light was extinguished Flynn chose the latter option and opened the car door. She walked casually down the street, ensuring she kept a discreet distance between herself and the tall woman with long blond hair. The woman stopped and looked around, before entering a car and pulling away.

Flynn had time to note the license plate, before returning to the warmth of her own car to continue her vigil. She would check out the number in the morning.

Sixteen

The undercarriage of the 747-400 lightly kissed the tarmac of runway 19L at Washington Dulles International Airport, but the impact was enough to rouse Alex from his slumber. Alex glanced at his watch and saw that it was still on UK time, but quickly calculated that the flight was over half an hour late. Still, that wasn't bad considering the chaotic state of air traffic control over America's eastern seaboard. The problem was that there were simply too many flights chasing too few slots, and capacity was still growing. In five years' time there would be total aerial gridlock over Washington and New York, however that was someone else's dilemma. He had his own problems to think about.

The aircraft had to wait a further twenty minutes for a gate to become available at the main terminal, irritating several of the more volatile passengers who had already begun making for the exits, before being told to return to their seats by flight attendants accustomed to dealing with 'difficult' passengers.

When they finally disembarked, Alex saw Leon Baptiste waiting for them at the gate. He had half-expected his American counterpart to have given up and left.

'What the hell sort of time do you call this?' Baptiste was only half joking.

'Blame Yankee Air Traffic Control.'

'Beats the crap outta' anything you Limey's have got.'

'Good to see you too, Leon. This is Samantha Shore. I believe you two met in Wales?'

'Hello,' she said, her voice drowned out by the hubbub of the terminal building.

'Hey, Sammy. Good to see you again.' He offered his hand, which she dutifully shook, and gave him a vague approximation of a smile. 'Your first time in the States?'

'Yes.'

'Then we'll have to make sure we show you a good time. Alex, where you planning on staying?'

'The Dupont Plaza.'

'To hell with that idea. You can stay at my place. Beth's dying to meet you. I told her she's in for one helluva big disappointment.'

Alex rolled his eyes towards the ceiling. Baptiste hadn't changed one bit. The antagonism was relentless.

They made their way to the short-term parking lot and began the journey to Baptiste's salubrious Georgetown address, taking the opportunity to discuss the investigation.

'So, what do you make of those plans, then?' Alex asked, voicing the question he had been aching to ask for the past week.

'I wouldn't read too much into it. I agree it is a little odd, but it isn't the first time that a manufacturer has supplied us with the wrong schematics. I remember an Ilyushin that went down off the Seattle coast a few years back. Had us foxed for weeks until we went to Russia and saw the discrepancy at the factory.'

'You don't think it was deliberate, then?'

'Ha! Not a chance,' Baptiste paused for a moment as he negotiated the labyrinthine interchanges from the Dulles Access Highway onto Interstate 66. 'What makes you say that?'

'Just a funny feeling, that's all.'

'As far as *that's* concerned, Dramar Aerospace are clean. Their finances are another matter, though.'

'Oh?' This was a complete surprise to Alex.

'I've got a friend at the FBI. They've been running a covert investigation into the company's affairs for some time. The Internal Revenue Service have been doing the math and at Gunpowder Falls two and two make five – or, more accurately, three and a half.'

'That's interesting. Who is this friend of yours?'

'Guy named Scott Eagle – special agent in charge of the investigation. If you're free for dinner tonight, I've invited him over. Thought you might like to talk to him.'

'I would.' So Dramar really weren't as squeaky clean as they made out. The DAC Skysystems site just north-east of Baltimore was also the company's financial administration centre, one of Alex's ports of call tomorrow. Whether this fresh piece of information put a new complexion on things, he did not know. Financial irregularities and inaccurate aircraft schematics. Was there a connection? Time would tell.

Alex was looking forward to dinner tonight.

'So you didn't get any pictures, then?' Kramer asked.

Flynn clenched her fists at her sides. What the hell did she have to *do* to please this guy? 'No, it was dark, and if I'd used a flash she would have spotted me.'

'I suppose so,' he grunted dismissively. Photographs would not have been much good for a broadcast anyway, but he would have liked to *see* this woman he was dealing with.

'It shouldn't be too hard to find out who she was. I checked the license plate with a contact at Philly PD. The car is registered to WCN. That's gotta' be our girl.'

'Obviously.' This meant that he would have to talk to Oscar Reece, and after the brush-off he'd given him on the plane to England, Reece might not be too forthcoming. 'Get me a list of all the female reporters and producers at WCN. Pictures too. Think you can handle that?'

'*I'll try*,' she replied in a cynical tone to match Kramer's, leaving the office and closing the door a little more forcefully than was absolutely necessary.

Another thought occurred to him. If Reece and his segment producer were running the story of the crash, where the hell did this woman fit in? It didn't make any sense. He was missing something. There was a big piece of the puzzle that he couldn't see, but Kramer consoled himself with the knowledge that he was, at last, making progress.

Seventeen

Ken Stanley glanced over at the wall isolator to check that it was in the 'off' position before attaching the wires to the detonator. C4 was perfectly safe until exposed to an electrical current. The plastic explosive could even be held over an open flame and it would not explode, just burn with a dull yellow flame. Once he was satisfied that all the necessary safety precautions had been taken he connected the wires to the detonator.

Bernie Cheadle and Damian Beaumont looked on from behind the blast barrier, the pangs of nervousness they had felt after the first few test detonations now banished. This would be the one hundred and seventh test they had conducted on the lower main stringer and they had made little progress over the past week. By varying the quantities of explosive, the distance from the stringer, and the amount of resistant material in between, they should have been able to reproduce the effect of the original bomb on the section of stringer. However, although they had been able to mimic the effect to some degree, there were still discrepancies that they could not account for. The pattern of cratering and the magnitude of destruction were the problem. No matter what they tried, the discrepancies were too pronounced. They had even attempted tests in a depressurized environment, but this had not greatly affected the results.

Stanley joined them inside the protective cubicle and flicked the lever on the isolator. Their 'bomb' was now live and primed. Even he was not immune to the tedious nature of these experiments. 'Three, two, one, fire.' He lifted the safety cover on the control box and pressed the firing switch.

The plastic explosive erupted in a flash of liberated energy, swiftly followed by a cloud of gas and smoke. Fragments of debris rained against the laminated glass screen that protected the three investigators and each of them flinched, despite the number of times they had gone through this procedure.

'Good,' Stanley said with satisfaction, shutting off power to the test area. 'Let's check the results.'

The tattered stringer was badly damaged but still intact.

'That's got to be the closest yet,' Beaumont said optimistically.

'Still not right,' Cheadle replied in a despondent tone. He was losing hope of ever achieving their objective.

'How much explosive did we use this time?' enquired Stanley.

'Two hundred grams at twenty-five centimetres,' Beaumont replied, 'with just the baggage hold alloy between.'

Stanley withdrew a magnifying glass from his lab coat and began to closely examine the material. 'Pitting is dispersed quite a bit, but you're right, Damian, it is the closest that we've come.'

Beaumont surreptitiously glanced at his watch. It was gone seven and his girlfriend was due to come over at eight.

'Go on home, lad,' Stanley said, noticing the young man's agitation. 'You too, Bernie. I'll finish up here.'

The two junior investigators offered half-hearted protests, but eventually left Stanley to his work.

Once he was alone he began the laborious task of cataloguing the results of this latest test, but was just going through the motions, his mind elsewhere.

After one hundred and seven tests, why had they not adequately recreated the effects of the original explosive device? What was it that they were doing wrong? They had used quantities of explosive from two hundred grams to one kilo, which had been a really big bang. They had recreated the effect of the blast wave passing through several layers of luggage, or no luggage at all, with the bomb fitted snugly against the baggage hold. Nothing seemed to work – unless the bomb was not inside the baggage hold after all, but closer to the stringer, with nothing to impede the course of the shock wave.

Stanley stopped what he was doing. Could that be it? Could the answer really be that simple? Since the discovery that a bomb had been responsible for the loss of the aircraft, the entire investigation team had been obsessed with the idea that it had been amongst the luggage, in the number two cargo hold – a psychological legacy of the Lockerbie bombing. What if this assumption was incorrect? He needed to check the wreckage from the baggage hold, which was being kept in the main hangar.

He grabbed his overcoat and made his way over to the aircraft graveyard, as he liked to think of it. The hangar was still illuminated but devoid of people.

On one side a specially designed scaffolding framework had been erected by a local construction firm, and the AAIB engineers had begun to reconstruct the area of the airframe that had been at the centre of the break-up. Many of the internal components had already been attached, including the discrete fragments of the number two cargo hold which was what interested Stanley. Fortunately, none of the skin panels had, as yet, been connected to the framework, which made his inspection easier. A star-shaped pattern of tearing was evident on the compartment bulkhead, and he studied the rips and folds. Someone, ignorant of the importance of the piece, had bent them back roughly into place in order to make all the pieces fit; probably an overzealous amateur at Sennybridge Camp. He concentrated on the fold lines in the alloy. The skin of the bulkhead was blackened, and displayed signs of the blistering heat that it had been subjected to. He removed the magnifying glass and a flashlight from his pocket and looked more closely. The inside appeared double folded, which was promising, and the outside was…

'There it is,' he breathed. Whereas on the inside of the bulkhead the metal had curled over in folds, the outside showed a minute crack running along its length. If the explosion had occurred within the hold, then the cracks should have appeared on the inside of the tear.

He briskly made his way back to the test laboratory to begin a new experiment, switching on one of the wall isolators which would power the control booth. Removing a section of the carbon fibre stringer from the storage rack, Stanley clamped it onto its cradle. He paused momentarily. Strictly speaking he should not be conducting another explosive test alone, but this was too important to be left until morning. The next step was to position the C4 charge above it. How much to use? A hundred grams should be enough to prove, or indeed to disprove his theory. He carefully cut a slice of the plastic explosive from the main block and weighed it before fixing it into position. A four-inch long cylindrical detonator was pushed into the compound and he began to attach the wiring. The green and brown wires were connected—

With the circuit completed, the C4 detonated, hurling the old investigator across the room like a rag doll to be slammed brutally against the unyielding glass screen of the control booth, shattering frail bones and finishing the job that the shock wave had started.

Ken Stanley's heart beat for several seconds more before giving up the uneven struggle to keep his devastated body alive.

Leon Baptiste's house was broadly what Alex had expected: large and ostentatious in the colonial style favoured by many of Georgetown's wealthy inhabitants. Inside, the house was a mixture of styles, reflecting the various tastes of the family. Paintings and miniature replicas of aircraft from different eras stood alongside beautifully intricate tapestries of mid-western farmyard scenes and African statuettes, reflecting the Baptistes' cultural heritage. Children's paintings adorned one corner of the entrance hallway, and images of the family pets dominated many of the walls. It could easily have been a confused mishmash of genres, but Beth Baptiste had successfully gelled it all into a harmonious blend of elements. It must have been her work; Alex knew his NTSB colleague possessed absolutely no artistic inclination.

She had greeted the pair from the AAIB with a warmth that Alex had seldom experienced, and would even be cooking English muffins for breakfast the next morning, just to make them feel at home. Alex thanked her graciously, politely failing to mention that he hadn't eaten English muffins since the last time he was in the States.

After dropping off their luggage they proceeded on to the NTSB's headquarters for a meeting with Dan Cole, the agency's chairman, which went on for almost two hours as Alex explained the progress that his own organization had made, and voiced his concerns about the design of the D500. Cole made no mention of the financial irregularities at Dramar Aerospace, and neither did Alex. It seemed that Baptiste had not even included the head of the NTSB into the small group of people who knew about the FBI operation.

That evening at seven Scott Eagle arrived, and Baptiste introduced his other two dinner guests. Eagle shook their hands firmly, his manner the complete antithesis of the easygoing Baptiste. The dour special agent regarded Alex and Samantha with suspicion, unhappy to discuss his work with anyone outside his own agency, let alone a couple of investigators from a foreign organization.

The conversation over dinner was stilted, despite Beth's attempts to breathe some life into the evening with her jovial banter.

After they had finished the delicious four-course meal and unanimously congratulated their charming hostess, the three accident investigators moved into the study to discuss the situation at Dramar Aerospace with Eagle in a more suitable environment.

The man from the NTSB was the first to break the ice. 'Listen, Scott, don't be an asshole. I told you these guys are all right. Whatever you tell me, you can tell them.' He opened the bottle of twelve-year-old Balvenie that Alex had brought with him and poured four generous glasses. 'Now get some of this down your neck and quit worrying.'

'The operation's been running for about six months,' Eagle began. 'Three months ago we managed to put an agent into their financial department at Gunpowder Falls, Maryland. So far, he hasn't uncovered anything particularly useful. A few questionable practices, but nothing more than any corporation of that size.'

'So how did the Internal Revenue Service become involved?' Alex asked.

'Tax. Dramar have recently adopted a system where capital is moved on a regular basis between DAC Skysoft, DAC Skysystems, and the production plant at Crystal Lake. It all looked fine on the surface, but some of the money was being siphoned off for something or someone else. It's only a tiny percentage, but even a fraction of a percent of a multi-billion dollar turnover amounts to quite a few millions of dollars. It just didn't add up, so that's when the IRS launched a joint investigation with the Bureau.'

'Where do you think the money is going?'

'We haven't a clue. We're talking about fifty million dollars every quarter. I can't see any of the top people at Dramar needing to embezzle *that* kind of money.'

'Have you involved the FAA?'

'Hell, no! We might as well go in there with red flashing lights on our heads. Security within the FAA is… not what it might be.'

Alex concealed his smile by taking a swig from the tumbler of whisky. 'I don't know if it has any relevance, but Dramar don't seem to have been completely honest with *us*.'

This got Eagle's attention.

'Careful Alex,' Baptiste interjected. 'You've got no evidence of wilful deceit on Dramar's part.'

'I know,' Alex waved his hand with irritation. 'I just don't like the feel of it. You may not agree, but don't dismiss the idea out of hand.'

'*What* idea?' Eagle demanded testily.

'The technical schematics of the D500 that Dramar Aerospace originally supplied us with did not correspond to the wreckage we recovered from Wales. When I informed them of the discrepancy, I got this invitation from Douglas Harrington.'

'Harrington? Why would he involve himself? I'd have thought he'd want to distance himself from the investigation as much as possible. He's not a technical guy. From what I understand, he'd have trouble changing a light bulb.'

'That's my point. Another thing that may or may not be related is that Dramar told Pacific Atlantic to fit their D500s with inferior analogue flight recorders. Now any one of these things taken individually is not that noteworthy, but as a whole they are enough to arouse suspicion – my suspicion, anyway.'

'Who have you spoken to about this?'

'No one outside the AAIB except my colleague here from the NTSB and Dan Cole. As yet there's no evidence of—'

Alex was interrupted by the house phone and Baptiste lazily reached across to answer it. 'Hello? Speaking. Just a minute. Alex, it's for you.'

Alex took the receiver from Baptiste, a look of confusion crossing his features. No one in the States would be calling him, and it must be two in the morning in England. 'Jamieson.'

'Alex, it's Stuart Davenport. There's been an accident…'

Eighteen

Clarence Grant double-locked his front door and made a cursory check that all the front windows were firmly secured. The Plymouth hated this cold weather and was even more reluctant to start than usual. After seven attempts the engine resentfully spluttered into life and he pulled away.

A dull feeling of nausea rolled through his stomach and throat. He detested himself for what he was about to do, however his conscience had eventually won the internal conflict. The story of the crash had now been relegated to the back pages, and the British investigators seemed blissfully unaware of the design fault. He had to do *something*.

Diana would understand.

Alex and Samantha arrived at the DAC Skysoft building on Canal Street at nine in the morning, the Investigator-in-charge at the wheel of the NTSB staff car loaned to them by Dan Cole.

The news they had received the previous night had hit them like a hammer blow. Ken Stanley was dead. Alex could not comprehend what the old man had been thinking. To work with high explosives, alone, at night, went against all reason. He must have had some motive, though, which begged the obvious question: what could have seemed so important to the experienced investigator that he would ignore procedures like that?

An elegant but stout wrought iron gate, at least fifteen feet high, by Alex's estimation, blocked the entrance as he stopped at the security office and lowered the window.

'Hi there,' he said in a friendly tone. 'Alexander Jamieson and Samantha Shore, AAIB. We have an appointment with a Ms. Kosinski.'

'Oh, yeah,' replied the uniformed guard who poked his head in the window to study the two guests from England, his eyes remaining on Samantha a fraction longer than was necessary. 'We were told to expect you. Do you have some identification, sir?' He beckoned one of his colleagues who walked over from the squat security checkpoint brandishing a pair of visitors passes.

Alex handed him their passports, which the guard gave more than just a cursory examination.

'That's fine, sir,' he said with an ingratiating smile, returning their passports and handing them the passes. 'Wear these at all times, please. Follow the track around to the main entrance, and Ms. Kosinski should be waiting for you.'

'Thanks.'

The gate swung open automatically and the car moved away slowly, the tires crunching on the thick gravel. Trees lined the roadway, their evergreen branches towering into the atmosphere and creating an arched tunnel that Alex negotiated the car through. The transition from the dirt and pollution of downtown Baltimore to this lush paradise was striking.

'I get the feeling,' he muttered to Samantha, 'that these people have a lot more money than sense. You're the engineering expert here, Sam. You'll have to be my eyes today.' He waited for an acknowledgement, but none seemed to be forthcoming. 'Is that okay?'

'Okay, yes. Sorry, I was miles away. Thinking about Ken.'

'Yeah, me too,' he said. 'We'll deal with that when we get home. Right now we need to stay focused.'

'I'll try.'

Alex looked across and she gave him a small smile.

The track opened out and the building came into view, a large stately home dating from the early nineteen hundreds, which had been tastefully converted and now housed the company's corporate offices. Six yellow stone pillars that matched the masonry of the structure rose as far as the second level, supporting a large section that overhung the entrance.

Standing on the steps stood a tall, slim woman in her early thirties. Masses of auburn curls cascaded over a pale blue business suit, and the unnecessarily high heels accentuated her stature. Standing deferentially a few feet behind her was another uniformed man, this time unmistakably a chauffeur.

Alex brought the car to a halt and they both got out. He proffered his hand to the stunning woman.

'Mr. Jamieson, I presume,' she said in a confident Texas drawl, displaying a set of brilliantly white, perfectly aligned teeth. 'I'm Jacqui Kosinski. Welcome to the corporate headquarters of the Dramar Aerospace Corporation.'

'Thank you. This is Samantha Shore, accident inspector – engineering.'

Samantha shook her hand and nodded with a nervous smile, the Public Relations Officer towering over her.

'I hope you had a pleasant journey across the Atlantic?'

'We did,' Alex replied, hoping to get the pleasantries over with quickly.

'Joe will take your car for you. We've got a helicopter waiting on the pad if you'll follow me.'

The two investigators followed the public relations officer along a path, which led through the trees to the helipad. A Bell 407 – Dramar Aerospace did not produce their own helicopters – emblazoned in the company colours awaited them and they were soon in the air. Once above the level of the trees, Alex could determine the layout of the site. Perfectly manicured gardens surrounded the main building, and at the back of the area stood the DAC Skysoft wing. Within this structure two hundred computer software writers created and updated all of the computer systems used by the company, and also supplied systems to other manufacturers.

'Impressive, isn't it?' Kosinski said to Alex above the sound of the rotors.

'Yes, very,' was all he could think of to say.

'We have an airfield just outside the city,' she explained, 'where we'll transfer to a D220 to make the trip to the factory at Crystal Lake. I'll show you round the plant, then we'll go on to the DAC Skysystems site in Maryland before your meeting with Mr. Harrington and Mr. Koenig.'

'We're looking forward to it,' he said.

The woman began a recitation of the history of the company, and Alex settled down to listen to her lyrical monologue.

Artemis saw the car pass at a steady fifty miles per hour and she pulled away to tail him at a distance. As she expected, the black sedan passed by, the two occupants maintaining a short distance to the Plymouth. There were only a finite number of routes that Grant could take, and she had worked out five separate locations for the hit, once her prey had eluded his pursuers.

Grant came off Interstate 95 at the Claymont junction and proceeded down I-495. She continued along

I-95 and would see him when he rejoined the freeway at Newport. If he had managed to lose his tail, then it would happen at Christiana, while he was still in the state of Delaware.

Once they had transferred from the helicopter to the D220, the flight from Washington had taken just over an hour, the Dramar Aerospace executive jet cruising at an unhurried three hundred miles per hour for most of the journey. The pilot took a wide, sweeping bank as he over-flew the factory, giving the passengers a fine view of the site that stretched into the distance. Half a dozen D500s lined the runway, ready for delivery. Other aircraft, mostly D440s and D460s, seemed to be filling the gaps.

They were immediately driven to the largest structure on the site. To call the assembly wing impressive would have been a masterpiece of understatement. The giant hangar had been constructed specifically to accommodate the D500 program, and the building alone had cost the company over a billion dollars.

Inside, four D500s were under construction, each with a wingspan of over two hundred feet, and yet they appeared almost puny within the giant edifice of the assembly building. All four had been painted in green primer to protect them before they reached the paint shop, a relatively small structure adjoining the main building to the north of where they stood.

'Kind of takes your breath away, doesn't it?' Kosinski said quietly.

Alex simply nodded, words seeming inappropriate.

The aircraft at the centre of the hangar was still in pieces, and the central segment of the fuselage, with the wings already attached, suspended seventy feet above the ground, ready to be lowered into position.

Gantries and stairways surrounded the aircraft, with hundreds of engineers and technicians working directly below the unattached section.

'That's airframe number forty-four,' Kosinski explained. 'At the moment we have an output of five aircraft per month, but we're hoping to increase that figure to eight per month within the next year.'

A passenger tractor arrived and they began a chauffeur driven circuit of the building, Kosinski bombarding them with trivial facts and figures regarding the D500 program.

'This is the first Dramar 'paperless' aircraft, the design being worked out on computer long before a single screw was turned. This meant that we didn't have to bother with expensive and time-consuming mock-ups. Every component was modelled on the computer to test how it would interact with other systems.'

'I see. Were there any problems with the static test aircraft?' Alex knew that there had been, and wished to test the guide.

'Nothing too serious. The carbon fibre horizontal stabilizers *did* develop a crack during endurance testing, so we had to reinforce them with alloy struts. However, you must bear in mind that the static test airframe had been through over one and a half lifetimes of cycles before the crack appeared.'

He glanced at Samantha who simply nodded, confirming the woman's explanation.

'What about the Fuel Management System?' Alex asked. 'I understand there have been some problems there.'

'Oh, you mean that Quamar Airways D500 that had to put down in Abdu Rasaba? Yes, that was actually due to the flight crew draining the port tank too quickly. They still had plenty of fuel to make it to Barakat, but to compound their error they misread the fuel gauges and made the emergency landing. To be fair, the Fuel Management System *was* overcomplicated, so we're simplifying the system.'

Samantha knew that she had also simplified the explanation, but that was understandable, so she kept quiet about it. She would have a word with Alex later.

'Can we have a look at one of the partially completed airframes?' the senior investigator asked.

'Sure, take your pick,' the public relations officer smiled.

'That one.' Alex pointed to the aircraft which seemed to have the most work left to do on it, barring the one in pieces at the centre of the hangar.

Kosinski leant forward and shouted to the driver. 'Take us over to forty-three.'

The shadow car trailed Grant's Plymouth Horizon through the backstreets of Claymont, Bellefonte, and Edgemoor, the twisting roads and frequent turnings making their covert pursuit virtually impossible.

'Where the hell *is* he goin', then?' the driver asked.

'Beats the shit outa' me,' his companion replied. 'Hang back, you dumbass! If he sees us—'

'I know,' the driver acknowledged irritably. 'This doesn't make any sense. D'ya think he knows we're here?'

'Hope to Christ he don't.' The Plymouth took a sharp turn to the right. '*Now* where's he going?'

'Talleyville's in this direction, ain't it?'

The car turned again.

'He's made us. No other explanation.'

The Plymouth indicated right and pulled in to park on the roadside.

'I can't stop here. Too obvious,' the driver said in confusion.

'Carry on and turn around further along.'

The driver followed the advice from his colleague and continued on for a couple of hundred yards before doubling back, but by then the Plymouth had disappeared.

The behemoth loomed above them as the tractor trundled beneath it at a slow but steady pace. As they passed below the starboard wing, minus its two engines that would be connected later, Alex took the time to marvel at its size and complexity. Ninety feet of shining, precision manufactured metal and composite material protruded from the fuselage, and he could not help but think of it as a thing of beauty; technology and aesthetics juxtaposed in perfect harmony, a purely functional device that possessed grace and elegance to rival anything that nature herself could produce. He really did hope that his suspicions would prove to be unfounded. The tractor continued along the fuselage towards the nose of the aircraft, and Alex remembered his walk along the side of another D500 eight days before. That aircraft in the main hangar at Farnborough had not been a thing of beauty, but a monument to the violent death of three hundred and eleven individuals – three hundred and twelve now – and this thought dragged him from his reverie.

The vehicle wove its way carefully between gantries and ladders, the driver gently massaging the controls like a concert pianist. They pulled up at what appeared to be some kind of staging area. A couple of dozen technicians were milling about, presumably waiting to be given the assignments for their shift.

Kosinski saw Samantha staring absently in their direction. 'Dramar Aerospace employs over a hundred and forty thousand staff, who enjoy the best facilities in the business…' She continued expounding the virtues of the company, but by this point neither Samantha nor Alex were really listening.

At the predicted time, the car once again came into view, and a careful study of the following traffic confirmed that Grant had successfully shed his tail. She accelerated and within a few moments was directly behind the Plymouth.

The timing was critical, and she would probably only get the one chance. This situation was far from ideal, however she had little option. She could not afford exposure at this time, the entire operation depending on her anonymity.

Artemis squeezed the accelerator, the car edging closer, and rolled the passenger window down.

Visitors were not normally taken inside the partially completed airframes, so Kosinski and the two investigators had to use the general access ladder, as used by the technicians. The inside of the aircraft was vast, and devoid of any interior furnishings, seemed even more cavernous. They had entered around the mid-section of the aircraft, just aft of the wings. Ahead of him, Alex could see arched beams stretching off into the distance toward the flight deck. If it were not for the number of obstacles blocking the view, he should have been able to see all the way through to the cockpit windows. A riveting machine moved ponderously along the bulkhead, every ten seconds firing a bolt into the superstructure before moving on to repeat the process. The noise within the confined space of the cabin was deafening, and he and Samantha gratefully accepted the earplugs that were handed to them.

'See anything interesting?' he discreetly asked Samantha, not wishing Kosinski to overhear. But the young engineer shook her head.

'With the floor beams in place, there's no way to see the lower stringer. We need to come up from below.'

They exited the airframe and Kosinski arranged to have a forklift raise them to the level of one of the lower maintenance hatches.

An eighteen-inch space separated the pressure hull from the outer skin and Samantha shone a flashlight into the space. The inverted 'V' shape of the stringer was instantly visible along with the KX-7 supports, which were what she really wanted to investigate.

But something was wrong.

She had expected to see a spacing of around eighteen inches, which would match the erroneous schematics they had seen over a week ago, but these appeared to be double that, the same as the wreckage back at Farnborough.

She looked down at her boss, who was waiting expectantly. 'One meter separation, Alex, just like the wreckage.' She saw his face drop, knowing what this meant.

Alex considered the implications of this discovery for a moment. What did it mean? Certainly his embryonic theory that the plans were correct and that it was, indeed, the wreckage that was wrong now lay in tatters. Dramar appeared to have been telling the truth all along, and his fanciful theories regarding a conspiracy by the company now seemed unfounded.

He should have prepared for this eventuality, however he had been so sure – so absolutely sure of himself. Now he would have to approach the meeting with Harrington and Koenig presenting a more affable exterior, and later would be forced to face a very smug Leon Baptiste.

Despite the apparent evidence before him, something still niggled at the back of his mind, but he could not pinpoint exactly what. Ken Stanley's results would have been invaluable, however the old man may now be taking them with him to his grave.

Grant glanced in his mirror and noted the silver Ford begin the overtaking manoeuvre, his foot releasing the pressure on the accelerator by a fraction.

Artemis removed the Sig P226 from the space beneath her seat and held the automatic pistol at arm's length, but kept it below the level of the window. With her attention focused on this task, she had failed to notice that the

Plymouth's speed had dropped, meaning that she was now passing it at a faster rate than she had intended.

Grant looked across as the silver car drew level. His eyes met those of the driver and a look of recognition was swiftly followed by confusion, a puzzled but polite smile crossing his features. His eyes darted back to the road ahead to check the positions of the traffic in front of him.

She lifted her arm by ten degrees and fired three shots in quick succession before burying the throttle, catapulting the car forward.

The first bullet entered his cranium through the left temple and exploded out of the right to leave the car through the far window. Grant was already dead when the second projectile punched a hole through his neck to follow the first. The third shot went high, a result of the disparity in speed between the two vehicles and her subsequent lack of preparation time, the shot ricocheting off the door frame and ending its short journey buried in the passenger door on the far side of the car.

The worst case scenario would have been for the Plymouth to veer left into her own car and directly involve her in the 'accident', but it continued ahead. Keeping a careful eye in her mirror, Artemis saw that the car was maintaining its course, but was accelerating, Grant's dead weight pushing down on the gas pedal. It slowly drifted across the four-lane highway as the road arced to the right.

When the front wheel hit the barrier the tire exploded, sending the car out of control. The impact initially pushed it to the right before the missing wheel forced it back to the left, the second collision much more violent than the first. Other drivers on the freeway belatedly realized what was happening, and swerved to avoid the vehicle as it careered along.

Hitting the barrier one last time the old Plymouth was spun around, flipping over when the two right tires found some purchase and bit the tarmac. It somersaulted through the air, and the nose hit the ground heavily, splitting the car in two and launching the engine skyward to crash onto the opposite carriageway, causing mayhem with the northbound traffic. The remains of the vehicle rolled several times, each impact with the unyielding ground increasing the damage until it eventually came to a halt, the corpse within battered to such an extent that it was barely recognizable as having been human.

Artemis reduced her speed to a sedate fifty miles per hour and continued serenely on, moderately satisfied with her morning's work.

The Tin Kicker

Nineteen

A lex spent the flight from Crystal Lake pondering the issue of the KX-7s, and said little during the journey.

The DAC Skysystems site at Gunpowder Falls was much smaller than Crystal Lake, but no less impressive, however as the afternoon wore on Alex found himself wishing to get things over with.

'These guys are the real magicians,' Kosinski whispered reverentially. 'Our computational fluid dynamicists aren't *among* the best in the world, they *are* the best in the world. We've followed a tradition by concentrating our design teams on improving aerodynamic efficiency, rather than depending upon the engine supplier to simply produce higher power output. The better the aerodynamics, the better the fuel consumption, the better for the environment, which is essential in today's market economy. Our co-founder, Samuel Drake, was probably the world's first true aerodynamicist. He had an intuitive feel for how air moves around a wing.'

Alex nodded appreciatively. He knew the history, and Sam Drake had, indeed, been a genius.

'This is Claude Brodeur. He's the senior aerodynamicist at DAC Skysystems,' Kosinski introduced the striking West Indian scientist. The man looked up from his computer console, two-foot-long dreadlocks swinging from side to side as if with a life of their own.

'Claude, this is Alex Jamieson and Samantha Shore from the AAIB.'

'Hi,' the scientist said, gleaming teeth revealed behind a genuine smile. 'You've come at just the right time. Take a look at this.' He pointed to the monitor.

The investigators looked at what appeared to be a section of an aircraft fuselage with computer generated 'smoke' trails running over it. Brodeur moved the mouse to one of the peripheral icons and the image shrunk to reveal more of the aircraft, now unmistakably a D500.

'You see how the airflow is disturbed once it passes the cockpit section?'

'Yes.' Samantha said, feeling this was closer to her field of expertise than her superior's.

'Well look at this.' He clicked the mouse again and two tiny red 'horns' appeared just aft of the flight deck windows. Immediately the airflow looked smoother. 'Those winglets smooth the flow and redirect some of it down. Smoother airflow equals less power requirement, which in turn equals lower fuel consumption. What do you think?'

'Looks impressive,' Samantha said with genuine admiration, trying to assimilate what she was seeing, 'but if the airflow is being vectored down, wouldn't that affect some of the movement over the wings?'

'You don't miss much, do you? Yeah, but that's just a question of integrating the two. It'll need some more tweaking but we should be able to include the winglets on the next generation of D500s.'

Samantha was as impressed by the man's enthusiasm as she was by this design innovation.

'That's brilliant, Claude,' Kosinski interjected, obviously feeling a little excluded from the conversation, accustomed as she was to being the centre of attention. 'Should give the guys at Boeing something to think about, eh?'

She moved them on to see some of the other sections of the design shop. 'Computational fluid dynamics is just one tiny aspect of the design process. This is where cooperation with our customers is vitally important. During the design of the D500, the airlines we deal with offered all kinds of ideas, which we were happy to take on board.'

Alex felt they were getting the full sales blurb and, despite the charm and sexual appeal of his guide, was looking forward to their meeting with Harrington. She was still talking, but Alex had mentally switched off again, merely nodding occasionally and laughing when he sensed she had cracked some puerile joke.

Samantha was not even bothering with that level of courtesy. The only thing that she had found of interest today was her conversation with Brodeur, but the airhead tour guide had soon put a stop to that.

After the death of Ken Stanley, they both found it hard to stay focused. One thing was certain: if Dramar Aerospace had contributed to his death, Alex Jamieson would get them.

The helicopter came to rest on one of two pads at DAC Skysoft on Canal Street in Washington, and the two weary investigators followed the unflagging PRO into the main building's front entrance.

The elevator doors slid open and Alex and Samantha found themselves staring down a long, spacious hallway. The lighting was more subdued than in the reception area, and the young engineer became aware of the scent of freshly cut flowers, but could not, as yet, identify the source of the aroma. They walked slowly down the passage, Kosinski speaking in hushed tones, as if to speak aloud in this inner sanctum were an inviolable taboo. After passing a number of closed doors on either side, they arrived at a crossroads and for the first time in over an hour, Alex actually took the trouble to listen as she spoke.

'Directly ahead of us is the boardroom, to the right is the lounge area where informal meetings are held and visitors entertained, and to the left is Mr. Harrington's office where we are to meet the chief executive.' She motioned for them to stay where they were as she walked over to speak to one of the secretaries.

Alex looked around, taking in the full scene. Chandeliers hung from the ceiling and original paintings of aerial scenes adorned the walls. A lavish floral display dominated the node, which explained the scent they had detected upon arriving on the top floor a few moments earlier.

He had seldom in his life experienced such an unashamed display of opulence; money and power obviously being used to impress and at the same time intimidate the chosen few who were invited into this area. Although his remuneration from the AAIB was by no means insubstantial, Alex had not been born into wealth, and found affluence flaunted in such an arrogant manner distasteful.

Kosinski returned and informed them that "Mr. Harrington" was now ready to see them. The secretary led the pair to the office and opened the door.

'Mr. Jamieson, I am so very pleased to meet you. My name is Douglas Harrington.'

'Alex Jamieson, and this is my engineering specialist, Samantha Shore.'

Samantha shook the proffered hand.

'I trust Jacqui here gave you the full tour?'

'I think we've seen enough,' Alex said cautiously. He was still unsure as to why they had been given the tour in the first place, unless all this was just a pantomime designed to allay his suspicions. Perhaps…

'If there is anything else you would like to see, then don't hesitate to speak to Jacqui after the meeting. She is completely at your disposal for the rest of the day.'

'Thank you,' was all he could think of to say.

'Good. Now, shall we go through to the lounge and discuss your investigation?'

'Certainly.' Could all this merely be an excuse for Harrington to pick his brains? Surely a man as powerful as this had his own discreet sources of information, and the chief executive would know that a senior AAIB investigator was legally bound not to reveal anything that was not already in the public domain. Something about this entire situation just did not add up, and he felt a sense of unease rising within him.

The secretary led the two of them to the lounge and opened the door, while Kosinski remained in Harrington's office. Obviously, she was not to be privy to what would be discussed during the meeting. The room was decorated in a pleasant Edwardian style, with not a hint of the nature of the company's business on show. Alex found this mildly surprising. Boeing and Airbus Industrie always seemed to be falling over themselves to remind anyone and everyone of just what it was that they actually produced.

'Take a seat, Mr. Jamieson, Miss Shore.' Harrington gestured to the elegant chairs that formed a circle around a low mahogany table. 'Greg Koenig will be with us soon. Would you like coffee or tea?'

'Coffee would be fine,' Alex answered.

Harrington sent the secretary away, leaving the AAIB Investigators alone with the chief executive. 'Now tell me, Mr. Jamieson: how is the investigation going?

You understand, of course, the gravity of the situation and the effect that this disaster is having on our company.'

'Yes, I do understand, but you must appreciate that I have to be careful what I say at this stage. As things stand, we have discovered that an improvised explosive device was used to destroy the aircraft.' Alex looked into the older man's eyes as he spoke, attempting to fathom his motives, but the chief executive simply stared back impassively. 'C4 was the explosive used, and it was contained within the number two cargo hold. To be frank, there's still a lot that we don't know. The investigation is an ongoing process.'

'It cannot be easy. There is one thing I really do need to know,' Harrington paused, clearing his throat before continuing. 'Was there any aspect of the design or manufacture of the plane that could have contributed to the disaster? Dramar Aerospace has staked its future on the D500, and I have the livelihoods of a hundred and forty thousand people to consider.'

Alex spoke slowly, cautiously searching for the right words. 'There is no evidence, at this juncture, to suggest that there was any deficiency in the design or construction of Flight 4401.' It was time to put Harrington on the spot. 'Is there anything that *you* are aware of that may have been a contributing factor?'

Harrington shook his head slowly. 'No, nothing. As far as we are aware,' he smiled, 'the D500 is a perfectly sound airplane. I just needed to hear you confirm this.'

'It wasn't a confirmation. I said there was no evidence.'

'That's—'

A knock on the door announced the arrival of Koenig, immediately followed by the receptionist bearing a tray of coffee and light pastries.

'That's good enough for me, for the time being. Greg Koenig – Alex Jamieson of the AAIB, and his assistant: Miss Samantha Shore.'

The investigator stood and shook the designer's hand. 'Good to meet you at long last, Mr. Koenig.'

'Likewise, Mr. Jamieson.' He handed Alex a hefty looking briefcase. 'These are the *correct* schematics for the D500, on hard copy as well as in digital form. I hope this will clear up the misunderstanding.'

'As do I.' He opened the case and peered inside at the three-inch thick folder.

Harrington spoke up. 'Mr. Jamieson was just telling me that he believes the D500 to be a sound airplane. That's good news, don't you think?'

'Very good. I had no idea that your investigation was far enough along for you to make a judgement like that.'

The designer possessed none of his superior's charisma, and Alex could feel the man sizing him up; testing his reactions. 'The investigation is progressing at a steady pace, but apart from the evidence of an explosive device, we have not reached any conclusions yet.'

'The death of your metallurgy expert must have been quite a blow. My condolences. Will it have much of an effect on the investigation?'

How the hell did he know about that? News of the accident had not, as yet, been released publicly. Alex tried not to let his emotions show. 'Ken Stanley was an outstanding investigator, and a good friend. He will be greatly missed, but the investigation *will* continue without him.'

'That's good to hear.' Koenig allowed a furtive glance in Harrington's direction, and for the briefest of instants, Alex thought he detected a hint of a smile on the designer's lips.

He'd been set up. Koenig had needed confirmation of Stanley's death, and Alex had just inadvertently provided him with it. There was little doubt in his mind that this information would now be leaked to the press, and the unwelcome attention of the media could throw the investigation into disarray – unless he could find a way to avert it.

'Changing the subject,' Samantha intervened, sensing the air of hostility that had descended upon the room, 'could you now clarify something for me?'

'I'll try,' Koenig replied with a gracious smile.

'What *is* the correct spacing for the KX-7 supports?'

'Ah, yes. One metre throughout their length, as is shown in the plans I have just given you.'

'I see,' Samantha nodded. 'Why did the original plans show them to be so much closer?'

'Originally we'd thought that the extra strength that they provided would be necessary, but subsequent testing of the upper and lower main stringers indicated that the extra supports were superfluous. I'm afraid there was just a simple mix-up and some of the earlier designs got left in.' The technical director let out a brief burst of awkward laughter. 'Just one of those things, I guess.'

'Accidents will happen.' Alex stared at the rim of his cup, assiduously ignoring the designer's gaze. Something about his demeanour was not right. The man seemed nervous, defensive, and ill at ease. A degree of apprehension would have been understandable, but Koenig's unease seemed to border on the neurotic. Harrington, on the other hand, displayed the cool confidence of a man who was completely comfortable with the situation.

Alex took a sip from his coffee as he formulated the next question. 'I was a little surprised to learn that Pacific Atlantic had opted for analogue flight recorders on their D500 fleet. I'd have thought that digital units would have been more appropriate, wouldn't you?'

'Well, as you know,' Harrington said, setting his cup and saucer on the table, 'digital recorders are a lot more expensive, and at the end of the day the choice is down to the airline.'

'Indeed it is, but on a brand new wide-body jet?'

'It is, perhaps, a little odd, so I suggest you contact Pacific Atlantic and ask them.'

'We did. They said they were acting on your advice.'

Harrington allowed himself a small chuckle. 'I don't know where they got that from. It really would make little sense for us to make a recommendation like that.'

'One would think so,' Alex paused, 'unless Dramar wanted to hinder a crash investigation.'

They sat in silence for a few seconds, the only sound being the muffled rumble of traffic filtering through the window, and Koenig's laboured breathing from the chair to Alex's right.

'Mr. Jamieson,' Harrington leant forward, 'if that is an accusation you are making, then it is a serious one, and I suggest—'

'It was not an accusation, merely... a thought,' Alex interrupted, and drained the last of the coffee from his cup, never taking his eyes from the chief executive's.

'Thoughts like that can be dangerous. Now, naturally we like to cooperate with the AAIB and CAA, but if you make wild allegations of that nature in public, then we will have to involve our lawyers. I don't think either of us want that, do we?'

'Of course not,' Alex replied, smiling without humour. 'If news of Ken Stanley's death is released prematurely, though, it may be unavoidable.'

Harrington considered this for a moment. 'I think you can rest assured that no information on that subject will come from us. You have my guarantee. More coffee?'

'Please.' Hopefully, that was one potential disaster averted.

The meeting lasted for a further twenty minutes before they left. Kosinski led them to the NTSB car and watched as Alex negotiated his way out of the administration building's car park and through the trees.

Once they were well on their way back to Washington he called Leon Baptiste and briefly described the day's events.

'You see?' Baptiste said. 'I told you there was nothing going on.'

'I don't care,' Alex replied edgily. '*Something's* not right. I'll tell you about it when I get back.'

Twenty

'Jesus, what a mess,' Detective Karl Vance said to the traffic cop. Wreckage had been strewn over the full width of the southbound highway, but some had now been cleared away, allowing one lane to be re-opened. At its worst the tailback had stretched eight miles, almost to the west Wilmington junction, but as traffic was now being diverted along Interstate 495 and the trapped vehicles filtered through the one available southbound lane, the jam now stretched for just five miles. Even so, it was still a major headache for the State Highway Patrol.

'It certainly is that, sir,' the uniformed man replied. 'Happened about eleven this morning.'

'It's a big accident, I know, but I don't see why I had to be called in.'

'Well, it looks like it could be a case for homicide.'

Vance gave the sergeant a dubious look. 'How'd you work that out?' he asked, the irritation clear in his voice. Four days without a smoke certainly wasn't improving his disposition.

'Have a look at this.' The traffic cop led him over to the largest chunk of wreckage that remained on the freeway. Vance poked his head into the irregularly shaped hole, which, a couple of hours before had been the front passenger's window.

'JESUS CHRIST!' he yelled, yanking his head from the window. 'Couldn't you have cleared that up first?' The detective gagged into his handkerchief, just managing to retain his lunch.

'Sorry, sir,' the sergeant apologized. 'We didn't want to disturb anything until forensics had finished going over it.'

Vance took several deep breaths to settle his stomach. 'Okay, what am I supposed to be looking at?'

The junior man pointed to the inside of the doorframe. 'There's a bullet lodged just about here.'

Vance's eyes followed the man's finger and saw what he was indicating. He looked across to the driver's door, ignoring the brutalized corpse. 'Any of the glass from the driver's window left?'

'Yeah, it stretches for about two hundred yards down the freeway,' was the cynical reply, 'but there is a mark on the other frame that looks like it could've been caused by a gunshot.'

Vance moved around to the other side of the hulk and gave the mark a cursory examination. 'Yeah, looks like you're right.' He slowly strolled down the freeway to the point where the 'accident' was believed to have begun, the sergeant walking silently alongside.

'Look up there,' Vance gestured towards the embankment that enclosed Interstate 95 along that stretch of the road. 'If there was someone taking pot shots from up there, then a bullet hitting the top of the window frame would be deflected downwards, *not* across.'

The sergeant was confused. 'So?'

'So unless this gunman was sitting on the side of the freeway, the shot had to come from another vehicle, and that sounds like a professional hit to me.' Vance smiled dryly. 'This wasn't just your average, everyday drive-by shooting. This was an execution.'

Madison Flynn gently replaced the receiver in its cradle and exhaled heavily. 'Well, well, well.'

'Well?' Kramer demanded.

'Well,' she replied at length, 'that was my contact at Philly PD. The car was registered to WCN, all right, and in particular to a researcher named Nicholas Romani. But get this: there was a car accident on I-95 today. Guess who just died?'

'Romani?'

'Guess again.'

'Not Grant?'

She nodded with a smile. 'Bit of a coincidence, don't you think?'

Kramer did not answer. Grant was being – had been – covertly followed by security staff from Dramar, and if they had found out that he was selling company secrets, then it was perfectly conceivable that *they* had killed him. Not for an instant did he believe that the car crash was an accident, but what company information could be so sensitive as to require the death of one of their own designers? 'Did you get those photos I asked for?'

'Right here.' She tossed a flash drive over to him. 'These are our files on all the principal and secondary staff at WCN. Romani is in there, but the woman I saw the other night isn't. I've made checks on just about every woman who works for the station, right down to secretaries and even cleaners. No good. I tried other stations and freelancers, too, just in case Mr. Romani wasn't being entirely honest with his employers. Still nothing.'

'Our mystery lady becomes ever more mysterious,' Kramer muttered. His earlier conversation with Oscar Reece at the rival station had also been fruitless, his opposite number being less than cooperative, although he suspected that the reporter knew as little about her identity as he did. For now, they would have to concentrate their efforts on the researcher. 'What do we know about this guy?'

Flynn removed the personnel file from the folder. 'Nicholas Romani: originally from Brazil – São Paulo to be precise. Recent immigrant. Started working for WCN two months ago. Lives alone in downtown DC, but has numerous… shall we say female companions? Educated at the University of São Paulo. Worked for three years—'

'Quite a ladies man, then?' Kramer interrupted, looking his segment producer up and down several times. 'I think I may have another little job for you. You're not the shy type, I trust?'

She smiled. 'Would you be proposing a honey trap of some kind, Lewis?'

'With a sting in the tail.'

The politics of a murder investigation such as this were a nightmare. Clarence Grant had been travelling from Cherry Hill, a suburb of Philadelphia in Pennsylvania, to DAC Skysystems where he worked in Gunpowder Falls, just north of Baltimore, Maryland, but had been killed on the short stretch of Interstate 95 that passed through the northern spur of Delaware. Not one of the local law enforcement agencies really wanted the case, preferring to attribute it to an audacious drive-by shooting, with Grant merely in the wrong place at the wrong time.

Vance didn't believe a word of that, and had spent the past two days fighting to be assigned the case, but had eventually been told that due to the 'unique' nature of the death, it was now to be taken over by the FBI. He'd spent a large part of that afternoon turning the air blue in his captain's office as a result, but to no avail. The Feds *would* be taking over.

But he was not a man to be put off so easily. He was sure that this was not just some random killing. Thirty years of homicide investigations had heightened his sense of intuition, and he was not wrong, of that he was certain. Thankfully, during those thirty years he had forged reciprocal alliances with operatives from various agencies in the Maryland, Pennsylvania, and Delaware regions. One of these was from the Baltimore field office of the FBI, and he had managed to get himself 'invited' to inspect Grant's house. What he had not expected was that for some reason the Bureau was investing some serious resources into the case.

When he arrived at the house in the quiet, leafy suburb of Cherry Hill, he found that it had been completely sealed off, and more than twenty agents were swarming over the property. Who the hell had this guy been? Aircraft designers were not normally accorded this kind of treatment, alive *or* dead.

After a brief but heated argument with the agents guarding the door, he was permitted to enter the building, but would have to remain escorted at all times – not the sort of welcome that a detective of thirty years standing would normally expect.

Once inside, the FBI agents eyed him with suspicion, as FBI agents always did, but on this occasion the mistrust seemed even more focused than usual.

'Vance, up here,' a familiar voice beckoned him from the top of the stairway.

'Burnett,' he shook the Philadelphia field agent's hand when he finally made it up the short flight of stairs, his breathing laboured, and was surprisingly pleased to see a familiar face. He had not had a smoke for six days now, and was impatiently awaiting this fitness dividend that all the reformed smokers he knew were always telling him would make his life so much better.

'What the hell is goin' on here? We start off with a nice little murder on I-95, next thing I know, the Bureau takes over and all this shit starts hittin' the fan.' He gestured to the agents in sight.

'Keep it down.' Special agent Gerard Burnett pulled Vance aside so they could talk a little more privately. 'The Washington office has taken over. Philadelphia doesn't know what is going on. Rumour has it that the director himself is taking a personal interest in this one.'

'Stone? Who was this guy, a friend of his?'

Burnett looked around nervously. 'It may go a little higher up than that.' He spoke so quietly that Vance had to strain to hear him. 'I got a look at the financing for this case. It's part of an ongoing investigation.'

'So where is the money coming from, then?' Vance had little time for this cloak and dagger stuff.

'It pretty much amounts to a blank cheque, and the Executive Office is picking up the tab.' Burnett glanced around again to make sure no one had overheard him.

'Presidential approval? Jesus, that ups the stakes a bit. A friend of the President's, then?'

'What would Bob Archer be doing with an aircraft designer from Philadelphia?' Burnett asked rationally, shaking his head. 'Besides, this investigation has been going on since long before Grant was killed.'

'Good point. So, what does that leave us with?'

'Maybe he was involved in something a lot bigger than he could handle. Mafia; drugs, perhaps.'

'If it was just Director Stone we were talkin' about I'd say yeah, but not the White House.' A pair of forensics agents walked past and the conversation was halted for a few moments, giving Vance a brief opportunity to think. Once they were well out of earshot, he continued. 'There's nothin' we can do about that, now. What have you found in the house?'

'Loads of stuff in one of the bedrooms from Dramar, but that'll take weeks to go through.'

'Maybe the guy used to get off on pictures of planes.'

'No, this is all technical stuff. Designs, memos, lists, part numbers, that kind of thing.'

'Secret stuff?' Vance asked, an embryonic idea forming in his mind.

'Maybe. Yeah, I guess so.' Burnett would not know one way or the other, but presumed no manufacturer would want technical information like that to get out.

'So what if,' Vance ventured, 'this guy Grant was selling stuff to a rival? Maybe Boeing or the Europeans, and Dramar found out. They had to stop him somehow…' He shrugged his shoulders, leaving the sentence unfinished.

'So instead of firing him, like any normal firm, they put a contract out on him. Come on, Vance, that's a bit of a leap.' Burnett made no attempt to conceal his cynicism.

'Maybe they couldn't just fire him. If we're talkin' about company secrets, anything's possible. Anyway, a workin' theory is better than no theory at all.' Vance knew that the FBI agent could not argue with that logic.

'Okay, so it's a theory. I'm not sure I can sell it as 'working', but I'll put it to the guys upstairs. You'd better go, and don't forget that what we've spoken about today stays between *us*. Got it?'

'Got it. I'll see myself out.'

'No, you won't.' Burnett escorted him from the building and into his car, making sure the police officer's Pontiac had actually disappeared around the corner before he returned to the house.

Twenty-One

The bar on Connecticut Avenue was one of those chrome and glass establishments with pastel colours, soft lighting, and comfortable seats. The staff were smartly attired and polite in that formal manner, but completely devoid of character.

As was the case with many such places in Washington, Brookes' Bar was emptier on a Friday night than any other during the week, the bulk of their trade being affluent businessmen and women, or white collar government employees who were wealthy enough not to have to live within the capital.

The usual early evening rush had now dissipated as lawyers, government employees, media workers, consultants and advisers, architects and designers, joined the headlong charge to escape the choking city, leaving barely a dozen people in the bar.

Romani drained the last of the beer from his glass and beckoned the barman, who reluctantly tore himself away from the group of teenage girls out for their first drink of the evening. Brookes' Bar was never more than a meeting point for these kids, the bright lights and thundering music of the city's night-clubs a much more appealing attraction. The barman cracked the lid off the bottle of Molson and spun it through three hundred and sixty degrees. The resulting whistles and giggles from the group showed that he might be in luck later that evening. For a few moments Romani considered going over to the girls, but then thought better of the idea. He did not want some outraged father to come searching for him later.

Looking in the mirror behind the bar, he noted the door opening and glanced around, his eyes quickly darting forward again. Perhaps tonight would not be a total waste after all.

The woman came straight to the bar without looking right or left, so she was probably not meeting anyone here, he surmised, and that usually meant only one thing. She perched on the stool to his left, and since she'd had the barman's attention since the moment she had walked in, ordered a dry Martini with ice and a twist straightaway. Romani clicked his fingers and the young man behind the bar reluctantly pulled his eyes away from the new arrival.

'I'll get that,' he said simply, smiling to her and permitting his eyes to drift briefly downward, giving him the briefest of opportunities to appreciate the insubstantial black dress clinging to her slender curves.

'Why, thank you,' she uttered in a suggestively deep tone as she turned to face him. Beams of reflected light shot along every silken fold in the dress, and a thinly stockinged leg came up to cross over the other, a five-inch patent leather stiletto in full view.

'Nick Romani,' he said, offering his hand.

'You can call me Madison,' Flynn said, allowing him to gently shake her hand.

'I haven't seen you in here before,' he ventured.

'Just visiting. Here for a computer conference.' She sipped at the Martini, wishing she could drink more tonight, but had to keep her wits about her.

'Have you been to Washington before?' he asked.

'Yeah, a couple of times. You don't sound like a native, though.'

'I've been living in DC for a couple of months. Originally from São Paulo, Brazil.'

'Ah,' her eyes sparkled. 'Is it true, then, what they say about the Latin temperament?'

He allowed a brief, subdued laugh, and inched his bar stool a little closer until their legs were touching. 'Well, I'll let you decide that for yourself.'

Flynn finished her Martini a little more swiftly than she'd intended. 'Oh, my glass seems to be empty. Are you having another?'

He finished his own beer and clicked his fingers again to get the barman's attention, not taking his eyes from Flynn's. 'Molson for me,' he said, 'and a large Martini for the lady.'

Flynn reached into her handbag for her lipstick and a small vial of white powder, which she surreptitiously kept concealed in the palm of her hand. As she appeared to fumble with the lipstick it fell to the floor.

'Shit,' she mumbled, and made to move from the stool to retrieve it.

Romani, ever the gentleman, held up a hand and reached down to get it, his eyes moving along the long, shapely legs.

Flynn took the opportunity to drop half a gram of Amphetamine Sulphate into the bottle of beer, the fine powder slowly cascading through the alcohol, but obscured by the brown smoked glass. When Romani emerged from beneath the bar he placed the lipstick in her hand, and poured the beer into his glass. He failed to notice that the Molson was a touch cloudier than usual.

They talked for a while, Romani becoming progressively more loquacious, not to mention amorous, and Flynn was finding it difficult controlling the man. For the umpteenth time, she removed his marauding hand from her breast.

'Come on, Nick,' she giggled, 'what *are* these other business interests of yours, then?'

'Well...' he said drunkenly, running the chastised hand up her leg and inside her dress. 'It's big, honey. Really big. Biggest thing I've ever been involved in. Big, big, big. But it's a secret, so I can't tell. A big, big secret.' The index finger of his free hand was raised and swayed in front of his lips for a few moments.

Flynn could see that his pupils were now dilated, and was beginning to wonder whether she would get *anything* of use out of lover-boy here.

'It all revolves around... Diana. Diana, Diana, Diana. My good friend Diana.'

'Okay, so Diana's your friend.' Flynn was becoming exasperated. 'Is she a reporter?'

'A reporter,' Romani earnestly considered this for a moment. 'Yeah. Yeah, okay, she's a reporter.'

Flynn began to sense that she might be onto something, so she let the errant hand explore her stocking tops without argument. 'So Diana's a reporter. Who does she work for?'

Romani seemed to be deep in thought. 'Diana – Diana works for Diana.'

Flynn was about to pull the hand away.

'Diana is the leader.'

'The leader of what? An organization?'

'No – no – no – no – no.'

Flynn looked into those drunken eyes and attempted to ignore the hand as it continued to probe. A Pulitzer Prize was beckoning. 'Where might,' the hand slipped inside her panties, 'where might I find Diana?' she asked, keeping her voice even, despite the probing fingers.

'No one *finds* Diana,' he slurred, the mixture of Amphetamines and alcohol working against one another. 'No one except me.'

Her hand, until now employed purely to grasp the Martini, moved up his leg, the motion eliciting a groan of anticipation from him. 'You can tell me,' she said softly.

'Why do you want to know?' he asked, suddenly suspicious.

'Come on, Nicky. Aren't we supposed to be getting to know each other?' she breathed into his ear, moving her hand slowly and sensually in a rhythmic motion. 'But if you want me to stop…'

'No!' he said in a panicked voice, and then dissolved into giggles. 'Diana is… She's a babe.'

'But where can I find her?' Flynn pleaded, the urgency now plain in her voice.

'I don't know,' he shook his head loosely. 'Try her apartment.'

'Her apartment? Where's that?' She removed her hand and noted the look of dismay on his face with satisfaction.

'Okay, okay. New York. East 83rd Street. One of the old blocks on the Upper East Side. I don't know which. Will you carry on now?'

She removed his hand from within her dress. 'I don't think so. Sweet dreams, lover-boy.' She kissed him fully on the lips, but pulled away as she felt the searching tongue clumsily emerge from his mouth.

Madison Flynn gathered her belongings and left Romani to stare glumly after her as she disappeared.

Once she was gone he ordered another beer, and moved haltingly over to the group of giggling girls, much to the chagrin of the barman.

Romani blearily awoke on Saturday morning. He glanced at his watch, his eyes taking several seconds to focus on the numbers and he groaned, remembering that he should have been in work early that morning. A naked girl lay next to him, her chest rising and falling slowly as she breathed softly in her sleep. How old was she? Seventeen? Certainly no more than eighteen. More to the point: where the hell had she come from? He was damned if he could remember anything about last night. Never mind. It would probably come back to him later.

It never did.

Twenty-Two

'Flaps and slats now fully retracted,' Davenport said from the right-hand seat. 'Slight crosswind coming from the right.'

'FMC is compensating,' Alex said, to his left, as he piloted the airliner through the lower atmosphere, but the D500's Flight Management Computer was doing the real work, making minute adjustments to the aircraft's trim. 'Passing through 2-0-0,' he said as the jet reached twenty thousand feet and continued to climb.

All seemed well with the aircraft as it pierced the night sky, the only view from the cockpit windows the impenetrable blackness of the evening. Several more minutes passed before either man spoke.

'Passing through 2-5-0,' Davenport glanced across at the captain of the flight. 'Not long now.'

Alex was keeping one eye on the computer generated navigational display of the D500's 'glass cockpit'. 'Leaving Heathrow approach control. Okay, now getting the data-burst from Swanwick Air Traffic Control.'

'Passing through 2-8-0. Here it comes.' Davenport gripped the armrests on his chair.

They both started as they felt a slight jolt. A depressurization alarm began to ring, followed by others: a fire alarm, hydraulic pressure alarm, electrical failure alarm, an American voice saying in an urgent tone, 'STALL! STALL! STALL!'

Both control columns shot forward. 'Sticks forward and shaking!' Alex shouted over the noise of the warning klaxons and the shaking of the cockpit. Every indicator on the flight deck was flashing red. The nose of the plane was pitching up, and there was not a damned thing they could do about it.

Then the lights went out.

Then the lights came back on again, and the simulator returned to its normal horizontal position.

'You two still alive in there?' enquired the excited voice of Les Thompson.

Alex pressed the transmit button. 'Still in one piece, Les. Please standby.'

The two pilots sat rigidly in their seats, Davenport the first to break the silence. 'Quite a ride. Poor bastards never had a chance.'

'Makes you stop and think, doesn't it?' Alex took several deep breaths before unbuckling his seatbelt.

Faye Beresford and Samantha Shore had been monitoring the systems from the control booth, while Thompson had watched in fascination as the flight deck unit bucked and rolled and pivoted as it did its best to recreate the violent motions of Flight 4401, the information from the Flight Data Recorder having been fed into the simulator. The access gangplank was slowly lowered until it met the door of the simulator module and Thompson had begun to make his way along its length, even before it was in position. He was ebullient as the pilots emerged, shaking both by the hand to congratulate them, but was surprised by their sombre demeanour. Unlike the majority of personnel at the AAIB he was not a pilot, and failed to grasp the emotional impact that such an exercise could evoke. They had both flown seemingly countless thousands of hours in passenger jets, and knew that the event that had just been recreated could so easily have happened to them for real.

Alex swiftly put the simulator experience behind him and moved on to other matters. The rest of the team would remain at the BOA Flight Training Facility at Heathrow for the remainder of the afternoon, Davenport trying a variety of different procedures to test whether the break-up could be avoided, or at least delayed, and every test would be monitored and recorded. Alex had a date with a sadly neglected virtual in-tray at his office in Farnborough.

Oh, he thought, the never-ending glamour of an air crash detective's life. But Sunday was just a couple of days away, and he would finally get a distraction from the investigation.

He could hardly wait.

At seven-thirty, the sun finally crept above the level of the trees and a brilliant shaft of light pushed its way through the gap in the curtains to fall lazily onto the thickly carpeted floor. The elongated rectangle of light gradually moved across the room until it met the bed, where it came into contact with his naked arm as it hung limply over the side of the mattress. The warmth penetrated his skin, and began its slow assault on his subconscious.

Alex forced his eyes open.

It was Sunday, his first day off for three weeks, and by God, he was determined to enjoy it. He had arranged to visit his brother's family for lunch, and he was looking forward to seeing Tom and Tara again. Tom had always been a stabilizing influence on his life, and the family had given him vital emotional support during the separation and divorce.

The sun-dried grass crunched beneath Alex's shoes as the party, led by his brother Tom, tramped slowly across the open field. Tom's youngest son sat perched on Alex's shoulders with his pudgy little legs astride his neck, a high-pitched squeal of delight escaping from his lips every time he saw something new. Somewhere behind, Alex could hear Tara, Tom's wife of eleven years, laughing with their other two children. The kids charged around in frenzied excitement, covering at least three times as much ground as the rest of the group.

'Good,' Tom said with relief, 'this walk should wear them out.'

Alex shook his head. His brother had everything a man could want: the perfect wife, a picture post card cottage in a sleepy English village, three great kids. He was a senior captain for Virgin Airways, and yet he could still find something to complain about.

They stopped at a stile next to a stream and waited for the rest of the party to catch up. Tom leant back against the trunk of a convenient silver birch, studying his younger brother with an enigmatic smile.

'Come on, then,' Alex insisted, 'out with it.'

Tom burst out laughing. 'I didn't say a word.'

'You didn't have to.'

'Okay, what's up with the D500, then?'

Alex groaned, wishing that just one day could go by without him having to think about the investigation. 'Nothing, as far as we can tell, but it's still too early to say. We'll know more once further tests have been carried out.'

'That's the official line. Now tell me the truth. If Virgin decide to buy any of these, then I want to know that she isn't going to fall apart around me.'

'I've got a bad feeling. Something is going on at Dramar Aerospace, but I've got no evidence.'

Tom considered this for a moment. His brother was inferring that there was some kind of conspiracy going on at the venerable old aircraft manufacturer. He was about to ask Alex about it, but the rest of the group chose that moment to catch up with them.

'Who wants to stop for a drink?' Tara asked breathlessly. An enthusiastic response from the children gave her the answer she had been hoping for.

They sat in the shade of a small group of trees, sharing the lush, green canopy with half a dozen sheep, which Tara eyed suspiciously. She was a city girl at heart, and preferred to keep the joys of nature at a comfortable distance.

She retrieved her young son from Alex and gave him his plastic cup of orange cordial, the drinking spout disappearing into the boy's eager mouth. The older children took a few swift swigs from their own drinks before going to explore the upper levels of the trees. Alex and Tom settled against a sturdy stump and resumed their conversation.

'You were saying—'

'That Dramar are a bunch of crooks? Well, they are. Don't ask me how I know. I just do.' Alex took in a deep breath and slowly explained the progress that the investigation had made. He spoke of the erroneous schematics and the KX-7 supports, the composite tests and the death of Ken Stanley, the flight recorder analysis, the trip to Crystal Lake, everything he could think of, except the actual details of Dramar's tax embezzlement – he'd given his word to Scott Eagle. As he spoke, the outpouring of information and the emotions it elicited acted like a catharsis, bringing all the events of the past three weeks into perspective. He knew he had been affected by the crash, but speaking to an informed industry insider brought it home to him just how much his psyche had been transformed.

After a few minutes, the monologue came to an end. Alex felt fatigued, as if the lifeblood that he relied upon had been drained from his body. He waited for Tom to say something, but his normally garrulous brother sat in contemplative silence for several moments.

'So, what do you think?' Alex prompted.

'It's scary,' Tom said at last. 'It's bloody scary.'

Alex breathed a sigh of relief. If his own brother agreed with his suspicions, then that was enough for him to continue to dig. He'd found Leon Baptiste's staunch opposition to the idea of a cover-up at Dramar demoralizing. Now that he had Tom on his side, he felt rejuvenated.

'There's something I don't understand,' Tom queried. 'Do you think that this conspiracy at Dramar contributed to the crash?'

'I don't know. Damned unlucky for them if the bomb happened to go off in the very place that there was a weakness.'

He watched Tara as she sat cross-legged on the grass, playing absently with a stalk of grass as she cradled her young son in her arms. He saw her delicate fingers manipulate the shoot, bending and twisting it almost to breaking point, and then relaxing the stress on it.

'So you *do* think there is an inherent weakness in the airframe, then?'

Tara pulled on the stem, but it was strong.

'I've got a feeling. Not very scientific, I'll grant you, but there's something in that design.'

She bent the stalk in two until it formed a right angle, and pulled at it again. This time the piece of grass snapped easily when she pulled it.

'Something in that design,' Alex repeated distractedly. 'There's a weakness.'

'Yes,' Tom said, staring at his younger brother, 'I think we're in the process of establishing that.'

'No, you don't understand. What if…?' Alex tried to find the words to describe the idea that he had just partially formulated. 'What if there *is* an inherent weakness in the design of the main stringers. Not just the spacing of the supports, but maybe the material of the stringer itself.'

'The FAA does check on these things,' Tom added reasonably. 'It's all part of the certification process.'

'The FAA have been complaining for years that they are understaffed. For the most part, they have to trust the honesty of the manufacturer. Dramar carried out their own fatigue tests, just like everyone else. The FAA simply sign off the relevant certification sheets.'

'So, what are you saying? Dramar knew of a fault and *lied* to the FAA.'

'Yes,' Alex said simply.

'What about the bomb?'

'The bomb was the trigger, but at the end of the day, Flight 4401 killed herself.'

Several more moments elapsed before Tom spoke. 'Good theory. How do you prove it?'

How do you prove it? Alex thought. *How do I prove it?* 'We test that damned lower stringer. We finish what Ken Stanley was working on; then we nail those bastards.'

Tara plucked another stem of grass from the ground.

Twenty-Three

A lex parked in the usual spot and stepped outside. He felt a spot of rain on his hand as he locked the car, and another on his face. Looking skywards, he saw cumulonimbus clouds rolling in, and a brief gust of a chill, northerly breeze whipped at his hair. That one flurry of cold, arctic air acted like a death knell to the summer.

He was right about the fault. He knew he was. He just had to prove it. Somewhere overhead he could hear a plane going over, but it was invisible behind the cloud layer.

'Boeing 777,' Les Thompson read his thoughts as he climbed the steps outside the DERA building to join him. The sound of the jet diminished, to be replaced by the perpetual splashing of the fountain. 'Around twenty thousand feet, I'd say, with two,' he frowned as he listened, 'Rolls Royce Trent 800s, if I'm not mistaken.'

Alex shook his head in bewilderment. 'Morning, Les. I don't know how you do it.'

'When you've been listening to engines as long as I have, you begin to recognize some of the little quirks of these things.'

'I can imagine. How did you get on with the simulator tests after I left on Saturday?'

'Pretty much what you'd expect. We tried various approaches, but there was nothing revealed that we didn't already know, or suspect.'

Alex nodded. Sometimes he felt that they relied too heavily on the evidence of the flight recorders. They were the Holy Grail at a crash site, the small boxes of tricks that would be the answer to everyone's problems. Sometimes, though, they just could not answer the big questions.

'What's next, then?' he asked.

'Correlate the data with 4401's Flight Data Recorder, then begin work on the graphic reconstruction. That'll be a long job. Lots of work involved, there,' Thompson effortlessly dropped the hint that he did not wish to be rushed.

'Then I won't keep you any longer,' Alex smiled, and left the scientist to head for the analysis lab, while he proceeded to his own office.

Alex looked at the devastation with a mixture of guilt and horror. Traces of the scientist's blood were caked onto the glass screen of the protective cubicle, and the remains of the lower main stringer section still rested within its cradle, just as it had since that fatal explosion five days before. The local CID forensics team had finally left that morning, and the investigators were now allowed back into the explosives lab.

At last, to see it with his own eyes brought it home to him just what had happened, and how greatly the loss of the old man was affecting him. He looked over to Beaumont and Cheadle, who both avoided his gaze. They had been the last to see Ken Stanley alive, and were shouldering much of the guilt that he himself felt.

This had been the first death during an investigation in the AAIB's history that had not been attributed to natural causes; the first death of an air crash detective from *any* agency, as far as he was aware. This made him the first Investigator-in-Charge ever to lose someone during an investigation. Not a distinction of which he could be proud.

'What happened,' he asked quietly.

'The police say that water from the storage tank on the roof had seeped in and caused some kind of short circuit,' Stuart Davenport explained, speaking softly and with due reverence. 'We think that Ken switched on power to the test area instead of the control booth by mistake. As soon as the connections with the detonator were made, the C4 exploded.'

Alex accepted this brief explanation with a curt nod. 'Why was he working alone?'

After a pause, Cheadle spoke up. 'We'd finished what we thought was the last test of the day. It was getting late and Ken said he would finish up. He told us to go home.' The investigator shook his head loosely. 'We should never have left him.'

Alex looked at the junior investigator and pitied him. He would carry this guilt for the rest of his life. It did not matter that it was the senior metallurgist who had flouted the regulations, and subsequently paid the price; Cheadle would always feel that the responsibility was his. Beaumont was younger, and the emotional scars would heal, given time.

'Neither of you did anything wrong. In the same situation, I wouldn't have done anything different. Now,' Alex decided to move things on, 'has anyone got any idea of what Ken might have been working on?'

Cheadle began describing the tests that they had carried out during the previous week. He spoke slowly in a detached, emotionless voice, as if he wanted to isolate himself from the devastating episode.

Damian Beaumont listened for a while, but eventually moved over to the stringer to give it a cursory examination. The remnant of carbon composite lay innocuously within the cradle as Beaumont walked around it, occasionally stopping to look at it more closely. He ran a finger along its pitted surface, feeling the ridges of liquorice-like C4 residue. 'It's almost perfect,' he said quietly to himself.'

'Hmm?' Alex mumbled, aware of another voice interrupting Cheadle's. 'What's perfect?'

'The composite – It's almost identical to the section we found in the wreckage.'

Bernie Cheadle went to join his younger colleague, relieved that he was no longer the sole focus of everyone's attention.

'There's nothing to impede the blast wave. Look,' Beaumont continued, pointing with growing excitement at the empty area surrounding the cradle. 'We've been obsessed with the idea that the bomb was located somewhere within the number two cargo hold.'

'And it wasn't,' Alex said, realizing that he was becoming infected by the younger man's excitement. 'How close do you think the bomb really was?'

'I haven't a clue,' Beaumont admitted honestly. 'I'm not an expert in this field. My background is engineering. You'd need to speak to a composites expert to find out for sure.'

'This might tie in with something I was thinking about yesterday,' Alex said.

'What was that?' Davenport asked, feeling like the last to be told a secret.

'I'll explain later. I'll have a word with the guys at DERA. They've got a great metallurgy and composites guy over there named Pennington. I'll see if he's available, and we'll have a meeting in my office at eleven this morning. In the meantime, you two find out all you can about what Ken was doing. Anything at all could be helpful. Stu, you're with me. I want to run a couple of ideas by you.'

Alex and Davenport left the lab, the Investigator-in-Charge casting his eyes toward the ceiling. 'Thank you, Ken,' he whispered silently.

Twenty-Four

'The broad's just along for the ride', she had heard them saying quietly. The fact that her résumé stated that she held a first-class degree in aeronautical engineering, and that she was fluent in four languages, including Arabic, did not seem to affect their opinion of her. The bottom line was simple: she was a woman. 'Women don't know shit about engineerin',' Casey whispered when they thought she was asleep. 'Women are good for three things, and none of 'em involve holdin' a wrench. Right?'

'Right,' Woody replied.

'Ladies and gentlemen,' the British Mediterranean Airways captain began, 'we will shortly be beginning our descent to Barakat International. I can tell you that the weather there is a balmy twenty-eight degrees, and the sun is shining. On behalf of…'

The captain continued the announcement, but no one on the Dramar Aerospace engineering team bothered listening – except the woman who apparently slept soundly in their midst.

'I'm tellin' ya, it's bad news havin' a broad like that along,' Casey continued. 'How the rest of us s'posed to get any work done?'

'Too damned right,' Woody agreed again, allowing his eyes to roam over her slender, athletic form.

She could feel them scrutinizing her, their eyes moving over her body like the ephemeral hands of an apparition as she sat prone and immobile in the business class seat. Her chest rose and fell rhythmically, moving just as a genuinely sleeping person's would.

'D'ya think she's, like, available?' Woody asked.

'Nah. Frigid bitches like that never are – not to the likes of us, anyway. Career women, that's what they call 'emselves. That's code for sour-assed bitch who don't fuck the blue-collar workers.'

'Still, no harm in tryin'.'

He would be the one. Woodrow Lindsay, she recalled his bio: thirty-eight years old, single, rented an apartment in Baltimore, heavy drinker, no known female companions for two and a half years, baseball fan, parents were Jewish, but he was an atheist. All-in-all, a wholly unremarkable individual. However, in less than a week, the lovesick Woody would become a most notable person indeed. He would just require a little persuasion.

'Hey Woody,' she said sleepily, allowing her eyes to open just enough for him to see that she was looking at him. 'Stop talking about it and come and keep me company.'

Artemis lightly patted the adjacent seat.

Donatella Martinelli climbed the steps from The Mall, which led to the entrance of the National Gallery of Art, one of Washington's most prestigious cultural centres. She cast furtive glances around her as she searched for spies or familiar figures, something she felt she was becoming extremely adept at recently. She walked past the Founders' Room and through the Rotunda, before moving into the West Sculpture Hall. She kept her steps slow and measured, occasionally stopping to admire the bronze effigies that stared back at her. A couple of times she glanced around and caught other eyes staring, which were abruptly pulled away with embarrassment. These were not the stares of professional sleuths, though, merely the wishful lasciviousness of the casual admirer. She normally welcomed those, revelling in the attention of the masses that coveted her, but could never possess her. However, every look that she glimpsed today, every casual glance, every hopeful smile seemed threatening. She walked on, the rhythmic clicking of her heels on the marble floor and the constant, subdued hubbub of humanity acting like symphonic accompaniment to the treasures of this place.

Donatella finally arrived at the galleries and relaxed a little. These rooms were fairly small compared to the grandeur of the Rotunda and sculpture halls, which made it easier to keep note of any faces that appeared too frequently.

She finally reached the painting she had been seeking, and stood before it to wait patiently. Raphael's Alba Madonna stared off to one side. Every fold of the Madonna's gown hung perfectly, the material clinging to her form in the unique style of the period, every line of the naked infant's flesh mesmerized the observer, every wisp of cloud captured the perfect moment. She adored this painting, cherished it, desired it, but the masterpiece was beyond even her means. She had no idea how many times she had stood before the work, basking in its sensual beauty, and she didn't care. As long as she could be in its presence, that would be enough for her. But time was running out.

'Very nice.' Thomas Purcell's voice sliced its way into her thoughts. 'If her hair was darker, she might look a little like you.'

'She looks nothing like me, Thomas.'

'Sure she does, it's just that she hasn't got cosmetically enhanced breasts,' he laughed, aware of the disapproving glances from others within earshot, and once again relishing her discomfort.

Donatella shivered, feeling genuine revulsion towards the man. It had been wrong to meet him *here*, in this almost sacred place. She felt his hand on her back, and tried to suppress the bile that rose in her throat.

'Everything's organized. Hope you like cheese, chocolate, and cuckoo clocks.'

'Switzerland?' Donatella exclaimed. 'Couldn't you be a bit more inventive than that?'

'Of course I could, but I like skiing. I've also got some… business interests in Geneva that no one at Dramar knows about.'

'A man of many talents,' she mocked, relieved that she'd had the good sense not to choose Switzerland as her true final destination. 'When were you planning on us leaving?'

'Oh no, not so fast, Donatella. I need to know what you've been planning. Call me mistrustful, but I find it hard to accept that you would go along with this so easily.' He turned her away from the painting, keeping a powerful hand on each of her hips.

'The FBI are watching us,' she said, involuntarily glancing sideways. 'I don't know why, but if the corporation is attracting that kind of attention, then we need our plan to be ready to go as soon as possible.'

'How do you know the Feds are involved?'

'I have my sources within the Federal Triangle,' she smiled enigmatically without humour.

'Do they know about Harrington's subterfuge?'

'I don't know. My contact could not be specific, but eventually one thing will lead to another, and before you can say Federal indictment, we'll have our own little media feeding frenzy down on Canal Street. I don't think I would suit prison life.'

'Point taken. How much time do you think we have,' Purcell asked, releasing her from his grip.

'The FBI cannot have any evidence of malpractice, otherwise they would have acted already. All they have is the possibility of irregularities. They will not move until they have solid proof, and even then, they need a case strong enough to stand up in court. Jack Stone may be an arrogant boor, but he's not stupid. He knows we have the best lawyers in the country at our disposal. That gives us a breathing space – and an advantage.'

Purcell smiled, and looked deeply into her dark, sultry eyes. She was smart. Very smart. Dangerously smart. 'I see you've done your homework. How long does that give us, though, in real terms?'

She turned again to the Alba Madonna. 'I would say that we have a month, maybe six weeks. The Bureau will start putting pressure on some of our people before long. Someone will fold, sooner or later. When they do: I'll know about it. That's when we move, and not before.'

'Understood. I place myself in your hands, Donatella.' He made to leave, but theatrically turned back when he reached the doorway. 'Don't forget what I said before. No end-runs. Goodbye, Miss Martinelli.'

'Thomas,' she said quietly. 'If you ever lay a hand on me again, I'll cut it off.'

Donatella returned her attention to the painting as Purcell walked away, the familiar smirk returning to his face.

Twenty-Five

Howard Pennington tapped a bony knuckle on the door, which was opened almost immediately.

'Mr. Pennington?' Davenport asked.

'It's Dr Pennington, actually,' the rangy old scientist replied without a smile. He was not happy to be summarily ordered to abandon his research.

'Good morning, Dr Pennington,' another man said as he emerged from behind a cluttered desk and proffered his hand.

'Mr. Jamieson, I presume?' he asked, casting a disdainful eye around the office. If there was one thing he hated more than interruptions to his work, it was mess and clutter.

'At your service. Call me Alex. We're pretty informal around here.'

'So I had noticed.'

The Investigator-in-Charge could tell that Pennington's attitude might prove to be a problem, but continued in the same, upbeat and amicable tone. 'This is

Stuart Davenport, Operations, Bernie Cheadle and Damian Beaumont, Engineering.'

The three AAIB men offered a subdued chorus of greeting.

'We've been discussing the results of Ken Stanley's final explosive test and have come up with some interesting theories—'

'If you do not mind,' Pennington interrupted, 'I would rather see the evidence for myself. In my opinion, theories should be left to philosophers and theologians.'

'Very well, Dr Pennington,' Alex said patiently, 'you can just sit quietly until we have finished our discussion, at which point you will be escorted to the metallurgy lab.' He returned his attention to the rest of the group, leaving Pennington to stew for a few minutes.

'As I said, I was thinking about this yesterday. It may be that we have a flaw in the lower stringer itself, and not necessarily the support units. What is the stringer made from?' He looked at Davenport.

'An organic matrix composite compound. J13-25, to be precise.'

'A compound we're familiar with?'

'No, Dramar have their own composites research and development facility at Crystal Lake.'

'Convenient. Now, let's turn our attention to Ken's test. Damian, how much C4 did you say Ken used?'

'Difficult to be sure. I haven't checked the explosives inventory yet, but it looks like about a hundred grams, and it was close to the stringer.'

'How close,' Alex pressed.

'No more than half a meter.'

'So we've got around three and a half ounces of explosive, detonating eighteen inches from the stringer, a carbon composite that is specifically designed to be incredibly strong. What happened to the test piece, Damian?'

'We only had time to conduct a brief preliminary exam, but I could see fracture lines which seemed to go quite deep.'

'So, if pressure was being exerted on the piece when the explosion occurred, like the conditions found at thirty thousand feet, plus the possibility of a Mach stem effect, then it would not have held together. Right?'

'Sounds reasonable,' Davenport said, wondering where this line of thought was leading.

'If we put these two things together, what have we got?'

Beaumont was the only one who was beginning to grasp what it was that Alex was getting at. 'Jesus,' he whispered. 'You've got a mad bomber who knew *exactly* where to hit that plane, and how hard.'

'If we then throw in the 'faulty' schematics from Dramar, it becomes clear that the company knew of a weakness in the stringer, and was trying to conceal it.

'Dr Pennington,' Alex turned to the scientist, 'I want you to get samples of that stringer and start work on them. We need to know the exact stress tolerances of the J13-25 compound. Bend it, shake it, burn it, boil it, freeze it. Do whatever you have to, just find the answer. Time is an important factor here. There are around forty of these things flying at the moment, any one of which could come down at any time.'

'Why not talk to the CAA about this,' Pennington asked. 'I'm sure that they would be sympathetic – if your theory seems plausible enough.'

The suggestion was met by embarrassed chuckles from the investigators. The AAIB just didn't have that kind of leverage with the Civil Aviation Authority.

Alex shook his head, holding a hand up to quieten the rest of the group. 'Too many commercial considerations for them to act without solid evidence. Same problem with the FAA. You don't ground a whole fleet of aircraft without a damned good reason. Damian, would the extra supports have made any difference?'

'I don't know. Maybe they would have reduced the effects of accumulative stresses, but that would only have been a short-term measure. I can't see them having much effect, though, if a bomb went off nearby.'

'Okay, thanks. Could you escort the good doctor to the metallurgy lab and assist him with his experiments?'

'No problem.' The young engineer led the scientist out of the office.

'Dr Pennington,' Alex said just before they disappeared. 'Welcome to the AAIB.'

'Hmm,' the old man replied grumpily.

Alex sat in silence for a few moments as the two remaining investigators waited expectantly.

'Bernie, see if you can find out if any of the aircraft delivered so far actually have the extra supports fitted, and get me a full break-down of numbers and types, and who the respective operators are.'

Cheadle left for his own office.

'You know,' Davenport said, once they were alone, 'this whole exercise is dependent upon your theory.'

'The gamble is minimal. We keep this in the family until we're sure. If anyone asks, we're just pursuing a line of enquiry.'

'But if you're wrong, your credibility within the Branch will take a real dent, and I hardly think this Pennington chap will keep his mouth shut for long.'

'Leave Pennington to me.' Alex looked over to Davenport and flashed a wicked smile. 'Don't worry, Stu. I'm not wrong.'

Twenty-Six

A rtemis watched the airliner from the balcony of the Ramita Hotel as it circled the city in a wide arc, aligning itself with the airport VOR beacon. The four Fleetwing engines roared into life as power was applied to the throttles, keeping the glide angle at a comfortable four degrees as it approached Barakat International, twenty miles from the centre of the city. She felt the floor beneath her feet shake as the D500 passed over, the vibrations coursing through her body like waves of trepidation made manifest.

That would be Khalid's aircraft. He would be with her within the next few hours, and they could make the final preparations for the next stage of the plan.

It was good to feel the Mediterranean sun on her skin again as it softly caressed her face and arms. It was the same sun that had shone down upon her all those years before.

A burst of vulgar laughter from one of the rooms down the hall brought her thoughts back into focus. Woody was in there with them, no doubt boasting of how he had conquered the 'ice maiden'; of how his charisma had melted her gelid heart, and of the hours of passion that they had shared. She had let him take her the previous evening, and had played the role with the same commitment as all the rest, for it was a personal violation that was necessary if she was to succeed.

Her mission was all that mattered, and Woody could enjoy his fantasies for the next week.

After that time he would have little to feel joyous about.

'Where is he?' Eagle asked testily.

'He'll be here,' Burnett replied.

The senior FBI agent looked with agitation at his watch. 'Who is this guy, anyway?'

'Karl Vance. I told you, he's the best detective I've ever met. He knows a hell of a lot more than you or me.'

'He's not Bureau. I don't like talking to outsiders when a case is active. And another thing: if this guy's so good, how come he isn't working for us?'

Burnett shook his head. 'He's the best there is. He's just a little... eccentric.' Now he was getting worried. They had been waiting in the seedy Philadelphia bar for over half an hour, and his chances of promotion were looking increasingly slim. If the Delaware detective didn't arrive soon, he could kiss goodbye to—

'Who the hell's this?' Vance demanded, dropping heavily into the seat opposite his 'friend'. 'I got a message to meet *you* here. You didn't say nothin' about no one else.'

'Detective Karl Vance, meet Special Agent Scott Eagle. He's running the investigation into Grant's murder.' Burnett tried to disguise his relief, but failed.

'Detective Vance,' Eagle began, offering his hand which was shaken cautiously, 'Agent Burnett, here, tells me that you may be able to help us.'

'Feds want help from a regular cop? You must be desperate,' Vance chuckled into his beer.

Eagle shifted uncomfortably in his seat. This guy was obviously an arrogant son of a bitch. It remained to be seen whether or not he would be of any use.

'Come on then, Mr. FBI agent,' the detective goaded, 'what does the great Federal Bureau of Investigation want Vance's help with?'

Burnett cut in, afraid that the covert assignation might rapidly degenerate into a bar-room brawl. 'We've uncovered some information from Grant's house, and I thought you might give us your opinion on it.'

'Okay,' Vance yielded, 'show me what you got.'

'Detective Vance, I don't need to tell you the sensitivity of this information.'

'Just tell me one thing. How come this case has direct Presidential Approval?'

Burnett felt sick.

'All right, Mr. Vance. Dramar Aerospace have been the subject of an FBI investigation that has been going on for several months. Monies that should have gone to the

IRS have been disappearing. Nothing to get too worked up about, but three weeks ago one of their planes crashes.'

'But that was a bomb – wasn't it?'

'Oh sure, but then two weeks later, one of their senior designers is murdered in an audacious attack on I-95. One coincidence is unusual. Two are downright suspicious.' Eagle watched the detective closely as the man considered this.

'I knew all that before. *Now* tell me what's new.'

Eagle withdrew a sheet of paper from his pocket. 'These are diary entries which were recovered from Grant's home.'

Vance scanned the sheet. It was a photocopy of various pages from a small, personal diary. Several mentions were made of meetings with Diana.

'Who's Diana?' He asked.

'You tell me. You're the shit-hot detective.'

Burnett kept a low profile.

'He was supposed to meet her on the twenty-fourth. That's the day after the crash, but the entry must have been made sometime earlier than that,' Vance muttered as he mulled the problem over in his mind. 'And he was going to phone her on the seventh of this month. That's just two days before he was killed. Did he?'

'Not from his home phone. Not from Gunpowder Falls. He may have used an unregistered mobile phone that we haven't found or a payphone.' Eagle was beginning to wonder whether Vance was as good as Burnett made out.

'She's either a terrorist, or a reporter. Did Grant have any political hang-ups?'

'Grade A Republican, through and through,' Eagle replied absently. Why the *hell* had he not made that connection himself? It was obvious, now that he thought about it.

'So she's a reporter, Vance said. 'Probably local to the DC area. Find that reporter and you'll be three quarters of the way there.'

'I told you he was good,' Burnett said with relief. That promotion did not seem so far off, after all.

Twenty-Seven

As she had hoped, the fact that Woody was a heavy drinker had been little defence against the local *Araq*, an aniseed concoction not dissimilar to ouzo, but it had taken longer to initiate the process than she'd expected. However, within an hour he had begun slurring his speech, which was when she escorted him to her room where she opened another bottle.

He had looked at it gleefully, for the moment forgetting her charms. Like most alcoholics, he started drinking freely, with no thought as to the possible consequences.

He was barely able to remain conscious as he fumbled to remove his clothes, swaying with intoxication, and pushed her roughly onto the bed. One hand on her breast, groping roughly. The other on her thigh, hoisting the hem of the skirt up until it was around her waist. Panties were dragged down her legs which were forced open. She felt him enter her and closed her eyes, detaching herself from the experience. She was a bystander, dispassionate and divorced from the ordeal, watching this happen to another woman.

As she had so many times before.

His breaths came in short gasps as he blinked fiercely, desperately trying to focus on the task, however his thrusts eventually slowed as insensibility overtook him. He finally collapsed on top of her and began snoring loudly in a drunken stupor, and she had to exert considerable effort to extricate herself from beneath his prostrate body.

Artemis retrieved another bottle of Araq from the wardrobe and poured it down his throat, ensuring that he did not choke on the liquid, but guaranteeing that he would not awaken for several hours. Much of the alcohol spilled from his mouth onto the bed and the floor, but this was of no consequence. By the time he awakened she would be well on her way back to the United States.

She searched his pockets and found the Dramar Aerospace pass card that she had been looking for, which would give her access to the Quamar Airways maintenance hangar at Barakat International Airport. She then donned his work overalls, which still stank of stale sweat and the metallic smells of machine oil and grease. It was not by accident that they were a perfect fit: a similarity in their respective sizes had been a prerequisite of his selection as the subject.

'I hope you think it was worth it, Woody,' she said as she closed the door behind her.

The snores continued without interruption.

Several cars were parked on the road adjoining the hotel, but only one was occupied, the idling engine purring quietly. She could not see the driver's face in the darkness, but recognized Khalid's silhouette. The years had been kind to him. He had matured from the callow adolescent that he had been when she had first met him, into a strikingly handsome man with confidence, a keen intellect and a gift for tactical thinking.

'You are late,' he said simply, but without harshness.

'The subject took longer to subdue than I had anticipated. He will not be a problem now, though.'

'Did you have to—'

'Just drive, Khalid.'

Artemis stared out of the window, her colleague knowing better than to force the issue.

The road to the airport was quiet and they were able to travel unobtrusively, but nevertheless he felt the familiar pangs of trepidation begin to bite at the pit of his stomach. This was healthy, he reminded himself. An absence of fear would lead to overconfidence. Overconfidence would lead to recklessness, and recklessness would get you killed. She had taught him that, but she had also warned that the fear had to be controlled, for unchecked it could cause paralysis in a critical situation. Khalid kept his breathing constant, inhaling and exhaling slowly and rhythmically, never allowing an excess of oxygen to saturate his lungs. Hyperventilation would only feed the fear. He looked over at his passenger who continued to gaze absently at the lights of the city as they swept past, an image of serenity and calm.

Even at this late hour the airport seemed busy, and Khalid had no trouble merging the Nissan with the various maintenance crew vehicles that were arriving for the one a.m. shift change. So many airlines now used this facility that it was impossible for the understaffed and overstretched airport security to keep track of everyone entering and leaving – not that the poorly paid officers were that vigilant. Major carriers were now beginning to fly to Barakat, but were happy to overlook the inadequacies of the airport's infrastructure, just as long as it remained an inexpensive gateway to the Middle East.

They passed the terminal entrance and went on to the service and technical area where he stopped the car, and turned to his passenger.

'This is as far as I can go without arousing suspicion.'

'I know,' she said, staring intently at his silhouette, only the light reflected from his eyes giving a face to the shrouded portrait. She lifted a hand and lightly brushed his cheek. 'Soon, Khalid, soon.' She opened the door and stepped out into the cold night air.

'I'll see you in New York, then?' he asked.

'New York. Be patient – and vigilant.'

She disappeared into the darkness and he drove away, keeping a careful eye in the mirrors as he left the airport.

Her own apprehension simmered as she approached the maintenance hangar, though she consoled herself with the knowledge that Khalid was now safe.

Artemis held the credit card-sized key against the sensor. The light turned from red to green and was followed by a click as the door was automatically unlocked. Lighting within the hangar was subdued, the Quamar Airways D500 standing serenely above the gantries and ladders that surrounded it, like Lilliputians gathering around the inert form of Gulliver. By dawn, though, this giant would be free and ready to begin its journey across the desert.

She was now, due to Woody's initial resilience to the Araq, almost twenty minutes behind schedule, but she did not regard this as too much of a problem. The plan she had devised had an element of leeway built into it. She just needed to ensure that she lost no more precious time.

The underside of the fuselage towered above her and, as luck would have it, the access ladder that she had seen earlier the previous day was still in the correct position. She climbed it carefully, making sure of her footing in the poor lighting.

The access hatch could only be opened using a four-figure key-code, but the code was generic to all D500s and she had it memorized. The keypad was illuminated and she tapped the number in. With a mechanical clunk the hatch was unlocked and slid back, an internal light being automatically illuminated. She retrieved the device from her backpack and secured it into position with a generous amount of duct tape before arming it. This bomb, like the first, would operate using a barometric system, only detonating once the air pressure had reduced to a predetermined level: in this case, twenty thousand feet. As the pressure on the hull would be less this time, she had increased the quantity of explosive to one hundred and fifty grams to compensate. If Khalid's calculations were correct, the result should be the same.

The device was in place. The aircraft was ready to go. All she had to do now was make her escape, but that should be quite a simple matter.

The tractor slowly dragged the aircraft from the hangar, the vast sweep of her elegant wings barely clearing the doors, which were opened to their fullest extent. Like the fabled Roc emerging from its nest, the D500 was rolled onto the tarmac and the four engines ignited. The great bird was now free and moved with a sprightly vigour towards the terminal building where a crowd of eager passengers awaited, all watching the behemoth with excitement and the naive expectation of a child at Christmas as it approached.

As the group of over a hundred slowly climbed the steps and were directed to their seats by pretty flight attendants with painted-on smiles, the pilots went through the checklist.

'Maintenance status?' the captain asked, looking down the list.

'Checked,' the co-pilot replied.

'Circuit breakers?'

'Checked,' he repeated, examining the panel to his right.

'Battery switch?'

'On.'

'Standby power switch?'

'Auto.'

They continued through the list for several minutes, until they finally reached the end. With fifteen minutes until departure time the co-pilot left the cockpit and took one final walk around the exterior of the aircraft, giving it a cursory visual inspection to make sure all hatches had been properly secured, and probes and sensors were clear. While he did this the captain scanned the technical log to familiarize himself with the status of the maintenance that had been carried out at Barakat International.

All seemed well with the D500 and, at the appointed hour, the engines surged into life once more and moved her away from the terminal building to taxi toward the runway.

A crowd of onlookers watched the aircraft appreciatively from the viewing area as it moved to the far end of the runway, the slipstream from the engines displacing a cloud of dust as she went. Some watched through binoculars; many more had phone cameras trained upon it.

She stood within the group and watched impassively as the great D500 roared down the runway, gathering speed every second, passing the V^1 decision speed and accelerating on to VR, at which point the captain gave the order to 'rotate' the aircraft. The nose wheel lifted from the ground as the elevators in the tail were angled upwards. This increased the 'angle of attack' of the aerodynamic wing surfaces and the plane was lifted gently into the air, climbing steeply into the warm, clear sky of the northern Quamari desert.

With the spectacle now passed, the crowd began to drift toward the exit, and she moved unobtrusively among them, a dark shawl covering her head but leaving her face bare in the sunlight. Artemis prowled among them, like a lioness moving stealthily through the undergrowth as it stalked a herd of gazelle. The crowd moved slowly, as a disorganized mass. Some gazed back wistfully at the now tiny dot in the northern sky as it climbed over the desert, wishing their friends and loved ones well, many envious and longing to be travelling themselves. Others simply stared at the floor as they shuffled forwards. The man to her right was looking up, and she followed his gaze – straight into the lens of a security camera that was angled to observe and record the faces of all who came up to the viewing area. Instinctively she turned away, but knew that the unblinking electronic eye had registered her face beneath the shawl.

It was time to begin the long, fast drive to Beirut, and from there to catch the Lebanese flight to Frankfurt. It was ironic, but she would not feel safe again until she was once again standing on American soil.

The D500 had just passed the Azzril Manara 312 VOR beacon when the device detonated, fracturing the lower main stringer just as the previous device had. Passengers screamed; reached out for one another; began the opening words of prayers; stared in horror and disbelief as the two halves of the aircraft separated. The three fuel tanks exploded almost simultaneously, tearing the airframe apart and extinguishing the lives of the passengers and crew, their screams silenced by the conflagration that enveloped them.

The burning remains of the aircraft rapidly descended to the desert sands, a curtain of burning kerosene engulfing them and incinerating many of the bodies as they fell.

Soon the desert near El Abadan was awash with flame, the intensity of the heat turning the sand to glass and melting entire sections of the airframe until it had become part of the desert itself.

By the time a helicopter from El Zafir arrived at the scene an hour and a half later, there was little left of the great airliner and its complement of over a hundred. The molten mass of metal and plastic had simply been melted down to an amorphous whole, with little to suggest its origin.

The military crew of the helicopter looked down from their elevated vantage point with a mixture of horror and anger, mourning their dead countrymen.

Whoever was responsible for this would pay.

Twenty-Eight

The phone started to ring. Madison Flynn vaguely became aware of it through confused, dreamy clouds but tried to ignore it. It was far too late for phone calls. Whoever it was could wait until morning. Despite herself she glanced across at the alarm clock, the red figures flashing insistently, and she sighed with heartfelt irritation.

'One in the morning,' she said aloud.

The phone continued to ring.

'One in the Goddamned morning!' She reached over to pick up the receiver but it went silent as she did so.

'Typical.'

A few seconds later her mobile phone began to sing, and she walked unsteadily across the room to answer it, tripping over her baggy pyjama bottoms as she did so and cursing again.

'Madison Flynn,' she said, flicking unruly strands of hair away from her face and trying not to sound too groggy.

'Madison, it's Skip Thornton.'

Her disoriented mind tried to put a face to the name. *Oh yeah*, she thought, *newsdesk.*

'Skip, it's one in the Goddamned morning. For Christ's sake, get yourself a life, man.'

'I have a life,' he said defensively. 'But it's not one a.m. in Quamar.'

'And what has Quamar got to do with…' The words were beginning to make some sense. 'What's happened?'

'Remember that D500 that went down about a month ago?'

'Cut the crap, Skip. I'm not in the mood.'

'The D500 that got blown out of the sky?'

'Skip!' she said, the frustration and anger now clear in her voice.

'Another one just went down in Quamar. Just blew up in mid-air.'

'Jesus.' Flynn was now fully awake, her mind racing as she tried to make some instant connection. 'How many people were on board?'

'A hundred passengers plus crew, mostly Quamari nationals, I'd say. It was just a milk flight from Barakat to Istanbul. No one has claimed responsibility so far, but you know the way it goes. Every terrorist and his dog'll be jumping on this one.'

The shock of the news was not helping her to rationalize the situation. Why a Quamari airliner?

'Any statements coming from the Quamaris?' she asked.

'Hold it. I've got something else coming through.'

Flynn waited, picturing in her mind the Reuters website as it was updated second by second.

'Holy crap! They've arrested an *American* in Barakat. A mechanic.'

They had to move on this fast. 'Wake Kramer up. This is way too big to wait till morning.'

There was no knock on the door – not that Woody would have heard it – the Quamari secret police simply smashing it from its hinges and storming in. He lay sprawled across the bed, still naked after the previous night's drunken attempt to copulate. The agents, with the fiery thirst for revenge burning within their hearts, dragged him to his feet.

'Wha-what?' he cried as he groggily awakened. 'What's goin' on?'

Something was shouted into his ear in Arabic, but he did not understand.

'Filthy American scum!' He understood that, and also the butt of the assault rifle as it smashed into his ribcage. He tried to double over in pain, but was held upright by eager hands as foreign voices of hate rasped in his ears.

'Murder. Scum. You understand?'

Woody shook his head in confusion, which earned him another blow to his ribs, and also a rifle butt smashed against his forehead. He drifted momentarily in a sea of light until the pain from the blow invaded his consciousness, inducing a wave of nausea that threatened to engulf him.

'Please…' Tears poured from his eyes, mixing with the blood that gushed from the open head wound.

'Please, I don't know what you want?'

The pain in his head was almost overwhelming, and he would have welcomed the release of unconsciousness, but when a heavily booted foot made contact with his unprotected groin it became too much, the vomit and scream of agony and terror exploding from his mouth. Blows continued to rain down upon him and he was allowed to drop feebly to the floor, the shape of the foetal ball he adopted offering little protection as his pitiful form received blow after blow until long after he was once again unconscious.

When he awoke, Woody found himself sitting on a hard, stiff-backed chair and slumped over a metal table. His body was a nightmare of pain as he tried to sit upright, and the urge to vomit once again threatened to seize him, but he managed to keep the sensation under control. He was aware that he had now been dressed in prison issue trousers and shirt, but his feet were still bare. At least the clothing would offer a measure of protection if they decided to beat him again. The mere thought of another assault caused him to begin weeping, however the effort of sobbing openly increased the pain in his head, so he tried to keep the whimpers under control. He attempted to open his eyes, but could only see out of one, his vision blurred through the tears, the swollen flesh of the other eye forcing it closed.

Woody heard a door open and footsteps approach across the cold, unyielding floor. At the sound of a chair scraping on the bare tiles he looked up, endeavouring to control the pain that coursed through his battered body. A smartly suited Arab man sat down gracefully opposite him.

'Good day, Mr. Lindsay,' the man said in accented but fluent English. 'I am afraid you are in a lot of trouble.'

'No kiddin',' he managed to say, surprised at the strength of his own voice, although he realized that he had now developed a lisp, as he no longer possessed any front teeth. 'Why am I here?'

'Mr. Lindsay, you have been connected with the death of one hundred and thirteen people. Tell me: why did you destroy the Quamar Airways D500 that left Bakarat this morning?'

Woody's mind raced. *A hundred and thirteen people?*

'I'm an engineer for Dramar Aerospace.'

'Mr. Lindsay, you were seen entering the Quamar Airways' maintenance hangar at one a.m. this morning. The electronic pass that had been issued to you was used at around one a.m. Security cameras within the hangar saw you working on the aircraft soon after one a.m.—'

'I don't understand. It wasn't me.'

'And security agents have found Israeli designed bomb making equipment in your hotel room. The evidence is fairly conclusive. Do you deny the charge?'

'I – I… didn't kill anybody,' he pleaded.

The Arab sighed theatrically with disappointment. 'Mr. Lindsay, where were you last night at one a.m.?'

'I was…' What *had* happened last night? Some fragments were beginning to come back to him. 'I was with a woman.'

'Ah,' the interrogator said, 'one of the local prostitutes?'

The memory was still unclear as his thoughts struggled through the pain and the after-effects of the alcohol. 'No, she was part of our team.'

'Would this be Miss Diana Ames?'

'Yeah, that's her. She'll tell you.'

'She was your accomplice?'

'No, she was my… We'd started a relationship.'

The man shook his head. 'Unfortunately, Miss Ames cannot be found.'

'But she was *there*,' Woody whimpered plaintively.

The suited man continued to shake his head sorrowfully. 'Mr. Lindsay, unless you help me, I cannot help you.'

'But I'm tellin' you, she was there. If you can just find her, then she'll tell you, for Christ's sake!'

The man shook his head once more with resignation. 'It would seem, Mr. Lindsay, that Christ has deserted you.'

The interrogator stood and walked towards the exit as the guards approached the terror-stricken American.

When Kramer walked into the office at CTVN Flynn was already there. She was not wearing the usual business suit that he was accustomed to seeing her in, just tight denims, high-heeled boots and a baggy old sweater, devoid of make-up and her long blond hair a dishevelled mess. He did not feel he looked much better himself, the crumpled charcoal suit that he'd hurriedly thrown on the same one he had worn the previous day, his shirt unbuttoned at the top with no necktie. He could feel a day's growth of stubble as it scratched against the silk.

'Morning Madison,' he said briskly.

She looked up at him with astonishment. She had never seen him look anything other than immaculate, even in the rain and windswept hills of Wales, but what surprised her was the familiarity of his greeting. This was the first time that he had addressed her by her forename and she found herself finally beginning to warm to him.

'Morning Lewis. Rough night?' she asked with a twinkle.

'I can see it's going to be. What else have we got?'

She read through her notes quickly and succinctly. 'The Quamar Airways D500 left Barakat at nine a.m. local and exploded at twenty thousand feet near a place called El Abadan.' She stumbled over the pronunciation. 'One hundred and three passengers and ten crew confirmed on board. An American maintenance engineer, Woodrow Lindsay, was arrested shortly afterwards. Apparently he was seen entering the maintenance hangar during the night, and what has been described as 'bomb making equipment' was found in his hotel room.'

'Interesting. I take it that it was an American maintenance firm?'

'This manufacturer insists on doing its own maintenance.' She waited about a second and a half for the penny to drop.

'You mean this guy was a Dramar employee? Oh, this just keeps getting better and better! What do we know about him?' Kramer asked, slumping into the opposite chair.

'Not much. He's the original invisible man: lives alone in Baltimore, worked for Dramar Aerospace for fifteen years, Jewish, no known political affili—'

'Jewish?' Kramer interrupted. 'Could be an Israeli sympathizer, then.'

A pretty research assistant entered the office at that moment, brandishing a sheet of paper with the Associated Press logo at the top. Flynn snatched it from the girl and waved her away.

'You don't think there could be a connection with Israel, do you?' she asked as she began to read the sheet.

'If I've thought of it, then you can bet your sweet ass I won't be the only one.'

Flynn's eyes widened as she scanned the sheet. 'You're not. That 'bomb making equipment' was manufactured in Israel.'

Kramer sat in quiet contemplation for a few moments. 'I take it you've made our travel arrangements?'

'We can't go,' she said.

'What?'

'They're not allowing any western journalists into the country. Dramar and NTSB investigators are also being denied access.'

The young girl barged in again with another sheet of paper which Flynn took, not bothering this time even to wave a dismissive hand. 'Oh, my God. Quamar is expelling all the US personnel from the embassy. American citizens are being urged to leave. They are recalling their own diplomats from Washington, and their military have gone to a higher state of readiness. Lewis, you know what this means?'

'Of course,' he said flatly. 'They're gearing up for war.'

President Archer raked his long fingers through a mane of thick, unnaturally dark hair, the motion giving him a few moments to think through the haze of his weary brain. He had been awake and active now for over twenty-seven hours, barring the hour of sleep he had managed before the news had broken.

The initial furore following the first crash had eventually died down to a reasonable level. The FBI investigation seemed to be moving at a slow but steady pace, despite the political obstacles of liaising with the British security services.

He stared once again at the FBI file on Woodrow Lindsay, which did not even fill a full page. He shook his head and looked up at his Chief-of-Staff.

'This is all we have on him?'

'Yes, Mr. President,' Kenton replied awkwardly. 'Nothing about him has ever suggested that he would have the will, means, or ability to carry out an act of terrorism of this kind. As for his motives, well…'

FBI director Jack Stone spoke up. 'It wasn't him. I'd stake all our reputations on that. His profile doesn't come anywhere near fitting the bill. Not only that, he wasn't even *in* London to plant the bomb on 4401. He's just the patsy, taking the fall for someone else.'

'Who?' the President asked.

'If we knew that, we'd probably know the answers to everything.'

'Jack, I've got the entire White House press corps down the hall demanding answers; the probability of terrorist attacks on American interests at home and abroad; Quamar has done all but declare war on the United States, and that's the best you can give me?'

'I'm sorry, Mr. President. We just have very little to go on. Given time—'

'I haven't got time, Jack. I need answers now! I need to be able to tell *them* something.' Archer gestured vaguely in the direction of the White House press corps. 'I need to be able to tell the Quamaris categorically that this crash was nothing to do with us.'

'It wasn't us,' Kenton interjected. 'Mr. Lindsay is, at the moment, just a public relations problem.'

Archer stared at him incredulously.

'He's an American citizen being held for a political crime in a foreign country,' Kenton continued. 'What is of greater concern right now is the destabilizing effect of military action in the Middle East. If there's going to be a war with Israel, then you can bet that other Arab countries will be drawn in.'

The President closed his eyes and exhaled deeply, expurgating some of the surface anger that had built up within him. 'You're right of course, George. Tell me what *you* think.'

'What if this report of Israeli involvement is accurate. Obviously it follows that they would have been responsible for the first bomb. Think about it. If Israel destroyed an American airliner packed with US citizens, that's tantamount to a declaration of war. We're just a year away from an election, sir, with a low approval rating. If we do anything to assist the Israelis then we'll be crucified at the polls.'

Archer thought about this for long moments before speaking. 'If that does turn out to be the case, then Israel is in this on her own.'

The ramifications of this line of thinking were huge. If they did nothing to aid Israel in a military conflict, it could result in all-out war in the Middle East, every country with a grievance against the Jewish state taking advantage of the situation. But, if they were seen to be helping an aggressor against the United States, then it would be political suicide for the Archer administration. A classic Catch-22 scenario.

In his present state, the President did not trust himself to make an instant judgement.

'What assets do we have in the area?'

Twenty-Nine

The throng of people moved slowly along al-Wehda, edging as one toward the Israeli Defence Force troops who waited pensively a hundred yards away. Galil assault rifles were trained upon the crowd, each of the soldiers trying to pick a target, hoping that their first shots would not hit one of the young women or children that made up almost half the mob. The commanding officer ran his binoculars over them, hunting in vain for leaders to present themselves, but all he could see was ordinary Palestinian people moving with slow determination towards him.

The demonstration had not been expected, and its cause was apparently unknown to his superiors, so his orders had been left somewhat vague. "Contain any rioters. Use only necessary force. Shoot to kill only if containment is breached. Concentrate fire away from women and children". That was easy to say when cocooned in the safe environment of the platoon's barracks. The reality of the situation was a little different.

The crowd was now just fifty yards away.

Samir threw the first of the Molotov cocktails from the third floor of the tower that overlooked al-Wehda, and then ducked back into the shadows. It landed ten feet in front of the soldiers, liquid fire spreading in a flaming blanket before them. He heard a shot as an over-eager soldier accidentally fired, followed immediately by a furious rebuke from the commanding officer. A second petrol bomb landed ten feet behind the platoon, which turned *en masse* to face this new threat.

The crowd continued to move forward, just twenty-five yards from the troops, but the women and children had now moved within the rabble, their positions taken by young men, the backbone of the Intifada.

The third Molotov cocktail landed squarely within the group of soldiers, engulfing one unfortunate soul in flames. His screams acted like a rallying call to the mob, which now surged forward.

The Israeli officer knew for sure now what a bloody exchange this would be. 'Fire at wi—'

Samir's first shot silenced the soldier, his body dropping to the ground, limbs flailing in spasm. With their leader dead, the troops began firing wildly at the rooftops and into the crowd. The women within the multitude began screaming a high-pitched, uniform squeal, further confusing the soldiers. From the mass, individuals would dart forward to launch a volley of stones before retreating back within the group. Firebombs rained down upon the troops, while Samir picked off individuals with the AK47 assault rifle.

The platoon was in total disarray, and a trickle of men began to run. The trickle soon became a flood as more and more soldiers joined their fleeing comrades. Samir quickly identified the stubborn ones that held their positions and each was systematically felled by a round from the assault rifle.

The boldest young men of the mob pursued the retreating soldiers, and Samir cursed them, knowing that it would be a total mismatch and only death awaited them. However, with the fire of hate burning within their hearts and the thrill of the hunt overcoming reason, there was no way that they could be stopped.

When he came down and viewed the street it was littered with bodies. In all, eighteen Palestinians had been killed, including a thirteen-year-old boy. The Israelis had suffered even greater losses. Twenty-seven Israeli soldiers lay strewn across the width of the street.

The crowd waited a short distance away, unsure of what to do next, and awaiting his orders. They had bloodlust in their eyes, and wished to continue the fight, but he knew this victory was just a false dawn. The Palestinian people would pay a heavy price for this attack.

'Go. Now!' He commanded, but was met by a wave of recalcitrance. 'Go quickly, or this victory will mean nothing.'

The mob began to disperse and move away, the sound of an approaching helicopter quickening their pace until they had disappeared into the enclosed backstreets of the Old City.

Samir crouched over the body of the commanding officer, his limbs splayed out at unnatural angles, a small pool of blood framing the ground around his head.

From his pocket Samir withdrew a sheet of paper and pinned it to the soldier's tunic. It conveyed a simple, two-word message in Arabic, Hebrew, and English.

It said: FINAL INTIFADA.

The Apache helicopter gunship swooped low over Al-Shajaia Square, its cannons spewing metal death into any pocket of Palestinians that the pilot could see were exposed and vulnerable. However, the battles on the ground were mainly at close quarters, and for the most part all the flight crew could do was hover impotently over their targets, firing only when the enemy was far enough from the troops on the ground so they would not hit their own people.

Samir watched the helicopter nervously as it drifted over the square. When it came close enough to his position he fired three shots from the Kalashnikov, but they simply ricocheted off its armoured hull in a shower of sparks, dulled by the brightness of the sunlight. He returned his attention to the Israeli troops on the ground, picking off targets as they presented themselves. The wall he crouched behind suddenly came alive as it was pelted with bullets, and he realized that his position had been identified. It was time to move. The Zionists were winning this battle, and there was nothing to be gained by the wholesale slaughter of his people.

Samir gave three long blasts on the air horn, signalling the retreat, and the young strike force fighters did their best to disengage. The scene was chaotic as the Palestinians scrambled for cover, some deciding that it was best to continue the fight. Running would merely leave them exposed.

As the architect of the assault, Samir wanted to stay and fight with them, but it was hopeless. He scrambled along the ground, keeping low as bullets continued to fly in his direction. Once he was a safe distance away he peeked over the wall, and was horrified to see the Apache bearing down on him. He barely had time to fling himself to the ground before a missile struck the wall. The flimsy structure seemed to erupt around him. The wall, the ground, the entire world seemed to be tearing itself apart, and for a brief instant a strange sensation enveloped him. He seemed to be falling. The ground had opened up and swallowed him, and he waved his arms wildly to fend off debris as it struck him. Then, an instant before the impact, he realized that he really was falling. The explosion had flung him more than thirty feet, and he hit the ground heavily, hearing bones snap as unimaginable stresses were placed upon them. Pain shot through his entire body, and was compounded by the rubble of the demolished wall as it continued to pound him. He lay there for a few moments, unsure of what had happened. Only aware of the pain.

He opened his eyes and saw the blurred image of the helicopter moving away to find another target. Even through the agony his mind continued to work. He knew that the war was over for him. Even if the injuries that he had sustained were not fatal, he would not be able to re-enter the conflict as an activist again. Tears of frustration blended with those of pain as the realization hit him.

If the Quamaris were going to strike, then they had to do it soon. The Palestinians could not withstand this level of punishment for long.

Thirty

A lex stared at it with mixed feelings. He was weary; drained; tired. Five weeks of intense stress had taken their toll, and a small corner of his mind wondered how much longer he could carry on like this.

The reconstruction of the fuselage in the area of the detonation was finished – or as finished as it was going to be. They had been lucky to recover and identify eighty per cent of the wreckage, and this was largely due to the skill and professionalism of the AAIB inspectors. These were the best people in the world, he thought proudly. The American National Transportation Safety Board may be the most experienced, but the real talent was here at Farnborough.

The structure, mounted on a scaffolding skeletal framework, measured seventy-five feet in length, even larger than the Pan Am 103 assembly had been. For how many years would this monstrosity be taking up valuable space within the hangar? How long would it take to bring the murderers to justice this time?

Howard Pennington's lanky form was crouched beneath the structure like a praying mantis as he made a final inspection of the lower main stringer, satisfying himself one more time that he had overlooked nothing. Stuart Davenport slouched against the scaffolding, ready to assist the metallurgist if necessary, but wishing he were somewhere else.

The sound of approaching footsteps forced Alex to turn away from the obscene monument. Sir Roger Coombes, director of the AAIB, approached. He was resplendent as always in a pale grey Savile Row suit, waistcoat buttoned to conceal his middle age spread, gold cufflinks glinting in the amber light of lamps as he passed. A brightly coloured bow tie completed the ensemble, and Alex was reminded of how unkempt he invariably felt in his superior's presence.

'Good morning, Sir Roger,' he said formally, however the director was not a man who demanded formality.

'Good morning, gentlemen,' he greeted them warmly. 'So, Alex, why are we here, then?'

Alex cleared his throat before beginning, feeling that he had already given this explanation countless times before, but tried to inject some vitality into the monologue.

'We now have positive proof that this design is faulty. We also believe that Dramar Aerospace were aware of the deficiency, and have attempted to conceal it. The KX-7 supports that you can see here,' he pointed out one of the 'V' shaped fittings that were visible, 'were spaced at one-meter intervals throughout the length of the airframe. Dr Pennington has calculated that, based on an average fifteen-hour operational day and number of cycles for this type of aircraft, a failure would have occurred within two to three years of service, perhaps even less. The schematics we were originally supplied with showed the KX-7s to be fifty centimetres apart. This may have increased the life of the stringer by another couple of years, but was only ever going to be a temporary stopgap. The real fault lies in the construction of the lower stringer itself.'

'Hold on a minute,' Sir Roger interrupted. 'What makes you think there was a conspiracy at the factory?'

'Several things. Firstly, only the original eleven aircraft that were delivered have KX-7s in this configuration. The next seventeen aircraft have the extra stringer supports. Dramar then seem to have gone back to the original separation of one meter. This means that their technical director lied when he said that we had been supplied with the wrong plans and that the extra supports were superfluous. Secondly, Douglas Harrington specifically asked me whether we had found any inherent faults in the aircraft, which struck me as suspicious.'

'It's a fairly natural question to ask. He might have just been worried about the possible effects on his company.'

'Maybe, but that's not how it sounded to me at the time. Thirdly, there is the fact that they tried to blackmail me over the issue of Ken's death, not to mention the issue of the analogue flight recorders.'

'So all you really have is the same discrepancy in the plans that you had a month ago, and some educated guesses regarding a half-baked conspiracy theory. Come on, Alex, you've got to do better than that if we're going to take this to the CAA.'

The Investigator-in-Charge felt stung. The evidence was right there in front of them. He opened his mouth to speak but no sound came out.

'Sir Roger,' Pennington interjected. 'I was asked to join the investigation team a week ago. At that time I fully shared your sceptical view, however since then I have come to agree with Mr. Jamieson's conclusions. The J13-25 compound that the main stringers are constructed from does have an inherent weakness. That has been proven in the laboratory beyond any reasonable doubt. As for the conspiracy theory…'

Alex waited for the damning assessment of his paranoia.

'…I am forced to agree. Dramar Aerospace appear to have supplied us with misleading information; they have blatantly lied to us; they have advised their customers to fit the D500 with inferior flight recorders; they have altered their original design twice without explanation.'

'Blackmail, deceit, misappropriation of funds,' Alex continued, counting off each allegation on his fingers, his confidence rejuvenated.

'What misappropriation of funds?'

Davenport looked up, equally puzzled.

'I'm sorry, I can't be any more specific about that at the moment. None of these things taken individually are enough to ground the D500, but taken as a whole it forms a disturbing picture. Two of these aircraft have now been lost. If we fail to act now, we could be indirectly responsible for the loss of a third. The D500 can pack in four hundred people. I don't want their deaths on my conscience. Do you?' He shot a glance in Pennington's direction, his expression of gratitude saying more than mere words ever could.

'I have a meeting with the Minister of Transport at three this afternoon. He is going to want some concrete answers, Alex. The budget for this investigation has skyrocketed. I need to justify the expenditure with evidence.'

'But we *have* evidence. The first nine aircraft that are left are death traps. Pretty soon the next seventeen will not be far behind.'

'But the Minister—'

'To hell with the Minister! Tell him whatever he wants to hear. It's the CAA that we need to convince, and the laboratory evidence of the J13-25 compound is undeniable. *You* can see that as easily as I can. For God's sake, Roger, stop acting like a politician and look at this from the moral perspective. If the stringers had been strong enough, then four hundred and twenty-five people would still be alive. *We* can stop this from happening again.' Alex finally ran out of steam. His outburst could easily earn him an official reprimand, and his eyes dropped to the floor. There was nothing more that he could add. It was up to Sir Roger now.

The director stood in silence for a few moments as he contemplated the arguments that had been put to him. A lesser man would have censured Alex for an uncontrolled, unprofessional display like that, but he respected someone who was willing to put his reputation, indeed his entire career on the line simply because he thought he was doing the right thing.

Officially approaching the Civil Aviation Authority would be the first step in grounding the D500 fleet. If the CAA were sufficiently convinced by the AAIB's evidence, they would then approach the International Civil Aviation Organization in Montreal.

The Air Accidents Investigation Branch had a proud tradition of excellence that he had been entrusted to uphold and protect, and if Alex's theory was wrong then the Branch might never recover from the stigma that would result. However, the evidence regarding a fault in the design was overwhelming. His own career was on the line, and to involve outsiders now would be a gamble.

'Get your coat, Alex,' Coombes sighed with resignation. 'We're going to the CAA. And let's hope to Christ that they don't laugh us out of the building.'

The Civil Aviation Authority is based at Aviation House, a substantial structure to the south of the Gatwick Airport complex.

The knot inside Alex's stomach tightened as he and Sir Roger entered the building. This confrontation would be bloody, he was sure. The director had been right: much of their evidence was open to various interpretations, and the CAA would fight tooth and nail against grounding the D500 without approval and reciprocal action from the FAA and IATA. They had to find an argument that would be unequivocal. The deficiency in the J13-25 compound would be the key; it was the only aspect of their research that had proven categorically that the D500 was unsafe. But even so there was a safety margin of two to three years to be taken into consideration, meaning the proposal could be bounced from one committee to another almost indefinitely before any positive action would be taken.

Their visit had been unannounced. They were told that the safety regulations director was unavailable, and that they would have to see the deputy director instead. Alex groaned inwardly as he heard the news. He had butted heads with Deputy Director Kingsley Appleton on a number of previous occasions, the stuffy bureaucrat blocking him on each of their previous encounters.

They sat in silence outside the deputy director's office for a full twenty-five minutes before they were finally summoned. The antipathy that existed between Alex and Appleton was palpable the moment he opened the door and welcomed them in.

'Sir Roger. What a pleasant surprise, and Mr. Jamieson, so very good to see you again.'

Alex smiled without humour or affection, and shook the deputy director's hand, the flesh soft and flabby, the grip as weak as a nervous child's.

'What brings you here, then?'

Alex was about to speak, but Sir Roger jumped in before him.

'Mr. Appleton, we wish to discuss the situation regarding the D500. My accident inspectors and I are greatly concerned about the safety of the aircraft, and we have discovered some disturbing evidence to justify these concerns.'

'I see. Won't you sit down?' Appleton gestured to the chairs facing his desk as he sunk heavily into his own seat. 'Tell me about these concerns of yours,' he said, as if speaking to a naïve young nephew, 'and this evidence that you have.'

Alex noted the cynicism emphasized on the word 'evidence'.

Sir Roger explained how the J13-25 compound had been tested and the results achieved. The deputy director listened attentively. Alex said little during his superior's monologue, merely confirming technical details or correcting minor errors.

'I see,' Appleton nodded slowly with false comprehension. 'So you think that this stringer is the cause of Flight 4401's demise, and not the bomb, which you yourselves have ascertained brought down the aircraft.'

'The bomb was the trigger,' Alex said, 'but the weakness of the lower main stringer is what caused such a catastrophic failure.'

'You know,' Appleton leaned back in his chair, 'laboratory tests such as the ones you and your colleagues have conducted are all well and good, but the results can be manipulated to say just about anything. How can you be sure that this alleged fault is as dangerous as you believe? Surely such a weakness would have been detected prior to certification, would it not?'

Alex felt himself being drawn into an avenue of debate that he did not wish to be. 'As you know, Dramar Aerospace conduct their own fatigue tests, just as all the American manufacturers do. It's possible that they… missed something.' To openly accuse Dramar of deliberate deception at this point could be suicidal to their cause.

'Perhaps, but it is unlikely, wouldn't you agree?'

'Unlikely, yes, but perfectly feasible.'

'And did not Sir Roger, here, state that it would take two to three years for this alleged failure to occur naturally?'

'He did,' Alex sighed.

'So why are you pushing to have an otherwise perfectly airworthy plane grounded so quickly? The AAIB report has not even been written yet, let alone published. I believe that any precipitant action on the part of the CAA would be,' Appleton paused, searching for the right words, 'premature and reactionary. Have you any idea what the media would do with a story like this?'

'We're not part of Dramar's public relations team, and bad publicity for a manufacturer should not be allowed to affect the CAA's safety policy. The laboratory evidence is conclusive. Even you should be able to see that, Kingsley.' Alex regretted the jibe even as he said it.

'I beg your pardon?'

Sir Roger intervened. 'Ahem. What we must not lose sight of is the fact that the first eleven aircraft, at least, carry a fault which can result in a catastrophic failure. Such a fault must be investigated.'

'Which we have done,' Alex added, earning himself a glace of rebuke.

'Do you not think,' Appleton said, 'that perhaps you are a little too close to the problem? I'll tell you what I see: the first eleven aircraft—'

'Two of which have already been lost,' Alex interrupted.

Appleton did not disguise his irritation. 'The first eleven aircraft had a possible fault. The next twenty or so aircraft off the production line carried extra supports to compensate for this, but when Dramar Aerospace discovered through their own research that they were superfluous, they reverted to the original design.'

'Oh, yes,' Alex said sarcastically. 'Why didn't any of us think of that? Come on, Kingsley, look at the facts. If the—'

'I haven't seen any facts. You show me one piece of evidence that the D500s flying today are faulty, then I will back you up. Show me that any of those aircraft are unsafe, and you will have the full support of the CAA. But at the moment all I can see is what appears to be a campaign by the AAIB to discredit an aircraft and manufacturer that has been the victim of two terrorist attacks.'

'We've given you evidence. Get your own experts to check on our results. I guarantee they will come to the same conclusions.'

'Very well, however I think our people will conduct a more thorough investigation, and not make the mistake of revealing their findings before they are certain of the results.'

Alex wanted to break the supercilious oaf's nose. 'The tests will not take longer than a week to conduct. Your experts will tell you that. If they confirm our findings, can we assume the CAA will move to ground the D500 in this country, and make strong representations with IATA and the FAA?'

'The reality of the situation, as you well know, is somewhat more complicated than that. The test results will have to be evaluated thoroughly. Not just by ourselves, but also by the other JAA member states and the FAA. If there does indeed appear to be a design flaw, we must then consider all possible courses of action. An Airworthiness Directive would seem to be the most likely solution. We cannot simply ground an aircraft based on little more than malicious hearsay.'

'If we wait that long, how many more D500s would have been lost? How many tombstones will it take to get the CAA to act?'

'I have already explained to you,' Appleton said patiently, 'the CAA cannot ground an aircraft based on a single test. You need to present more evidence. If you can convince me that this fault is a genuine threat to public safety, then you will have the support of the CAA. Is that clear?'

'Perfectly,' Sir Roger said, rising from his seat and straightening his waistcoat. 'I think that concludes our business for today.'

They left, the AAIB director thanking Appleton for his time, and made the slow walk to the car. It was raining again, droplets of water splashing onto Sir Roger's umbrella as they made their way through the car park. Alex walked several feet away, the raindrops that hit his face and hair feeling refreshing after the enclosed atmosphere of Aviation House.

'I think that could have gone a little better,' the director said.

Alex didn't need to be told that his own conduct had been counter-productive. 'Sorry, Roger. The guy just pisses me off. What are you going to tell the Minister?'

'I haven't the foggiest, but that's for me to deal with. Appleton may have been right about one thing, though. You *are* very close to the problem. Perhaps you should consider taking a break.'

Alex shot a look at the director, who continued to stare ahead through the sheets of rain. 'I can't. I have to see this through. If I were to leave now, even for a few days, then the whole team could lose focus.'

'You need a break. Davenport can take over in the interim.'

'Please, Roger. Don't force this on me. I can handle it.'

The senior man pondered this for a few moments, as raindrops ran down his glasses in small rivulets.

'All right, I suppose we're stuck with you then – for the time being,' he added pointedly. 'Now, we need more evidence. Where do we get it?'

'Dramar produced eleven aircraft, then changed the design. Now they seem to have gone back to the original specification, but they can't have. I think we should take a look at one of the newer aircraft. If there has been an alteration to the design, then it'll not only prove that there was a fault on the original aircraft, but that they're guilty of concealing that fact from the public, the regulatory bodies, and probably the airlines that they've sold aircraft to.'

'It may not be enough to convince the CAA.'

'But if we keep pushing hard enough, we may be able to shake loose the truth.'

'Fair enough. The chairman of British Occidental Airways is a friend of mine, and I believe they have just taken delivery of a number of D500s.'

'Five were delivered last month,' Alex confirmed.

'I'll see if he will make one available for inspection.'

They reached the car, Alex's hair stuck down on his head and face by the rain. He just needed some more time and a little luck. Getting any airline to take an aircraft out of service, even for just a few hours, was a tall order. Such an interruption would cost British Occidental tens of thousands in lost revenue. As favours went, this was a big one. The company chairman would have to be a very good friend indeed.

That could be the piece of luck he needed. Now he just needed the time to capitalize on it.

Thirty-One

'Burnett,' the FBI agent said as he plucked the mobile phone from his jacket pocket.

'Scott Eagle. You got anything new on the Grant case?'

'How the hell would I know anything. This is a Washington office operation now – sir.' The deference to his superior was a little late, but he hoped it had been enough.

'Same here. We've been through every reporter in the DC area. Nothing. We extended the search to take in New Jersey, Pennsylvania, and Maryland. Nothing. New York. Still nothing. We've spent thousands of hours going over the information we have. I've got twenty analysts studying the data, and profilers working on Grant and Diana. I think we're gonna have to start thinking of going into Dramar and just hope that we come up with something.'

'Sounds risky. If we don't find anything, their lawyers could crucify us.'

'Tell me about it. I've got to clear it with the director. When I get that clearance, I want you to handle the raid on Skysystems at Gunpowder Falls. Washington can handle Skysoft on Canal Street.'

'Thanks,' Burnett said, wondering why Eagle was promoting him so rapidly. 'When do we go?'

'Thursday. That's just three days away. Can you be ready in time?'

'Don't worry about us. My team'll be ready.'

The water was cool enough to be rejuvenating, but not so cold as to leave her shivering as she hoisted herself from the pool in one swift, graceful movement. Donatella rubbed herself down gently, not trying to scrape every last drop from her body; the ultraviolet lamps set into the ceiling would soon finish the job. She could have bathed naked if she had wished, the wide panoramic windows mirrored to prevent the intrusion of prying eyes, but she preferred the security and feel of the Versace swimsuit. Besides, she never felt comfortable swimming nude with fewer than three Martinis inside her.

She relaxed on the soft lounger, the warmth of the lights making her drowsy, and she did not fight the lethargy that descended. If there was a better cure for stress, then she hadn't heard of it. Donatella was a creature of the sun, never happier than when lazing on a secluded beach, allowing the sunlight to slowly evaporate the droplets of water that glistened on her body. This artificially generated illusion was the next best thing, and she rarely spent fewer than three hours a day in her own private paradise.

Occasionally she would feel a passing pity for those who could not afford such luxury, or had the means but not the time. Poor things. She floated in that glorious place between sleep and consciousness as the lamps caressed the last of the water from her golden skin.

The sudden music scythed its way through the layers of sleep and into her mind. Taylor Swift. She immediately sat bolt upright. The song from a cellular phone. It was *that* phone; the mobile that was reserved for just one caller, the sound that she had hoped she would never hear again. She answered it with a shaking hand.

'Donatella Martinelli speaking.'

'Hello Miss Martinelli. This is Gerard Burnett.'

'What can I do for you, Agent Burnett?' she asked, hearing the quaver in her own voice and cursing herself for it.

'It's going down. I spoke to Eagle an hour ago. Dramar is to be raided on Thursday. This is it. The fat lady's singing.'

She paused a moment too long before replying. 'I understand. One hundred thousand dollars will be deposited in the Cayman account in the morning. You may not contact me again unless the situation changes before Thursday. Is that understood?'

'Perfectly. Nice doing business with you.'

This was it. This was the end of her life as she knew it. In two days Donatella Martinelli would disappear, and the wealthy recluse, Dominique De Paz, would emerge from nowhere.

Five years: that was how long she estimated she would be exiled from America. The furore following Dramar's collapse would have abated by then, and it should be safe for her to return. Not to Washington, of course. Not even anywhere on the east coast. Southern California would be her destination, and she could once again mingle with the idle rich, this time in the affluent Balboa Park district of San Diego. A little cosmetic surgery would be required, but losing her own face would be a small price to pay for freedom. She couldn't help but smile at the thought of becoming a blond. Imagine that, she thought. Her black hair had always defined her, and now she would be abandoning it. These were strange times, indeed.

Her hand had now steadied and she felt capable of making the next call.

'Mr. Levitt, this is Nina Ferroni. I need you to be ready to leave at nine o' clock this evening.'

'No problem, Princess. I'll be waiting for you.'

Thirty-Two

The White House chief-of-staff greeted the Israeli Ambassador with customary familiarity, shaking his hand and gesturing to the leather chair opposite his desk.

'Mr. Kenton,' Gerald Solomon began, 'we have a mutual problem.'

'We do?' Kenton feigned ignorance. 'What's that then, Ambassador?'

'Yes. The escalating hostility by Quamar against the state of Israel, and the continuing terrorist campaign against an American manufactured aircraft. The two issues are inextricably linked, and we need to discuss a solution which would be beneficial to both our nations.'

'Mr. Ambassador,' Kenton said, toying with his pen, flipping it end over end. 'The two issues may seem closely linked from the Israeli perspective, but to the US government they are very different. As yet, there is no evidence to suggest a link to these two tragic air crashes. It has not even been proven that the Quamari disaster was deliberate. The American citizen who has been arrested for planting a bomb couldn't have been responsible for the attack on Pacific Atlantic Flight 4401, and the charge that Israeli-made equipment was found in his hotel room is questionable at best. I sympathize with your position, but can't see how we can be of help.'

Solomon knew his hand was pretty weak, and that this game of diplomatic brinkmanship would be costly, but he had at least one ace up his sleeve. Humiliating concessions would have to be made, and would have far-reaching consequences that Israel would feel for years to come. But the alternative was unthinkable.

'We are facing possibly the greatest threat in our history. Several of the more volatile Arab nations have openly declared their support for the Quamari position. There has been a violent upsurge by the Palestinians. We have the strength to defend ourselves against a single enemy, but if several Middle Eastern countries are arrayed against us, I fear we may not prevail. I have been asked, by my government, to request American military intervention to end this dispute. What is required is a show of unified strength against the Arab aggressors. Quamar would not dare start a war if they face not only the Israeli army and air force, but also the might of the American navy.' A little ego-boosting flattery never did any harm when negotiating with the Americans.

Kenton considered the request for long moments before giving a measured response. 'If hostilities are initiated by Quamar, then the United States would make strong representations within the United Nations. Economic sanctions against any aggressor are virtually guaranteed, and I am sure would be supported by the majority of UN member states. Furthermore, it may be possible for us to consider covert military assistance on a limited scale. But to be blunt, Mr. Ambassador, the risks of open military action on our part outweigh the possible benefits.'

Solomon nodded slowly. He had expected this to be the American position. If the tables were reversed, then he would have done nothing different. But diplomatic discussions were always about posturing: a process of gambits, refusals, concessions, and compromises.

'What if I were able to offer you something that might make the proposal a little less one-sided?'

'What do you propose?'

'The identity of the terrorist responsible for the destruction of both Dramar Aerospace D500s, along with a string of other bombings and assassinations over the past decade.'

Kenton hadn't been expecting that. 'Such information might be useful… But a simple name would not be enough for us to alter our stance.'

'My government will make available all the information we have on this individual: photographs, aliases, known associates, security profiles etc. Plus a recent videotape, taken in Quamar just prior to the destruction of the Quamar Airways jet.'

This was indeed a tempting proposal. Solomon had been right: Quamar would not dare attack Israel if the United States threatened military action in response to hostilities, especially if such a warning was backed up by a strong show of force by the American navy. A UN resolution would be required before the United States could enter into the conflict, but that could be easily bought for the right political price. This was one of the benefits of being the most powerful nation on the planet.

'I will need to speak to the President before any decision can be made.'

'Of course, but would you also remind him of how the destruction of the state of Israel would destabilize the balance of power within the Middle East, threatening the supply of oil to the West? He should also bear in mind the political cost of having seven million Israeli refugees suddenly requiring resettlement, many of whom I'm sure would wish to come to America.'

'I will pass on your comments.' Kenton stood to see the Ambassador to the door.

'When can I expect a response, Mr. Kenton?'

'If it is convenient, Mr. Ambassador, could you return in,' he glanced at his watch, 'three hours? I know the President has a window in his busy schedule at five p.m.'

'Five o' clock would be satisfactory. Good afternoon, Mr. Kenton.'

'A pleasure as always, Ambassador.'

As the door to the Oval Office was opened, Solomon could see George Kenton standing ready to greet him.

Two Secret Service agents flanked the door, hands behind
their backs, and both could have had a Browning nine
millimetre ready to fire in under a second. The Israeli
Ambassador knew that, since arriving at the White House,
he had already passed through ten security devices that he
could see, plus at least a dozen discreet sensors that he
couldn't; everything from simple metal detectors to infra-
red scanners. No one came near this room without the
Secret Service's say-so, and the most elite of agents –
Presidential protection – were ready to meet any threat to
their Commander-in-Chief. It was just possible that he
had been able to smuggle some kind of weapon in, even
this far, and if that failed the Ambassador could still try to
throttle their boss with his bare hands. Vigilance at all
times was the motto.

Behind Kenton, Solomon could see Harry
Macfarlane – the National Security Adviser, Jack Stone –
Director of the FBI, and seated behind the ancient oak
desk was the President himself. All stood graciously to
greet him and Kenton led the Ambassador to a chair, alone
in the centre of the room and facing his hosts with the crest
of the United States of America embroidered into the
carpet beneath him. The seating arrangements, indeed the
very surroundings, were designed to intimidate, but he
had faced far worse during his long and chequered career.

Kenton cleared his throat before speaking. These
opening rounds were clearly going to be his show. 'Thank
you for being so punctual, Mr. Ambassador. We have
discussed your proposal, however the offer is not
sufficient for us to risk the lives of American servicemen

and women. We will require considerably more from the Israeli government.'

That was all Solomon needed to know. Those last two sentences were confirmation that America was willing to aid Israel in a military conflict. The agreement was wreathed in diplomatic language, but it was now just a matter of negotiating terms, and they would not make demands that would be totally unacceptable to his government, of which he was now the sole representative with full Executive powers.

'What more does the United States require of us?' he asked with his hands spread in a gesture of openness.

'We have noted over recent months that Israel has been… less than cooperative within the UN towards the United States. We would like this trend to be reversed. We will also require full financial recompense for the expenditure of military involvement, and a more favourable attitude towards American companies wishing to trade with Israel.'

'Those terms are extremely harsh. We believe that it is in America's best interests to help preserve the state of Israel, as our small country is an enclave of friendship in an otherwise hostile region. American companies are given the same opportunities in Israel as any other country, but we could discuss initiatives that would be beneficial to America in the free market.'

The diplomatic negotiations continued for a further twenty minutes, with not a word from the rest of the group, just a slight nod or shake of the head from the

President when Kenton looked to him for agreement or refusal. A deal was finally struck.

'Ambassador,' Harry Macfarlane said, not bothering to address him as 'Mister', a convention he never paid attention to, 'I think we're all intrigued as to how you know so much about this terrorist when the CIA have no leads. Would you care to enlighten us?'

For the first time during the meeting, Solomon felt uneasy. He was quite happy with the terms of the agreement they had brokered, but the next few minutes would be uncomfortable.

'I regret to inform you that… the reason we know so much about the identity of the terrorist, is because she is a former Mossad field agent.'

'She?' Macfarlane said.

Solomon heard a whistle escape from Stone's lips.

'Her real name is Mosa Ahmed. She was a Palestinian, recruited and trained by the Israeli Secret Service. It was our intention for her to infiltrate the upper echelons of Hamas, identifying and eliminating the strike force commanders. For a time, we believed that all was well. She killed four of the leaders, but then disappeared. Since then she has worked as an assassin and freelance terrorist for a number of organizations. We have been able to track her movements over the years, but have never succeeded in apprehending her. You may know her by the code name we gave her, and continues to use: Artemis.'

'Ah,' Stone said with recognition.

'You know her?' the President asked.

'Yeah. Tough bitch to nail down. No pictures, no regular *modus operandi*, no history.'

Solomon reached into his jacket pocket, making the Secret Service agents nervous, and withdrew a single flash drive. 'This is a copy of all the information we have on her, and this,' he pulled an SD card from his pocket, 'is a video that was obtained by Mossad at Barakat International Airport.' He handed it to Stone. 'It is the only recent image we have of her. Needless to say, this information is something of an embarrassment to Mossad, which is why we have not shared it previously.'

'I can imagine,' Macfarlane said with a wicked grin, barely able to contain his amusement. 'Nice to know even Mossad ain't perfect.'

The President did not share his sentiment. 'Mr. Ambassador, a lot of lives might have been spared if you'd come to us sooner.'

'My government is aware of this, and we apologize unreservedly for the deception. Perhaps, if we can put the past behind us, we can now begin a new era of openness and cooperation between our two great nations?'

'Don't count on it,' Macfarlane muttered.

'Now that we have a workable agreement,' Solomon said, ignoring the jibe from the National Security Adviser, 'When would American forces be in a position to offer assistance?'

Archer pressed a button on his desk. 'Admiral Harper, would you come in please?'

The side door to the Oval Office opened almost immediately and a uniformed senior naval officer, festooned with medals and ribbons, entered the room.

'Admiral, what assets do we have in the Middle East right now?'

'Mr. President, we have the Eisenhower battle group standing by in the Persian Gulf, the John Stennis and the Ronald Reagan in the Mediterranean, and the British have the carrier Queen Elizabeth at the mouth of the Red Sea. Two squadrons of F-15s are based—'

'Thank you, Admiral. That will be all.'

'Thank you, Mr. President.'

'Does that answer your question, Mr. Ambassador?'

'It does, sir.'

'Unless hostilities break out beforehand, we will begin aerial manoeuvres along the Quamari border in seventy-two hours.'

FBI director Jack Stone excused himself from the meeting at the earliest opportunity, clutching the briefcase which contained the priceless security details that had been provided courtesy of Mossad. Things must have been bad, he thought, for 'The Institute' to give up information like that. They were well known throughout the profession as being the most secretive of secret organizations, and to admit to a *failure?* This situation was totally without precedent.

As soon as the motorcade arrived at the J. Edgar Hoover building on Pennsylvania Avenue, the innocuous-looking flash drive and SD card were rushed upstairs to Scott Eagle's waiting team of agents. Pretty soon the Director of Central Intelligence would be beating the FBI director's door down, desperate to claim the material for his own agency, so Stone wanted to get as much of a lead as he could. As far as the Constitution was concerned, the lines of responsibility here were a little blurred. It was merely good fortune that he enjoyed a better relationship with the President than his CIA counterpart.

It took an infuriating forty-five minutes for the data to be downloaded, decrypted and translated into English from Hebrew. The Anti-Terrorism division would also have a central role to play, but for the moment Eagle wanted to scan the information for himself and hear the gut reactions of the eighteen-strong team who had been directly involved with the case from the beginning. In all, over two hundred and fifty FBI agents had been working on the Dramar Aerospace investigation, but these were his top people: men and women handpicked by himself whom he knew to be extraordinarily gifted in their various fields.

Copies of the fifty-page dossier were distributed among the agents, and Eagle sat down to study his own hastily assembled copy of the document.

Mosa Ahmed had been a strike force commander when she was captured by an Israeli Defence Force undercover unit, which in itself was unusual. Although the Palestinians were among the more progressive of the Arab peoples, it was still unusual to see a woman achieve a position of authority. Not only that, he read, but she had also been the mastermind behind a number of strategic initiatives.

'Christ,' Eagle whispered loud enough for others to hear. The final assignment set by the Unified National Command for the Uprising had been to seek out and destroy undercover units on the ground, and twice she had been successful. It had taken three bullets to bring her down, including a glancing blow to the head.

When Solomon had said that Mosa Ahmed was recruited from the UNC, he had been using polite diplomatic language to hide the true nature of her enlistment. The eighteen-year-old girl – the same age as his own daughter – had been tortured, both mentally and physically, sexually assaulted, undergone sleep deprivation, and then shared cells with Israeli criminal prisoners, who despised the Palestinians as strongly as their captors, which led to further abuse.

When they believed her spirit had been well and truly broken, and the pathetic wretch who had been Mosa Ahmed teetered on the brink of madness, she was offered a way out, which she had accepted without question.

Eagle stopped reading for a moment. He was sickened by the coldly graphical descriptions of orchestrated gang-rape, systematic physical abuse and psychological manipulation designed to tear away an individual's humanity. These were the matter-of-fact details that had dehumanized that young woman all those years before. Not for the first time it was brought home to him that in the real world there *were* no good guys and bad guys. She had been a freedom fighter in the eyes of her own people, but a terrorist in the eyes of the Israelis. However, it was they who had turned her into the monster that she had become.

The brutalization continued once she was in the hands of Mossad, but was carried out in a more coordinated manner, the rape of her psyche sustained for months until they were certain she was unquestionably theirs. Mosa was trained as one of them in all aspects of assassination, terrorism, demolition, explosives, infiltration, concealment, and a range of other 'black' procedures. She was eventually released back into the occupied territories, and successfully eliminated four Palestinian terrorist leaders.

But Mossad had not taken into account the spirit of Mosa Ahmed. They hadn't beaten her entirely, merely focusing her hatred and resentment and furnishing her with the tools and abilities to continue her campaign.

A predator had been released into the wild.

The next page listed assassinations and terrorist attacks that she was known or suspected to have carried out, many of which had been true masterpieces of the craft.

Photographs filled the next few pages, all of them showing a pretty eighteen-year-old girl. She was quite beautiful, and for an instant he found it difficult to accept that this almond-eyed Venus could possibly be responsible for the acts for which she was accused. But this, he quickly realized, was just the basic hormonal reaction a man felt when confronted with an image of this kind. She was a cold-hearted killer. That was all that mattered, he kept telling himself.

The last twenty or so pages contained psychiatric profiles from when she had been recruited by Mossad – which were practically useless as she had fooled the intelligence service's finest for so long – a possible pattern of *modus operandi*, which was equally useless as her methods were too varied to classify, known aliases, and finally a list of associates. Eagle had to smile at that one. The list had only three names on it, and one of them had been shot dead in Nairobi the previous spring. The second was Samir Abdallah, a strike force commander who had been at large since before Mosa's capture, a decade and a half earlier. Last known location: Gaza City. The final name on the list was Khalid Al-Namari, who was also believed to have been an activist within the strike forces. Last known location: São Paulo, Brazil, four months ago. A single photograph accompanied each of the last two names, but both images were too indistinct to be of much use. Perhaps image enhancement and photo manipulation would help, but he had his doubts.

The hubbub within the room had risen to a substantial level when Eagle finished his cursory examination of the documents, indicating that the other eighteen agents had also finished and were bouncing ideas off one another in an unofficial brainstorming session. Eagle allowed this to continue for several minutes as he listened to various theories being expounded and courses of action proposed. Some were quite obvious, others were intriguing, and a few were downright bizarre.

It was time to view the video from Barakat International. How Mossad had obtained it, he had no idea, and didn't really care. The CIA could have the pleasure of trying to work that one out, and the best of luck to them.

The recording began, and Eagle took a few moments to assimilate what he was seeing. A readout in the corner of the screen displayed the date and time, and which camera was being used. The scene, he realized, was the roof of the Barakat terminal building. A crowd of people with their backs to the lens stood at the protective railing. All heads turned as one as they watched an unseen aircraft taxi at speed down the runway.

'Hope it gets better than this,' one of the agents commented.

When the spectacle was over and there was nothing of interest left to see, the assembly began to move toward the exit, passing directly beneath the camera. Just a few individuals passed by to start with, but soon the main group followed.

Eagle saw a woman among them, shuffling forwards with the rest. Her head was bowed as her eyes moved over the floor, the face obscured behind a dark shawl and a mass of obsidian hair.

'Is that her?' he asked no one in particular.

'Look up at us, baby.'

The Arab ambling along to her right looked up at the camera.

'Come on, sweetheart. Give us a peek.'

She noticed the man looking up and followed his gaze.

'That's our girl,' Eagle almost shouted, and clapped his hands in triumph.

She looked down again, not with the instinctive reaction that one might have expected, but casually in the perfectly natural motion of someone who has nothing to hide. She was a real pro.

Eagle shook his head slowly as the woman disappeared beneath the camera. She truly was beautiful, even more so than the photographs had shown her to be when she was just eighteen. The years since her capture and torture had been kind, the face now showing the graceful allure of maturity. Once again he had to remind himself that she was a merciless mass-murderer, directly responsible for the deaths of one hundred and sixty-three innocent Americans on one flight alone.

The playback was repeated another half dozen times before the image of those exquisite eyes was frozen on the screen.

'Well,' Eagle said at last, 'this bitch ain't gonna come knocking on the door, so we'd better work out how we're going to catch her.'

The faces that stared back at him did not look optimistic.

Thirty-Three

The airfield was almost deserted by the time Donatella arrived, more than three quarters of an hour late. The journey from Washington had been a nightmare of delays, frustrations, and petty irritations. The plane from Washington National Airport had been delayed due to a "slight technical problem", causing a knock-on effect on the rest of the journey, which meant that she didn't arrive in Tallahassee, on the Georgia/Florida border until nearly six in the evening. Once she had taken possession of the hire car, though, it had simply required a long, fast drive south until she arrived at Tampa.

Following her uncomfortable first meeting with the pilot, she had firmly decided to dress down for the final flight of the harrowing journey, wearing shapeless slacks and sweater, and the flattest pair of shoes she possessed. She hoped that this would be enough to dissuade Levitt from making any unwelcome advances, but was still nervous about spending several hours alone with him in the Learjet.

When she arrived at the drab, prefabricated hut she found it locked and darkened, as bereft of life as the rest of this God forsaken place. Donatella felt genuine fear begin to rise within her, which threatened to overwhelm the façade of composure to which she was so desperately trying to cling. The entire plan was dependent upon *him*. If he had given up waiting and gone off somewhere to get drunk…

She turned with a rising feeling of trepidation as she heard footsteps approaching in the darkness, and a powerful flashlight was shone directly into her face. It was impossible to distinguish the figure in the glare of the beam, and she shielded her eyes as best she could.

'Mr. Levitt?' she asked hesitantly.

'You took your Goddamned time. Just about given you up.'

'I was delayed. Are you ready?'

'Sure. You in a hurry, then?'

She ignored the remark. 'I have two suitcases in the trunk that need to be taken aboard.'

Levitt raised a bemused eyebrow. 'Only two? You're not planning on being away long, then?'

'That's none of your business.'

'Whatever you say, Princess.'

He stood close to her – uncomfortably close – and she could smell alcohol on his breath.

'I s'pose you want *me* to shift 'em into the Lear?'

'If you wouldn't mind.' Just a few more hours of this purgatory remained, and she would force herself to endure it, no matter how unpleasant it would be. What other choice did she have?

The reluctant pilot heaved the cases from the car and threw them, without a great deal of finesse, into the cargo hold before sealing it closed.

'Right, you got the rest of the money?'

'I have – but not until we arrive at Pointe-à-Pitre.'

'Don't you trust me?' he asked with a smirk.

'Is there any reason why I should?'

'Not really, I guess. I'll trust you, though. Besides, it's a long way to the island, and we can sort out the details later.'

It was twenty more minutes before they finally took off, Levitt filing a flight plan with the local Air Traffic Control and going through the series of pre-flight checks. A more reputable pilot would have been assisted by a co-pilot, but he was not a man who regarded FAA regulations as workable or fair on small privateers, and generally disregarded those rules which were an inconvenience.

All the time the plane sat immobile on the tarmac, Donatella stared anxiously from the window, half-expecting to see a train of FBI fleet sedans come charging down the runway to prevent the take-off. But eventually they took to the air, briefly sweeping across the Gulf of Mexico before crossing the Florida mainland and heading out south-east over the Atlantic.

Levitt kept well clear of Cuban airspace. All manner of problems might ensue if he were to stray too close without permission, something he occasionally did to wake up the local air defences. Once a fighter pilot;

always a fighter pilot, but the Lear wasn't an F-15, and his passenger looked restless enough as it was.

An hour passed as she looked down upon the blackness of the ocean before she saw lights below.

'If you're lookin' out the window,' Levitt said through the cockpit to cabin intercom, 'that's Andros in the Bahamas below us, and the next sight of civilization on our grand tour of the Caribbean will be Acklins Island.'

She made no attempt to respond. The stresses of the day had left her too weary to hold a conversation anyway (even if she wanted to), but she could not sleep. She was terrified of the pilot, terrified of being caught, even though they were now well clear of United States territorial waters, terrified of everything. She could not even begin to relax until she was safely in the beach house near Petit-Canal.

Levitt came back to see her a couple of times, trusting the autopilot to keep them on course. Donatella was genuinely grateful when he offered her a bottle of warm Bacardi and told her to help herself, which she did so eagerly, not giving a thought to the fact that she was drinking it neat from a coffee-stained plastic cup. The alcohol had the desired effect of calming her frayed nerves, but she refused to allow herself to relax or, worse still, believe that she was truly free.

However, she could not prevent her mind from wandering to a happier place. Could it be true? Had her escape really been successful? Donatella Martinelli's life had ended at Tallahassee. It was now Dominique De Paz who travelled south over the Caribbean islands to a new, simpler, and anonymous life. Could it really be true?

After several hours of flight, she felt pressure build in her ears, and swallowed several times to neutralize the sensation. They were descending. The penultimate leg of the journey was coming to an end. Ahead, she could see a few lights on the ground, and long before she expected, they had touched down at the small airport that served Pointe-à-Pitre, the large town which sat on the isthmus of land that connected the two halves of the island.

The Learjet taxied to the small, squat terminal building, an oasis of light in the sea of darkness. Levitt had been good to his word, she conceded, and had transported her safely to her destination without incident. He came back into the passenger cabin once the plane had come to a halt.

'End of the line, Princess. I think you'll agree I've played my part.'

'You have,' she said, allowing a gracious smile to cross her lips. Donatella was almost beginning to like this rogue of the skies, despite his overly familiar attitude towards a paying passenger, and regretted her earlier mistrust of him. She pulled a wad of notes from her handbag – plus a few extra – and handed them to him.

'There are taxicabs outside twenty-four hours a day. You won't have any trouble getting wherever you're going.'

'Thank you. Would you mind helping me with the cases?'

'Not a problem.'

Levitt hauled the hefty suitcases through immigration all the way to the taxi.

'You okay from here?'

'Yes, thank you. Goodbye, Mr. Levitt. I'll be sure to use your services again if I ever have the need, and recommend you if ever I'm asked.'

'Adieu, Mademoiselle Ferroni.'

After an hour in the taxi, conversing in broken French with the driver, she finally arrived at the small beach house. It was perfect. Her exile might not be too much of a trial after all, she thought as she waved regally to the servants who stood outside to greet her. Dominique De Paz stepped gracefully from the car, introducing herself to the three members of her staff, who had been waiting most of the night for her to arrive.

But Donatella Martinelli would return to haunt her, and much sooner than she might have expected.

Thirty-Four

Alex arrived at the DERA complex before the dawn, rain lashing down and his breath condensing in the frigid autumn air.

He spoke with Damian Beaumont for several minutes, discussing the effects of the Mach stem on the D500's lower stringer. This secondary shock wave would compound the effect of the incident shock – the original explosive detonation. The initial wave of energy would propagate outwards in an expanding sphere until it met any reflective surfaces, like the skin of the aircraft, which would absorb some energy by deformation. But as the blast front is moving at supersonic speeds, the skin cannot deform rapidly enough, and much of the energy simply passes through it. When this energy meets the outside air, the shock wave is reflected back into the airframe to recombine with the incident shock, creating a wave significantly more powerful than is originally released. It was this that had caused such devastating damage to the lower main stringer, as well as some of the smaller stringers which, along with the ring-shaped frame stations that supported the hull around its circumference, maintained the structural integrity of the aircraft.

As they now had accurate data on the size and position of the explosive device, it should be possible to precisely calculate the effects of the explosion. All this information was vital to the investigation, but was of longer-term interest. What Alex needed now was solid facts on the properties of the stringers. Only by proving beyond doubt that the J13-25 compound was flawed and a potential danger to public safety could they present a watertight case to the CAA.

The Investigator-in-Charge moved on to his own office, grabbing a steaming mug of coffee on the way. He was scanning through his emails before he had even sat down, his eyes going wide when he saw one from British Occidental Airways.

The door opened abruptly and Sir Roger Coombes strode in.

'Alex,' he said breathlessly, I've just had an e-mail from British Occidental. One of their new D500s is stranded at JFK. Some kind of rudder problem, I think it said.'

'I think I've had the same email. I'm just reading it now.'

'Anyway, that doesn't matter. It'll be grounded for at least forty-eight hours, and the airline's chief exec has granted us permission to give her an inspection. This is great, isn't it? It's what we've been waiting for.'

'Damn right it is.' Alex's mind raced. He'd had his doubts over whether Sir Roger could pull this off at all, let alone so quickly. 'I'll take Damian with me. Aside from Pennington, he knows more about the stringers than anyone else.' He paused as he weighed the situation in his head. 'And I'll take Samantha. She's a good organizer, and her engineering experience would be a big help to Damian. Davenport can handle things this end. We'll need a flight out today. I doubt we'll get over there in time to do any work this afternoon, though. Are you sure the plane is going to be out of commission tomorrow?'

'That's what the message says. Read it for yourself. I have to leave. Good luck, Alex. Bring us back a result,' Sir Roger shouted as he rushed out the door and down the hall.

Alex needed to think and act quickly. He'd vaguely formulated a plan, following the meeting with Kingsley Appleton at the CAA, but had mistakenly assumed that any inspection would take place within the UK.

He picked up the desk phone and dialled two-zero-seven. 'Samantha, have you got your passport with you?'

'My passport? Of course, it's with my emergency kit. Why? Where am I going?'

'Are you up to a trip to Washington?'

There was the faintest hint of a hesitation before she answered. 'Absolutely. What's happened?'

'British Occidental have a D500 grounded at JFK, which means we have a chance to give it an inspection. But it's got to be fast. Can you make the arrangements for you, me and Damian?'

'Sure.'

'Also, you'll need to liaise with the NTSB. I'll fire off a quick email to Leon Baptiste to let him know to expect us. Get things moving.' He hung up without waiting for a reply. Next on the list was Davenport. This situation was racing ahead too quickly for his liking.

Thirty-Five

'Uh-huh,' Madison Flynn said into the telephone receiver as she scribbled notes with her free hand. 'You got a name?'

Kramer watched her absently as he finalized the wording for tomorrow morning's broadcast.

'Cindy. Just Cindy, nothing else?' Another pause. 'Okay, Todd. I won't ask how you got this. Usual arrangements?' she asked, referring to payment for the illicitly obtained information.

'Anything useful?' Kramer asked once she had hung up.

'Yeah. I think we've got her.' She didn't expect too much of a reaction from the reporter. Flynn had lost count of the number of times that promising leads had resulted in nothing during this investigative report. There was no reason to believe that this scrap of intelligence would be any more fruitful than all the others, but she had a feeling about this one.

'Evidence? Real evidence?'

'This contact of mine says that he knows someone who was with a hooker in New York last week. It was obviously him, but he wasn't about to admit that to me. Apparently this girl was as high as a kite, and started talking to him. She mentioned a room-mate who has a long-term lease on this apartment.'

'East 83rd Street?'

'Yep. Goes by the name of Diana.'

'Sounds promising.'

This was a more favourable reaction than Flynn had expected. 'She was in New York the day before Grant's murder, and the day after the bombing of Flight 4401. She also, apparently, has a room in this apartment sealed tight. It all sounds a little suspicious to me.'

'And to me. The address tallies. The dates seem to correspond. What's your gut feeling?'

Flynn hesitated. If she were wrong, Kramer would destroy her. But if she was right… 'This is the one. I'm sure of it, Lewis.'

'I've been doing some checking of my own. I was thinking about Diana. Strange name to use as a pseudonym, don't you think?'

'I guess. I hadn't really thought about it.'

'Well, I did. 'Diana' is the Roman equivalent of the ancient Greek goddess of hunting. The Greek name is Artemis.'

'Artemis!' she exclaimed. 'We know that name. She's a terrorist.'

'Yep. It all fits, and now we may know how to find her.'

'I'll book the flight to New York—'

'Wait a minute.' Kramer held up a hand. 'It's still not enough. What we really need is first-hand information and interviews from the investigation team. There's no way the FBI will agree to that, but the British investigators might, given the right incentives. There's a team flying into Dulles this evening. I'm going to arrange a meeting with the Investigator-in-Charge.'

'Then we go to New York?'

'Then *you* go to New York, with a camera crew, and stake out that apartment. It'll be raided by the FBI tomorrow morning. It's your turn to get your face on TV.'

For a moment Flynn was completely dumbstruck. 'Thanks, Lewis. I won't let you down. Where will you be?'

'Meeting with Alex Jamieson.' He sat back with a contented smile on his face. 'Big day tomorrow, Ms. Flynn.'

A very big day.

Thirty-Six

B y the time the 747 touched down at Washington Dulles International, it was five in the afternoon, local time. The snow that had been threatening the city for the past month had now begun to fall, coating the airport in a thin white blanket.

As the jet pushed its way through to the terminal building, Alex could see snowploughs scurrying down the opposite runway, desperately trying to keep it open. But it was obvious that they were losing the battle against the elements. As soon as a section of tarmac had been cleared, a fresh layer would begin to form, even covering the salted grit that was supposed to prevent such an occurrence. The capital was notorious for its harsh winters, and was often virtually immobilized as a result, but it was unusual for it to come so early in the season. Alex realized just how lucky they had been to land at Dulles at all.

Unlike the previous visit, three weeks before, no one was waiting to greet them. Samantha had made the arrangements for a hire car, as well as negotiating with

British Occidental Airways for the inspection the next day, arranging hotel accommodation for the trio (which Leon Baptiste had immediately cancelled, insisting that the team stay with his family), organizing a schedule for tomorrow, along with a host of other seemingly trivial, but vital considerations.

Their first port of call was the NTSB administrative offices on L'Enfant Plaza. Cooperation with their American counterparts was essential if the two-way flow of information were to continue in the future.

The snow was, by now, becoming a serious impediment to travel around the city, and several smaller routes were already impassable, but Alex handled the unfamiliar car skilfully. On several occasions he felt the back wheels begin to slide from under him, but each time, with the reactions of a racing driver, collected it up and kept moving more or less in the right direction.

'Are you sure about this, Mr. Jamieson?' asked Dan Cole, the NTSB's chairman, after Alex had delivered a similar speech to the one he had delivered to Sir Roger, two days before.

'No, I'm not sure. We can't be, until we know how the third generation D500 differs from the first eleven. We do know the J13-25 composite is subject to a failure under certain stress loads. We know that the design of the KX-7 supports has been altered twice since the start of production. What we don't know is how the third generation configuration is an improvement on the original design.'

'Maybe Dramar went back to the original configuration because they believed there was nothing wrong with it after all.'

'But they would have conducted exactly the same fatigue tests that we have, and would have reached the same conclusions. It makes no sense for them to fit the newer aircraft with the same flawed material.'

'True.' Cole weighed the options for a few moments before looking over to Leon Baptiste, who had been listening silently to the conversation. 'What's your opinion on this?'

'I was sceptical. I *am* sceptical, but the evidence seems pretty conclusive. Either way, we need to test the theory and establish whether Alex's conclusions hold up. The FAA are going to be the problem.'

'Leave them to me. As far as the FAA are concerned, for the moment we're just helping our British colleagues conduct some research.' He returned his attention to Alex. 'What do you need from us?'

The Investigator-in-Charge had expected the support of Cole, but it was still a relief to have the NTSB director on his side. 'Some technical equipment to help with tomorrow's inspection would be a great help.'

'Fine. Leon, give 'em whatever they need. This now takes top priority. If there is a fundamental flaw in the D500, and I pray to God there isn't, then we need to be certain of it as soon as possible. I'll contact JFK and make sure there are no hold-ups tomorrow. Is there anything else?'

There wasn't.

Baptiste drove them to FBI headquarters for a brief meeting with Scott Eagle. By now, Alex was getting really worried about the weather. If this snow kept up through the night, there was no way they would make it to New York tomorrow. His two companions obviously shared his concern as they stared silently out of the windows, but kept their anxieties to themselves. Baptiste, as always, seemed totally unperturbed by the conditions, having negotiated his way through far worse than this.

The New Brutalist façade of the J. Edgar Hoover building came into view, its hard, uncompromising lines softened by the snow. Their visit was expected and the four of them were escorted to Eagle's office on the fourth floor, overlooking the central courtyard that Alex hadn't even realized existed.

The Federal agent looked tired, the stresses of the past five weeks mirroring his own appearance.

'Hi there, Alex,' he welcomed them amiably. 'Good to see you again Ms. Shore.' His eyes fell upon the young metallurgical and composites engineer. 'I don't know you.'

'Damian Beaumont, sir. It's a pleasure to meet you.' Meeting a genuine, real-life FBI agent was a dream come true for the awe-struck young man.

'Jesus, Alex, you look like shit. When was the last time you got some sleep?'

'Bad habit, so I gave it up. Sometime in September, I think.'

'Looks like it. Leon says you got something to show me.'

Alex opened his briefcase and produced a box of discs. 'This is all the information we have on the J13-25 organic matrix compound, along with the relevant sections from both sets of schematics, test results, data on shock wave propagation, explosive material and quantities used—'

'Enough,' Eagle cut him off. 'I get the picture.'

'But this is all unofficial. If my director found out I was passing on information this sensitive, he'd have me for breakfast.'

'Understood. We'll use it to corner the bastards, but none of it will be admissible in court. I'll see to it that no mention is made of you, or the AAIB. That okay?'

'Completely. Now, one good turn deserves another. Have you got anything that might be of interest to us?'

Eagle frowned with a crooked smile playing on his mouth. 'Ask me again this time tomorrow.'

'Oh?'

The agent glanced at Samantha and Beaumont, judging whether they could be trusted, but Baptiste noticed this and gave him an unobtrusive nod.

'We're raiding Dramar Aerospace tomorrow: Skysoft, here in Washington, and Skysystems outside Baltimore. It'll be a massive operation, with over two hundred agents involved, but I think it's worth the gamble. We've learned just about all we're going to learn now. We need to see their confidential files.'

'Is there *anything* else you've found out?' Alex asked, probing deeper.

'Well…' Eagle said at length. 'We know who planted the bombs.' He pulled the revised dossier from his desk. 'She's quite a character. Take a look.'

Alex flicked through the folder, and his eyes were drawn to the photographs of the eighteen-year-old activist, and the digitally enhanced stills from the security video.

'Wow.'

'I know. Difficult to keep your eye on the ball when it looks like that.'

'Who is she?'

'Mosa Ahmed, a Palestinian terrorist who's been active for years.' Eagle didn't mention her involvement with the Israeli secret service, or the manner of the information's procurement. He didn't trust the British investigator that much.

Alex passed the file to Beaumont, whose eyes nearly popped out of his skull when he saw the young woman in the photographs.

'There was one interesting thing,' Eagle continued. 'A designer who worked on the D500 at DAC Skysystems was murdered on the day you visited the facility. At first, we speculated that this was carried out by Dramar themselves, but now it looks almost certainly to be the work of Ms. Ahmed, or Artemis, as she is usually known. We know that he had been talking to a woman, and the manner of the death was consistent with a professional assassination. Maybe he was about to blow her cover. If she wants to start a war in the Middle East…' He let the sentence hang unfinished as he considered a new possibility. If the Quamaris were to learn that it was an Arab who had destroyed one of their civilian aircraft, then there would be no logical reason to begin hostilities against Israel. Blaming the Jewish nation for such an atrocity would have been fundamental to the success of the plan. If the truth were to be made public, assuming it was believed by the interested parties, then the entire Middle East would unite to hunt her down.

'We'll have to end the meeting there. I've got some calls to make.'

Samantha had gone to bed early, exhausted after the flight from Heathrow and the whistle-stop tour of Washington's Federal Triangle. She did not handle sleep deprivation well at the best of times, and after the stresses of the past few weeks, she was barely conscious when her head hit the pillow.

Damian Beaumont was too agitated to even think about sleep, as this was his first visit to the United States and he had wanted to take a drive around the city, but the conditions outside were too treacherous to contemplate venturing out. He grudgingly decided to go to his room and work on the plan for tomorrow – if they made it to New York.

Alex envied him his youthful vigour, wishing that he still possessed the stamina to keep going hour after hour. He too wanted an early night, but Baptiste had insisted that they take some time to enjoy the bottle of Balvenie that Alex had brought with him. This had become a tradition whenever one of them visited the other's country, a tradition that Alex would have been happy to break if it would give him a few hours of rest. The next time Baptiste visited the UK, Alex decided, he would keep him up for forty-eight hours straight. That'd teach him.

'Go steady, Leon,' Alex said ineffectually as Baptiste poured a tumbler halfway to the top.

'You need a drink.'

'Sure. Feel free to be as generous as you like with my whisky.'

'I will,' Baptiste grinned a row of pearly white teeth as he sat down opposite his friend, taking a sizeable swig.

They sat in silence for a few moments until Baptiste could hold back no longer.

'You look like crap, Alex. What the hell you been doing to yourself?'

Alex laughed. Baptiste had never been one to mince his words. 'I guess I've been burning the candle at both ends. It's been pretty tough, the past few weeks.'

'Stop it, you're breaking my heart. What's the plan for tomorrow?'

'Damian and Samantha will carry out the inspection. I'll just be performing a supporting role. That's assuming we ever get to JFK.'

'Don't worry. We'll get you there. Even if it's by helicopter, we'll get you there. When Director Cole says top priority, he means it.'

The phone started to ring, and a chill ran down Alex's spine as he recalled the last time he heard that sound in this room, informing him of Ken Stanley's death.

'Baptiste.' There was a pause as the NTSB investigator listened. 'For you.' He handed the receiver to Alex.

Was history repeating itself?

'Alex Jamieson speaking.'

'Hello Mr. Jamieson. My name is Lewis Kramer. I'm a reporter with Columbia Television News.'

Alex recollected the name from his time in Wales, five weeks previously. 'I'm sorry, Mr. Kramer. I have nothing to say to the press.'

'You'll want to hear this.'

'If you have something you wish to contribute to the Flight 4401 investigation, then please go through the proper channels.' His finger trembled over the disconnect button.

'It regards Artemis, or Diana, if you prefer.'

Alex said nothing.

'Do I have your attention now, Mr. Jamieson?'

'You do.' He should have hung up immediately, but, the inquisitive creature that he was, had allowed the conversation to continue. 'What information do you have, Mr. Kramer?'

'That is not something I wish to discuss over the phone. Perhaps we could meet tomorrow?'

What was going on? The criminal investigation was in the hands of the FBI. How had Kramer known that he was in Washington? More to the point, what did the reporter want from *him?*

'It's important, Mr. Jamieson.'

'I'm going to New York in the morning.'

'I know. Meet me at the Rock Creek café on 28th Street at nine a.m.'

'I'll be there,' Alex heard himself say. 'But this had better be good.'

'Oh, don't worry. It will be.'

And the snow continued to fall.

Thirty-Seven

Caribbean waves lazily kissed the shoreline, their dancing illuminated by the softness of the moonlight. The warmth of the evening was punctuated by the occasional sea breeze, which brushed tantalizingly against her skin.

The soft silk of the nightgown felt good against her bare flesh. She wore nothing underneath. There was no need. Her nearest neighbour lived two hundred yards along the coast and this was a private beach. Even the house servants, who had greeted her in the early hours of the morning had been dismissed, leaving her in total isolation.

This was a new sensation for Donatella. She was accustomed to the bustle and verve of the metropolis. The solitude that she now experienced was unfamiliar and just a little disconcerting. However, as she sipped at the dry Martini, her anxiety slowly ebbed away to be replaced by a warm feeling of contentment. She was finally free after weeks of apprehension and torment.

A flock of yellow-bellied sugar birds suddenly took flight and soared into the air, then, as one, swooped low over the waves until they came to rest on the rocks of the reef.

Paradise had its drawbacks, though. Once the novelty had worn off, how would she cope with the disconnection from society? Would the loneliness eventually become so unbearable that she would be tempted to prematurely return to America? This was uncharted territory for her, but she trusted her intelligence and resolve to see her through.

A cool breeze from behind her moved a stray lock of hair, tickling the follicles at the back of her neck. She had noticed a similar sensation a couple of times earlier in the day, whenever the front door had been opened, causing a light through-draught.

She lay perfectly still, suspending her breathing; every muscle in her body going taut as she realized that she was no longer alone. Donatella listened, however she heard nothing but the waves lapping onto the beach. She turned slowly. The first thing she saw was a glint of the moonlight on gunmetal.

'Sorry, Princess. Hate to have to do this.'

She sat upright, suddenly feeling terribly vulnerable in the insubstantial nightgown.

'What do you want, Mr. Levitt?' Her voice trembled with fear. She couldn't see his face in the shadows, her eyes transfixed by the Beretta 92 automatic pistol.

'I've got a message for you.' He handed her a single sheet of paper, which she unfolded and began to read through moistened eyes.

> *Dearest Donatella,*
>
> *I warned you not to double-cross me, but you went ahead and did it anyway. Now this is the result. I suppose I could have let Mr. Levitt kill you earlier, but I wanted to give you a few hours to believe that you had actually beaten me. It's a shame, really. A partnership would have made us extremely powerful, and would it have been so unbearable? But I guess it was never meant to be.*
>
> *Goodbye, Donatella. I hope the end comes quickly for you.*
>
> *Thomas Purcell.*

So this was it. Donatella Martinelli's life really would end on Guadeloupe, but not in the way that she had intended. Her only hope was to stall him, talk to him, make the act of cold-bloodedly murdering her impossible.

'Get up,' Levitt ordered.

She complied slowly, raising herself onto unsteady legs that felt like jelly.

'You don't have to do this, Mitch. We could come to an agreement.' She felt as naked as a newborn, light flurries of air from the open doorway moving the garment in rhythmic waves.

'Turn around.'

Her feet would not move, terror immobilizing her like a rabbit suddenly caught in the headlights of a car. A trickle of urine dribbled down her thigh.

'TURN AROUND!' Levitt shouted, the command jolting her body into compliance.

'I can make you rich. I can have ten million for you in the morning. You could go anywhere you like, be anyone you want, have any woman you desire.'

He pushed the Beretta into the belt around his waist, and removed two lengths of cord from his pocket.

'Think about it, Mitch. Whatever Purcell is paying you to do this is insignificant compared to what I can offer you.' She felt her hands pulled from her sides and held together behind her back. The first piece of cord was wrapped around her slim, tanned wrists and snapped tightly closed, which elicited a breathless shriek of pain. A tear rolled down her cheek and she licked it from the side of her mouth. It was probably the last thing she would ever taste. She could smell the latex of the gloves that he wore. Every sense had been heightened by the horror of the ordeal.

'Please Mitch, for God's sake, don't do this.'

'Kneel down.'

'You can't—'

'GET ON YOUR KNEES!'

She did so reluctantly. Her ankles were tied with the second piece of cord. The execution was to be a professional job.

'Twenty million,' she pleaded.

Donatella heard nothing for several seconds. Was he considering the offer? Could she really *buy* her way out of this?

'Sounds tempting. But if I were to let you live, then your friend Purcell would have me killed. Just not possible, I'm afraid.'

She felt the barrel of the handgun on the back of her head. It moved down and ran along her neck, pushing the strap of the flimsy nightgown aside to reveal a bare shoulder. Levitt was obviously contemplating having some fun with her first.

'Sorry, Princess.'

Her breaths came in tortured gasps.

'Thirty million.'

There was nothing but silence.

'Everything. You can have everything I've got,' she cried.

The gun returned to the back of her head.

'PLEASE, FOR GOD'S SAKE, PLEASE—'

The bullet entered the parietal bone of her cranium. Splinters of bone followed the projectile as it tore through the sagittal sinus, falx cerebri, corpus callosum, and entered the somatosensory cortex. Movements, both skilled and more basic, were disabled as it continued its onslaught through the prefrontal lobe. Hearing, touch, and smell were all shut off. The anterior cerebral artery was severed, creating a massive haemorrhage, compounding the effects of the bullet as it approached the ethmoid sinus. Emotion, awareness, and finally the speech centres were destroyed, the bullet erupting from her nasal cavity, and taking half of her face with it.

Donatella's body convulsed once, her back arching in spasm, before she fell heavily onto one side. Blood spattered the furniture and the floor, and Levitt cringed as some droplets hit his face.

The lifeless right hand still clutched the note from Purcell. He removed it as he had been instructed, and stuffed it into his pocket. The assassin walked around the body, avoiding the pool of blood that was gathering on the floorboards. But he was taking no chances. He fired two more shots into her head, and three into her back, just to make sure.

There was no reaction. No movement. The lifeless corpse stared unblinkingly ahead.

Donatella Martinelli, a.k.a. Nina Ferroni, a.k.a. Dominique De Paz, was now, unquestionably, dead.

Thirty-Eight

Eagle made a final check that everything was ready to go. The Bell 407 command helicopter was flanked by two National Guard UH-60 Blackhawks, ready to disgorge a dozen agents each, who would then make the charge into the DAC Skysoft corporate headquarters. Simultaneously, six FBI fleet sedans would storm the main gate, restraining the security guards who would, hopefully, be taken by surprise. That would be the flashpoint. If one or more of the guards decided to make a fight of it, then both sides risked taking casualties.

Sixty miles north-east a similar operation was taking place at the Gunpowder Falls design and administration facility. The agent who had been in place there for the past four months was ready to direct the operation and prevent the escape of senior staff who were suspected of being involved in the embezzlement arm of the case.

They moved swiftly along the Potomac, keeping low to avoid giving their quarry advance warning, only rising above fifty feet to avoid the many bridges that traversed the river. Ice floes drifted along the surface, and it wouldn't be long before the great waterway would be frozen over completely.

The Canal Street operation had been devised by Eagle himself, every conceivable eventuality being considered and prepared for, but he knew there were still about a thousand things that could still go wrong. According to their intelligence, there were no firearms kept within the Skysoft building, but intelligence could be wrong. Did Harrington and the directors have a secret means of escape? Would they be able to destroy any incriminating data before capture?

Too many damned variables, Eagle thought to himself. And then there were the eight directors they knew were not in the building. Seven of them were under surveillance and were, at that precise moment, being placed under arrest. The eighth had disappeared. Had Donatella Martinelli been forewarned? That suggested a security leak within the FBI, but he didn't even want to consider that possibility.

The Potomac rushed past below – not far enough below for his liking – as they neared their Canal Street objective. The Theodore Roosevelt Memorial Bridge came into view, and the three helicopters rapidly gained height, swooping over the trees to the north of the river, then dropping again swiftly as the on-board satellite navigation system informed the pilot of the command ship that he was over the target.

'Showtime,' the pilot said.

'Let's hope it's a good one,' Eagle replied, keying the mike. 'Shit!' he cursed as he looked down. One of the two helipads was occupied, which meant that only a single Blackhawk could land at a time. For ninety valuable seconds he would only have twelve men on the ground.

The 407 assumed a position a hundred feet above the courtyard at the front of the building.

The first of the assault team craft came in to land, and he watched the initial group with some measure of pride as they threw themselves from the helicopter and made the sprint to cover the four entrances to the building. The aircraft was on the ground for just eleven seconds before it rapidly pulled away and headed back to the river, allowing the second aircraft to dart in and repeat the operation.

Each agent carried an open mike, and Eagle listened to their reports intently, wishing he were down there with them.

'Levin secured,' one of the voices said. That was Louis Levin, director.

'Harding secured,' said another.

'Purcell secured.'

'Switchboard secured.' DAC Skysoft was now mute, and could not send a warning to Skysystems at Gunpowder Falls if the second assault had been delayed.

'Koenig secured.' What the hell was the technical director doing here? He was an added bonus.

'Harrington secured.' They had Douglas Harrington. He was the key, Eagle was sure.

'Resistance at the gate,' one of the ground team reported breathlessly. Then: 'Pacified. No more resistance.'

Two more calls came in, stating that they had the other two directors. It had been a clean sweep, with the only casualty being a Dramar security guard with a superficial bullet wound to the leg.

It could have been a lot worse.

'Take us down,' he instructed the pilot.

The 407 came to rest in the car park at the front of the Skysoft building and he jumped out, keeping his head low to avoid the rotor blades as they continued to windmill.

Once inside he took the stairs at a run, proceeding to Harrington's office. The secretaries sat at their desks in stunned silence as he strode past, the atmosphere of dread in the foyer palpable. Only one returned his stare, an older woman with the fire of hate in her eyes. Douglas Harrington's personal secretary regarded him with contempt, and his gaze lingered on her for a moment. If the corporation was as guilty of deceit as he believed it to be, then the other poor girls would be as guilty, in law, as those they had served. Some plea-bargaining was a distinct possibility, and would only serve to bury Harrington and the others more deeply.

He walked into the chief executive's office, noting with satisfaction the look of defeat on the man's face. He went to stand in front of the handcuffed entrepreneur.

'Good morning Mr. Harrington. I'm Special Agent Scott Eagle.'

'I hope you have some explanation for this—'

'Don't bother.' He gestured dismissively to one of the assault team. 'Get him out of here.'

Harrington was led away, a broken and fearful man.

A computer analyst looked up at Eagle.

'What've we got?'

The analyst grinned. 'Enough.'

The cleaning maid was the first into the beach house the next morning, surprised that Madame De Paz was so trusting of the local population that she had left the front door open. She ensured that she made plenty of noise as she moved through the house, singing a jaunty Creole tune so her new employer would not be alarmed.

But when she reached the veranda that looked out onto the expanse of the Caribbean the singing stopped. She stood stock still for over half a minute before she reacted.

The screams, when they came, were heard at the next house along the coastline, over two hundred yards away.

When the local police arrived a quarter of an hour later, the unfortunate woman was hoarse from screaming, dark skin framing reddened, tear-filled eyes. Another fifteen minutes passed before they could get anything coherent out of her.

'Poor Madame,' she cried. 'Poor Madame De Paz.'

The police officer shook his head. The crime rate on Guadeloupe had been increasing over recent years, following the collapse of the sugar and rum trades, but murder was still uncommon. Although his experience was limited, the officer could tell that this was no frenzied attack; no crime of passion. This woman had been professionally executed, deliberately and expertly with dispassionate skill.

'Poor Madame,' the woman continued to wail.

'Who was she?' he asked gently, glancing over at the corpse, hands and feet still bound.

'Madame De Paz. Madame Dominique De Paz.'

'Are you sure?'

She nodded. There was not enough of the face left to be absolutely certain, but the woman recognized the hair and nightgown, which was heavily stained with blood. 'It is definitely her. She was my new employer. Who could have done this? Why?'

The tears began again.

They knew that a Dominique De Paz had recently acquired a property and had moved here from New York, but that did not answer the question of *who* she was, or why she had been so brutally murdered. If they could not uncover this mysterious woman's history, it was unlikely that they would ever find her killer.

Thirty-Nine

When he awoke at six a.m., Alex had been relieved to see that the road outside the Baptiste residence was still passable, but even so it took him twenty minutes to dig the hired car out of the snow that had been deposited on the side of the street by snowploughs during the night. However, his problems were just beginning.

The drive from Georgetown to Rock Creek should only have taken a few minutes, but after half an hour of trying to get through he gave up, and abandoned the car at the side of the road to complete the journey on foot, trudging dejectedly through eighteen inches of snow. The cold penetrated his clothes until he felt numb and light-headed, his feet painful as icy fingers penetrated his shoes. But he eventually made it to 28th Street and found the cosy little café, and was just fifteen minutes late.

Kramer waved to him discreetly from a table in the corner.

'Mr. Kramer?'

'Pleased to meet you, Mr. Jamieson. Sit down.' He signalled to the waitress to bring a fresh pot of coffee.

'I don't have much time,' Alex said directly, 'so let's get straight to the point. What have you got, and what do you want?'

Kramer smiled at the investigator's candour. 'What have I got? The whereabouts of the terrorist who has plagued Dramar Aerospace for the past five weeks. What do I want? Access to you, your investigation team, and some of the AAIB's files relating to the Flight 4401 inquiry. Also, access to the reconstruction at Farnborough and the AAIB's laboratories.'

'Anything else?' Alex asked sarcastically.

'I think that's enough.'

'I don't understand. Why are you talking to me, and not the FBI? I'm just running the crash investigation. The British Security Service or their American equivalents are the ones who would be interested in your information.'

Kramer leant forward, clasping his fingers together as he explained. 'Mr. Jamieson, I'm a TV reporter. My viewers want to see something interesting, like shots of the wreck of 4401, and how the investigation has been carried out. If I went to the Feds, all I'd get is a variety of stuffed suits in a variety of nondescript offices saying nothing of much consequence. This way, I get the images and interviews I want, and you get to be instrumental in cracking the case. CTVN would also be prepared to pay handsomely for the AAIB's cooperation.'

Alex was thankful that the waitress chose that moment to arrive with the coffee. It gave him a few valuable seconds to evaluate the situation. What should he do? Hunting international terrorists was not in his job description. The AAIB were not glory hunters, and generally did their best to avoid publicity, but if Kramer really did have such information and Alex failed to act on it, then Scott Eagle would curse him to his dying day. More to the point, stopping this terrorist would save lives, and wasn't that the ultimate goal of any air crash investigator?

'How handsome would this payout be?'

'In the region of a million dollars.'

Shit. Funding for the branch was always an issue, and Sir Roger would kick him from one end of the DERA complex to the other if he turned down a sum like that. Was accepting payment even legal? The AAIB's legal department could decide that later.

'Okay, Mr. Kramer. You can have your interviews; you can have limited access to our headquarters, but not to our confidential files. Those are too sensitive, no matter how juicy a carrot you dangle.'

'Do I have your word on that?'

'You do.'

Kramer produced from his briefcase a single sheet of paper, which constituted a formal contract. 'Would you be so kind as to sign this?'

Alex read the document carefully. No mention was made of access to investigative material. The wily reporter had never expected that, and had achieved his objective precisely.

'Thank you, Mr. Jamieson,' the reporter said once the contract had been signed and returned.

'Well?'

'She has been using the name Diana Kearn, but is known throughout the intelligence community as Artemis. She holds a long-term lease on an apartment in New York.' He withdrew another sheet of paper from the case. 'This is her address.'

Alex scanned the sheet. The location meant nothing to him.

'East 83rd Street is on the Upper East Side of Manhattan Island.'

The investigator nodded. 'How did you get this information? Even the FBI don't have anything like this.'

'Like I said, I'm a reporter. It's my job to know.'

'Is she there now?'

'That, I can't tell you, but you can bet that she'll be back soon if she isn't. She sub-lets the apartment to a local prostitute: Cindy Mahler. *She's* almost definitely there now, and could tell the Feds quite a bit – if you feel like telling them.

'Of course I'm going to tell them.' Alex was hardly going to go after one of the world's most wanted terrorists himself.

'Then I think we're finished here, for the moment.'

Alex glanced at his watch. 'Nine-thirty. I have to go. I'm sure I'll be hearing from you.'

'You will indeed.'

Kramer left Alex alone to finish his coffee and ruminate over the deal that he had made. He would have to move quickly. This information was too important to hold onto.

Eagle stared over the analyst's shoulder, skim reading the letters, memos, e-mails, reports, and directives on the screen as they appeared, each click on the mouse revealing more incriminating evidence. Dramar's lawyers would have a hard time explaining all this away, he thought with relish.

His mobile phone rang and he answered it absently, more interested in the details he was seeing on the computer monitor.

'Eagle.'

'Scott,' Alex said, 'I've spent the last twenty minutes trying to get hold of you.'

'Who is this?'

'Alex Jamieson.'

'What's happened?'

'I've got some information for you. It regards Artemis.'

What did the AAIB man think he had? 'Tell me, Alex, but remember that this is an unprotected line.'

'I know where she is – or at least was – and I have an address in New York.'

'You're not screwin' with me, are you?'

'That's the last thing I would want to do.'

'How did you find out?'

'I've struck a deal with a reporter: Lewis Kramer. You know him?'

'Of course I know him. How the hell does he know?' If a rottweiler like Kramer had information like that, then he wouldn't sit on it for long.

'He's a reporter. It's his job to know these things.'

'He's a major league asshole. Where are you?'

'The Rock Creek café on 28th Street.'

'I've got a helicopter with me. I'll pick you up. We'll head straight for New York, and we can drop you off at JFK. By the way, Alex, we've found some information ourselves that you might find quite interesting.'

'Like what?'

'Tell you when I see you.'

'Okay. We need to stop off at the NTSB labs first to pick up some equipment. Is that okay?'

'It'll have to be. Go get Samantha and Damian. Be ready for us to make the pick-up from the parkland at the south end of 28th. Got it?'

'Consider it got.'

Eagle hung up and sat there for a few moments, mulling over what he had heard, considering its implications. This was huge, and probably, from what Jamieson had implied, time sensitive.

But first he had to question one of the many suspects he now had on ice.

Thomas Purcell stared at him with an expression of incredulity. 'Agent Eagle, are you seriously suggesting that there is an inherent fault in the D500, and that *I* and some of my colleagues have attempted to suppress this information?'

'I am, sir. And we also have reason to believe that the chief executive and several directors at least have diverted funds which should have gone to the Internal Revenue Service towards a massive program of retrofitting the original delivery of eleven aircraft. You deny this charge?'

'I most certainly do. Look, I'm a director of the corporation. My involvement in the running of the company is negligible. This would have been a policy decision and, generally speaking, those matters are left to Mr. Harrington. If these charges *are* substantiated then I will have a few questions for our chief executive.'

'I'm afraid that won't be possible. Your Mr. Harrington has been directly implicated in this conspiracy, and faces Federal indictment.'

Purcell shook his head. Conspiracy was such an ugly word. 'Well, that doesn't really surprise me. I've had my suspicions about him from the start. Him and that Martinelli woman. They always seemed far too close for my liking. But I can personally vouch for Harding and Levin. We are close friends, and if either of them knew that anything was going on, then believe me, I would have heard about it.'

'So,' Eagle said tiredly, 'I can take it that you also deny the charge of collusion?'

'Absolutely. I can't prove my innocence, but you'll find no evidence to implicate me, because there is no evidence. Harrington and Martinelli: they're the ones you should be concentrating your attention on.'

Perhaps he was telling the truth. Purcell certainly sounded convincing, but Eagle was too drained to make any judgements right now.

'Ms. Martinelli seems to have disappeared. I don't suppose you have any idea of her whereabouts?'

'I haven't. Donatella and I have never… been close. I wouldn't be surprised if she has engineered this entire situation herself. She's smart. If I were you, I'd check to see whether her accounts have been emptied.'

'We're already working on it, Mr. Purcell. We'll find her, don't worry about that. No one is *that* smart.'

'Agent Eagle,' Purcell asked, 'am I under arrest?'

That was an interesting question. Without a shred of evidence to implicate him, the Dramar Aerospace director would probably be free in twenty-four hours anyway, and his lawyers would be launching a suit against the FBI for wrongful arrest. Better to keep the director on his side, for the time being. 'No, you're not. But I wouldn't leave DC for the next few days.'

'That's fine with me. I have a corporation to salvage. Dramar Aerospace needs leadership right now, if we are to survive the next few months.'

Scott Eagle didn't have to be a genius to guess who that leader would be.

Forty

Alex stamped his feet on the ground several times to dislodge some of the snow that had built up on his shoes, and forced his hands deeper into his pockets. He shivered involuntarily as the bitter cold plied its way beneath the layers of clothing. Samantha stood immobile next to him, enduring the freezing conditions stoically and without complaint, as Beaumont kept moving in an irregular circle in an attempt to ward off the numbing effects of the arctic air.

Helicopters seemed to be everywhere, the only sure way of travelling through Washington DC today, but none approached their position as they waited.

For Christ's sake, Scott, hurry it up, Alex silently cursed the FBI agent. Not only were the frigid conditions affecting his reasoning ability, but every moment lost reduced the time they would have to inspect the D500 at JFK.

'That's it,' Beaumont said, nodding his head in the direction of a helicopter that seemed to be heading towards them.

The small helicopter passed right over them and pirouetted several times, low enough to stir up the virgin snow, and dropped gracefully to the ground twenty yards from where they stood. The trio of shivering investigators shielded their faces from the barrage of ice that was churned up by the downwash from the rotors, and it was several seconds before Alex could see Eagle's figure in the open doorway, beckoning them over.

'Took your bloody time.'

'Sorry about that,' the FBI agent shouted as they climbed aboard. 'Got a little held up at Skysoft.'

With the side door barely closed, the 407 surged into the air once again, and headed off in the direction of the NTSB labs.

'We've got 'em, Alex,' Eagle said. 'Harrington is in some big time shit.'

The investigator took a few moments to think as the cold-induced haze on his brain began to subside. 'So we were right? There was a design flaw? And they tried to cover it up?'

'Yeah, but we don't know exactly what it was. There may well be details buried in the files, but it'll take a while for the NTSB to go through it.'

'So we still need to check that D500 at JFK?'

'If you want a quick result.'

'We do. We've got to get that plane grounded as soon as possible, before any more are lost.'

Eagle pulled a folder and several discs from his case. 'Here, one good turn deserves another. This is the evidence we've dug up so far. It proves that there was a conspiracy at Dramar Aerospace. It should be enough for you to convince the CAA. Dan Cole will be getting an identical set any time now, and he can deal with the FAA.'

This was great, Alex thought, but they had to get it back to Farnborough as soon as possible. 'Samantha,' he said above the sound of the rotors, 'I need you to get this to Sir Roger. When we arrive at JFK, I want you to take the first available flight to London. Damian and I can handle the inspection. Can you do that?'

'Yes, no problem.'

The NTSB labs loomed below them, shrouded in a thick layer of snow, and the Bell 407 began its descent.

President Bob Archer flinched as the make-up artist completed the last few finishing touches. Masking the creases in the President's face had been particularly difficult today, the subject having been awake and working for many long hours.

'That'll do,' he grumbled, waving a hand in front of him.

'Just a few more touches, Mr. President. We want you to look our best, don't we?' she replied brightly.

'*We* have been sitting here so long, we no longer give a rat's stinking ass how we look.'

'There,' she said, pulling away to admire her handiwork. *Not bad*, she thought, considering what she'd had to work with.

'Time for one more run-through, Mr. President,' the broadcast's director said as he made a final check of the lighting levels. So many addresses to the nation had been made from the Oval Office over the years that there was little he could do to make improvements, but it was a matter of professional pride to ensure that this one was among the best.

'No more run-throughs,' Archer snapped. 'We're ready.'

'As you wish, Mr. President. Five minutes to go.'

The hands of the clock gradually crept around. George Kenton watched them nervously as he pondered the events of the past twelve hours. The United Nations resolution had been far more difficult to obtain than any of them had anticipated. It had been a close-run thing, and he'd had to call in more than a few favours to secure the necessary result.

'Thirty seconds,' the director advised everyone.

The only Arab state that had not been in opposition was Saudi Arabia, the wealthiest country in the Middle East exercising its veto.

'Ten seconds.'

The autocue began to roll.

'My fellow Americans, at ten-thirty this morning the United Nations passed resolution one-one-zero-four, authorizing a coalition of American-led forces to defend the state of Israel against military action by Quamar. This unwarranted aggression is based on erroneous intelligence regarding the destruction of a Quamar Airways jet, four days ago.

'I can tell you now, that we have evidence that not only exonerates Israel and the American technician being held in Quamar, but also implicates a Palestinian terrorist in this cowardly attack.

'Her name is Mosa Ahmed, but is usually known by the pseudonym: Artemis.'

The face of the President was briefly replaced by a digitally enhanced photo of the terrorist.

'She is also believed to be responsible for the bombing of Pacific Atlantic Airways Flight 4401, in which one hundred and sixty-three American men, women, and children perished. As of this moment, she tops the list of the FBI's most wanted. Immediately following this broadcast, I will be contacting the Quamari Prime Minister in an attempt to avert hostilities, but will make it clear to him that America and her allies are resolute and determined.'

Kenton had read the speech in advance, but was still impressed by his Commander-in-Chief's delivery. He may not have been a great President, but history would remember him as a great salesman.

He hoped it would be enough.

'Captain.' The communications officer of the carrier, HMS Queen Elizabeth, glanced up at his commanding officer. 'We have authorization to begin aerial manoeuvres.'

'Authenticate,' Captain Harris ordered.

'Authentication confirmed, sir. Verification of command codes match the list for today.'

'Very well, we have authorization for Operation Crescent Shield. Flight officer, begin take-off procedures. Weapons station, please advise Phalanx crews to stand ready. Radar station, any notable changes since the last update?'

'Negative, sir. Two bulk carriers about fifteen and eighteen miles to the south-east respectively. Another to—'

'Thank you, Mr. Lamb. Any aerial movements to be concerned about?'

'High altitude civilian only.'

A roar of jet engines drowned out the electrical hum on the bridge.

'Take-off in progress, sir,' the flight officer informed him unnecessarily, but following standard procedures.

The first F-35 Lightning II thundered down the flight deck and propelled itself off the ski ramp at the bow of the Royal Navy's flagship, its thrusters vectored downwards and aft as the pilot coaxed the plane into the air. The thirty-knot headwind gave the strike fighter just that extra lift it needed to get airborne.

Captain Marcus Harris watched the aircraft as it gained height and peeled away to give the next plane plenty of space for its own take-off. He observed it through binoculars as it circled, waiting for the other seven Lightning IIs to join it. His eyes came to rest on the horizon. A hundred and fifty miles away lay the coasts of Oman and Yemen. Once they were all airborne the fighters would assume formation and travel at low-level north along the red sea, sandwiched between Saudi Arabia and Egypt, then hug the Sinai Peninsula until they reached Israeli airspace. They would then gain height and skirt the Quamari border, alerting the Arab state's air defences. The wing commander's orders were explicit: fly no closer than two hundred meters of the Quamari border, and do not – under any circumstances – cross that border. The intention was to intimidate the Quamaris – not start a war.

To the east, the USS Dwight D. Eisenhower was conducting a similar operation, as were the John Stennis and Ronald Reagan in the Mediterranean.

Harris silently cursed his superiors in London, and the architects of the plan in Washington. Operation Crescent Shield may have appeared relatively risk-free from the comfort and safety of the White House, but out here with little support, the situation looked a lot more uncertain. His first duty was to his country, Harris acknowledged, but his next duty was to the sailors under his command.

Ten thousand Quamari troops now lined the Israeli border. If a shooting war began, then this intellectual game could rapidly degenerate into an extremely bloody conflict.

Everything would depend on the Quamari response.

Forty-One

The 407 had refuelled whilst at the NTSB labs before it began the long flight to New York, making a brief stop at the DAC Skysystems site to pick up Special Agent Gerard Burnett, whom Eagle wanted with him when they stormed the apartment on East 83rd Street.

The rest of the flight took another hour-and-a-half as they raced against the cold front, driving its way relentlessly northwards. Baltimore was now just as inaccessible by road as the nation's capital, and Philadelphia was beginning to feel the full effects of the snowstorm as well. It was only a matter of time before New York succumbed to the ferocity of the weather system.

Alex glanced at his watch, then nervously looked outside again at the clouds that churned above them. 'Samantha, when we get to JFK, you're going to have to move fast.'

'I know. I doubt I'll have more than an hour. It might be best if I grab the first flight to the UK, whether it's going to London or not.'

'Do whatever you think seems best.'

Alex recognized the marshlands of Jamaica Bay as they passed below, indicating that they were just a couple of minutes out.

'Nearly there,' he said as he gathered his belongings.

John F. Kennedy Airport appeared below them, and the small helicopter slowed as the pilot approached the heliport area, bringing it in for an expertly smooth landing. Burnett swung the door open and leapt out, a blast of cold air hitting him full in the face and carrying with it the first few flakes of snow to fall on the airport. A car waited on the tarmac for the two FBI agents, and Eagle held a finger up, telling the occupants to wait one minute.

'Alex,' he shouted above the noise of the rotors and the wind, 'this is where we part company. The British Occidental hangar is over there.' He pointed to a large structure about a hundred yards from them. 'Sam, jump in the car. We'll drop you at the terminal.'

'Thanks.' She turned to Alex, and for a moment they just looked at one another, neither knowing what to say.

'You sure you're going to—'

'I'll be fine, Alex. You work on that D500, and I'll get this stuff to the CAA.' She glanced over to Beaumont. 'Good luck, Damian.'

'You too.'

'Sorry to break this up, folks,' Eagle interrupted, 'but we gotta go.'

Woody became vaguely aware of the door opening, but could see nothing, the flesh around his eyes now so swollen that he was effectively blind. He tried to mentally prepare himself for the interrogation, but all he could do was cry.

The interviewer would ask him a series of questions, and he would answer them as best he could, but it was never enough. They would always attempt to trap him into saying something to incriminate himself, and he would unwittingly oblige. The beating would then begin. On the rare occasions that he managed to outwit the interrogator, the beating would be even more severe, and he had learned to cooperate after the first couple of occasions where he'd thought he may be winning. It was better that way, even though he knew that he was probably signing his own death warrant by doing so.

'Good evening, Mr. Lindsay. I trust you are well?'

'Never better,' he mumbled.

'I have good news for you. Fresh evidence has come to light regarding the terrorist attack, and it appears we may have been mistaken about your involvement. You are to be released this evening.'

Woody sat in silence as he tried to understand what the Arab was saying. Was he really going to be freed, or was this just some kind of twisted joke designed to toy with his emotions? Perhaps it was simply a new ploy in the interrogation process.

'Why?'

'The true identity of the murderer has come to our attention. Now, Doctor Hamira will give you medical attention, and you will have an hour to clean yourself up. It wouldn't do to return home in this state. Your countrymen may think that we have been mistreating you.'

'I'm going home?'

'Yes, in around two hours' time.'

The Arab knew how lucky they had been. If Woodrow Lindsay had died during the torture, the Americans might not have honoured the peace deal that had been agreed an hour earlier. The strike fighters that had been patrolling the Quamari/Israeli border were now safely back on the carriers, instead of pounding Barakat and El Zafir in revenge. Besides, it had been obvious from the start that the hapless technician was innocent. The interrogator had told his superiors this, but they had insisted on continuing the torture in the hope that something would be uncovered. It was much better this way.

'Come, Mr. Lindsay. It is time to go.'

Forty-Two

Madison Flynn watched from the 4th floor window as the two Fords pulled up outside. The apartment she had chosen was immediately adjacent to the property leased by Artemis, and the old man who lived there had readily accepted the two hundred dollars she had offered him, in exchange for providing accommodation for the news crew for a few hours. Flynn had brought two camera operators and sound engineers with her from Washington. The first crew was stationed at the end of the hall in the small utility room that served this floor, and would record the FBI agents when they emerged from the elevator or the stairs. The second crew was with her, and sat ready to follow the agents into Artemis' apartment.

'They're here,' she said into the mike as she watched the ten uniformed, ballistic vest-wearing figures appear from the cars and walk nonchalantly toward the entrance to the building. Even without the body armour and M4 Carbines, there would be no mistaking them as a SWAT team. 'Tony, are you ready?'

'We're ready.'
'Start recording.'

The ancient doors of the urine-soaked elevator creaked open, and Eagle led the assault team down the hall. Eight of the agents held assault rifles or Glock 9mm handguns at the ready. The other two carried the battering ram. Soon after his graduation from Quantico, Eagle had tried kicking a door down, and had learnt the painful lesson that it was not as easy as it looked on TV. There would be no polite knock on the door for this raid – not with the world's most wanted terrorist possibly on the other side.

Burnett crouched low as he led three agents past the door, keeping out of sight of the spyhole inset into it.

They were lucky that the lighting was so poor, the diffused beams casting only indistinct shadows on the walls and floor. The team moved as silent as ghosts into position, and Eagle soundlessly mouthed the count, using the fingers of his free hand to signal the other agents.

Five-four-three-two-one.

The ram was swung back, then propelled forward until it crashed against the door. Splinters of wood exploded from around the lock as it was torn away from the frame, and the team charged through the empty space.

'Federal Agents,' Eagle shouted as he threw himself against the wall. 'Get down on the floor.'

'Go,' Flynn said calmly, but with a racing heart. She swiftly led the cameraman and sound engineer out of the apartment, glancing towards the camera so the viewers at home would see her face. When she reached the door she found herself staring down a hallway. As she had expected, the layout of Artemis' apartment was a mirror image of the one she and the film crew had been occupying for the previous few hours. At the far end she could see a bedroom. Dirty, stained sheets hung loosely from the bed. The ten agents were still at the near end of the hall. Some crouched. Some stood. One lay prostrate on the floor. All had weapons drawn. She moved aside so the cameraman could get a better view.

Eagle didn't know what it was. He didn't hear anything. He didn't see anything. But he suddenly became aware of a presence behind him. He swung around, the barrel of the Glock following his eyes. He saw a woman. An attractive woman in a stylish business suit, and involuntarily squeezed the trigger, realizing too late that she held a microphone, and behind her a camera was watching him.

Flynn screamed as she grasped what was happening and flung herself against the doorframe. She saw the flash, but heard nothing. All she felt was pain as her arm erupted in fire once the bullet had passed through it. She sank to the floor, wailing in torment as she clutched the wound, staring in horror as her own blood seeped from between her fingers. The young reporter glanced upwards and, despite the agony of the wound, noted with some satisfaction that the camera was still rolling. This would make great television.

'Who the hell are you?' Eagle demanded.

'Madison Flynn, CTVN.'

The FBI agent shook his head in fury. 'Craddock,' he pointed to one of the agents. 'See to her, and get these cameras out of here.'

He returned his attention to the hall. This distraction would have given Artemis vital seconds to prepare. There was now no other option. He sprinted the few yards down the hall and threw himself into the living room, crouching and rolling as he did so, expecting to be met by a hail of bullets. Two other agents followed him, the other six taking the open bedroom, the bathroom, and the kitchen.

In less than a second he had analysed the arrangement of the furniture, despite the low level of lighting. Cabinets lined the walls to his left and right. A low coffee table dominated the centre of the room, piled high with fast food remnants and packaging. But his attention was drawn to the couch against the far wall, and the immobile woman draped across it.

Flynn forced herself to her feet, using the door frame for support. The pain was unbelievable, worse than anything she had ever experienced. She was aware of tears rolling down both cheeks, and cursed herself for them. Her first appearance on TV, and her make-up would be smeared all over her face.

'You're not going anywhere,' the agent said firmly.

'Oh yes we are,' she replied, focusing on him and driving the pain aside. 'You wanna get your face on TV, Agent Craddock? You wanna tell twenty million people how your boss, Special Agent Scott Eagle, is so trigger-happy that he'll gun down a CTVN reporter?'

'I'm sorry, Miss. You can't go in there.' He looked contemptuously at the cameras as they continued to film him.

Flynn tried to push past him, but was held firmly in place by a hand against her chest.

A flash, and the accompanying sound of a gunshot caused them all to jump and look down the hall.

Once the lock had been shot away, Burnett kicked the door open and quickly scanned the bedroom, but his heart sank as he realized it was empty.

The room was a total contrast to the adjacent bedroom. The bed was immaculately made; ornaments and cosmetics were neatly placed on the dresser. The only incongruous object was a coffee mug on the bedside table. Burnett put the back of his hand against it. It was cold, but there was no mould growing inside.

She *had* been here recently. If that self-serving bastard Kramer had come to them last night, they would have her now.

He looked around the room. No pictures decorated the walls. The small bookshelf supported copies of political biographies: Nelson Mandela, Saddam Hussein, Abraham Lincoln, Charles De Gaulle. There did not seem to be any pattern to the collection. He would have expected a terrorist to be obsessed by dictators and radicals, but what he saw was a cross section of the political spectrum. There seemed to be nothing to glean from this.

He searched through the drawers and cupboards, most of which were empty. There were some items of clothing, a few receipts and used travel tickets. He glanced at some of these. One was a ticket stub from a United flight. It was dated the twenty-third of September: the day of the 4401 crash. There was no doubt now that this was indeed her apartment.

They had missed her by less than an hour.

She lay unconscious on the couch, the discoloured dressing gown doing little to conceal her nakedness beneath. Her bare breasts rose and fell slowly, indicating to Eagle that she was, at least, still alive, but the bruises on her limbs, as she had searched for ever more elusive veins to inject herself, were proof that she would not survive for much longer. He was sickened to see that even her neck was not free of the marks.

Needles seemed to be everywhere, and he trod carefully as he approached. It was a miracle, he thought, that he hadn't jabbed himself on one of them as he made his dramatic entrance.

The FBI agent stood over her. The flesh around her eyes was dark, arms and legs unnaturally thin; skin grey and blotchy, the pallor of death. Eagle found her repellent, an obscene reminder (as if he needed one) of the pathetic excuse for a society they lived in, but at the same time he felt the sadness and pity of a father. She was not much older than his own daughter. *She* was at college now, however he wondered how much it would take to push her to this state. How fine was the line?

'Cindy,' he said firmly. His subordinates were watching. 'Cindy, wake up.'

Burnett walked in from the second bedroom. 'Sir, we've found something.'

'In a minute,' he dismissed the agent with a raised hand, and grasped the girl by the shoulders, pulling her upright into a seated position. Her head lolled from side to side as he shook her. 'Come on, Cindy. I haven't time for this. Wake up.'

She mumbled something incoherent.

After trying several more times, his patience found its limit and he dropped her back onto the couch, storming out to the kitchen.

Burnett heard the crash of crockery smashing onto the floor, then the sound of a tap running. Thirty seconds later, the senior agent reappeared carrying a bowl of water, its contents slopping over the sides and onto the dirt-encrusted carpet. He upended it over the girl's face and picked her up once again, this time with one hand, by the neck.

'WAKE UP!' he shouted, and slapped her hard across the face.

Her eyes screwed up as she felt the blow.

He slapped her again. And again. 'Wake up, damn you. Wake up!'

'Okay, I'm awake.' Her bloodshot eyes opened a fraction as she looked to see who was beating her this time, pupils dilated to such an extent that there was no way she could have focused upon him. 'Who're you,' she asked drowsily.

'FBI. I want to ask you some questions.'

'F – B – I?' She was trying to make some sense of the abbreviation, then finally made a connection. 'Oh. You want a freebie, yeah?'

He drew his hand back to slap her again, but stopped, the hand poised.

'Hey, quit it! No rough stuff.' Her voice seemed to be getting stronger.

'I need to know about Diana.' Eagle removed his hand from her neck, and she remained upright. Just. 'Was she here?'

'Yeah, she was here. She's gone now. Not comin' back for a long time, though. Long time.'

Her eyelids rolled shut again, and she began to fall back once more, but Eagle grabbed her head with both hands.

'Cindy, where has she gone?'

'Hmm?'

'Where has she gone?'

The girl's eyes snapped open again. 'Abroad. Didn't say where. You gonna arrest me, or you want that freebie?'

'Where is she?'

'Gone away. I told you. Had a job to do, then goin' away. Goin' away for a long time.'

He wasn't going to get anything else from her, and gently lay her back onto the couch, pulling the dressing gown together to cover the girl and at least give her some measure of dignity.

'Did anyone see any of that?' he asked the assembled group.

'Not me,' Burnett replied. 'I was looking the other way.'

'Same here,' said another.

'Slut deserved it,' added a third.

Eagle glared at him. He felt nauseous after hitting her like that, no matter how necessary it was; no matter how many lives were at stake. Such an act went completely against his own set of values, and he knew that the experience had dehumanized him and diminished him as a man. In the space of three minutes he had shot one innocent woman, and physically beaten another. In his entire life, he had never felt less proud of himself.

'Call an ambulance,' he said quietly.

'There's one on its way,' Burnett said.

'Not for the reporter. For her.' He took a final look at the feeble, defenceless girl. God alone knew what she must have gone through to drive her to this state.

'You said you found something?'

'Yeah,' Burnett said. 'In Artemis' room.' He handed over a sheet of paper. 'It's a Dramar Aerospace maintenance memo. Found it in the garbage.'

Eagle scanned the sheet. 'Maintenance on a D500. Well, we know this was her apartment. I don't see…' He read further. 'A British Occidental D500? And look at the date.' He thrust the sheet back at Burnett.

'I know. Routine maintenance on G-APSN. Is that the aircraft the British guy is working on?'

'No, that's in for emergency repairs. This order was signed on the tenth. That's three weeks ago. Cindy said that Diana had a job to do, then she was going away.'

Burnett felt butterflies form in the pit of his stomach. 'She's going to hit *another* D500. She's at JFK.'

'Mother of God.'

Forty-Three

S amantha slipped the ticket inside her passport and gripped the small booklet tightly. She had been lucky. Extremely lucky. What none of them had taken into consideration was the volume of human traffic wishing to escape New York before the weather system hit the city. After queuing for over twenty minutes, she had managed to get one of the last three seats on the flight to London Gatwick.

Alex would cringe when he heard the price she'd had to pay for the first class ticket, but there was no alternative. She had to get this information to Sir Roger Coombes as soon as possible, and then to the CAA.

Most of the passengers had already boarded when she arrived at the gate. She had no luggage to check in. That was still at Leon Baptiste's house in Georgetown, and would have to be forwarded later.

She rushed through passport control and along the ramp. A friendly flight attendant ushered her to her seat, and the airline concierge settled her in. Samantha breathlessly thanked him as she relaxed into the seat near the cockpit, and took several deep breaths to slow her heart rate after the panicked rush onto the aircraft. A glass of wine was held in front of her and she hesitated about half a second before accepting it. She may be on company business, but no one would blame her for drinking a single glass after the day she'd had.

She closed her eyes and took a sip as she tried to regain her composure. She'd done it. She was on her way.

Samantha opened her eyes again and looked out of the window, watching as the jet bridge was retracted, and heard the change in pitch as the engines increased in power.

The D500 began to taxi toward the runway.

The hangar was almost deserted as Alex Jamieson and Damian Beaumont entered, moving to one side to allow the final group of engineers to leave the facility. The British Occidental maintenance hangar was large enough to accommodate two high capacity transports, and it was obvious that one had recently been removed, leaving a giant empty space at the near end of the structure. The tail of the D500 they would be inspecting was still surrounded by gantries, following the work that had been carried out on its rudder assembly.

The brightly coloured aircraft, emblazoned in its patriotic red, white, and blue company style, rested silently on the concrete like a slumbering giant, and once again Alex was impressed by her design. However, this time he *knew* that the aircraft was flawed.

His job now was to establish how the third generation design differed from the first.

'Where do you want to start, Damian?'

'I think the best place would be the area of the break-up, around frame station one thirty-nine. That's the area we're most familiar with.'

They rolled an A frame ladder into position, directly below the access hatch, and hauled their equipment to the top. Beaumont punched in the four-figure key-code from memory, and the hatch slid back. The lower main stringer was immediately visible, as well as several of the KX-7 supports, and the young engineer hoisted himself through the aperture and into the crawl space.

'I can't see any difference so far,' he said. 'Hand the tool kit up here.'

Alex did as he was instructed. 'What about the other stuff?'

'Not yet. I can barely move in here as it is,' Beaumont said as he opened the toolbox, and removed a set of adjustable wrenches.

'Is there anything I can do to help?' Alex felt like a spare part.

'Not really. This'll be a one-man job, for the most part.' He tapped one of the tools against the stringer, and heard a dull thud reverberate through the crawl space. 'That's odd.'

'What is?'

'Pitch seems wrong. That sounded almost like metal. Hand me the URS.'

Alex heaved the ultrasonic resonance scanner through the hatch. 'You mean this stringer is an alloy of some kind?'

'No, it's a composite, all right. It just sounds funny.'

'Define 'funny'.'

Beaumont grinned down at him. 'Listen to this.' He tapped the stringer again. 'Did you hear that? The oscillation of the sound?'

'I'm not sure. Try again.'

Beaumont repeated the action.

'Sounds like a badly tuned guitar string.'

'Exactly. A composite shouldn't sound like that. Take this.' He handed the wrench to Alex. 'It'll take me a few minutes to set the unit up and get it calibrated. Go down to the hatch in the tail and try it. I'll do the same from this end. If we can hear the same sound from both ends, we might've cracked it. The access code is five-nine-four-one.'

'Fifty-nine, forty-one. Okay. Yell if you need anything.'

Alex climbed down the ladder and made his way aft, reaching up to run a finger along the aircraft's smooth underbelly. What this experiment would prove, he had no idea, but trusted the young engineer enough to go along with the exercise without question.

One of the Dramar technicians appeared from behind the framework encasing the tail section. He'd thought everyone from the team had left, but gave her a friendly smile as she approached. She didn't reciprocate, merely staring at him blankly. The woman looked oddly familiar, he thought as they passed. Did he know her? Something nagged at the back of his mind. The face he vaguely recalled was younger, without the lines of maturity. An old school friend, perhaps? No, not out here.

Alex stopped dead in his tracks as the realization hit him like a physical blow.

He turned slowly.

She stood ten feet away. Beautiful, but oddly menacing. She was as tall as him, and athletic, the bulky coveralls in the Dramar colours failing to completely disguise her femininity.

In one swift, flowing movement, she produced a handgun and pointed it directly at his chest, but continued to stare impassively into his eyes.

For a few moments, Alex was dumbstruck. What should one say to a mass-murderer with a gun?

'Good day, Miss Ahmed.'

'Good day, Mr. Jamieson.'

Forty-Four

S cott Eagle had the door open and was out of the car even before it had come to a halt. He bounded over to the entrance of the JFK control tower, a tomahawk-shaped finger of concrete reaching into the sky. He stopped briefly to shout down the protests of the airport security guards as he flashed his FBI ID card.

'This is a restricted area,' the senior guard said, blocking his way.

'I don't have time for this, mister,' Eagle replied. 'You wanna arrest me? Good luck.' He opened his jacket just enough for the man to see his shoulder holster. The guard looked over to Burnett, who had come up behind his boss, and had his hand inside his own jacket as he held the concealed weapon ready.

'Well... you'll need to be escorted. We can't have unauthorized—'

'Fine. Try and keep up.'

The guard chased after them as they made for the elevator. He had no idea what was going on, but was trying to do his best to think on his feet. After all, it wouldn't do to antagonize the Feds.

The main operations room of the control tower was smaller than Eagle had expected, considering the amount of air traffic the facility was responsible for. He and Burnett came to an abrupt halt as they emerged into the glass-encased area. The hapless security guard did not stop as quickly, and careered into the back of them.

'What the hell is going on?' demanded the tower supervisor.

'FBI,' said Eagle. 'Cancel any D500 take-offs.'

'What?'

He held up his ID. 'Stop any D500 from taking off. One is probably carrying a bomb.'

'A bomb?' A look of horror crossed the supervisor's face, the blood draining from his cheeks. He looked to one of the controllers, who himself looked as if he was going to be sick. 'That BOA flight. Wasn't that a—'

'Yeah. BOA 5552 took off about twenty minutes ago, heading for London.'

Eagle strode up to the supervisor. 'Get it back. We have strong evidence that a D500 leaving JFK today is to be destroyed. Get it back. Now.'

The supervisor turned back to the controller. 'Recall 5552, and clear a corridor.' He clicked his fingers to attract the attention of another controller. 'Alert the Coast Guard. If a plane is going down, I don't want people in this freezing water a moment longer than necessary.'

The supervisor looked grimly at the FBI agent. 'Let's pray to God we're not too late.'

The aircraft was well above the cloud layer, leaving the foul New York weather behind and below them, and the captain was about to extinguish the seatbelt sign when the call came through.

'BOA 5552 heavy, Centre. Immediate return to JFK. You have a possible explosive device on board. Over.'

He looked across at the co-pilot, who returned his stunned gaze.

'5552 heavy. Say again, Centre.'

'5552, Centre. Emergency return to JFK. Possible explosive device on board. Over.'

The captain took a full three seconds to evaluate the situation.

'5552. Acknowledged, Centre.' He cut the transmission and said to the co-pilot, 'Drop us to five thousand feet. One-eighty turn. Rate of descent: six thousand feet per minute.'

'Six thousand?'

'If a bomb does go off, I want equal pressure to the outside air. Explosive decompression could kill this plane if the bomb doesn't do it first.'

'Roger. Six thousand it is.' The co-pilot tapped the new numbers into the Flight Management Computer, as the captain switched on the cockpit to cabin intercom.

'Ladies and gentlemen, this is the captain. We have developed a minor technical fault, and are returning to JFK. Please remain in your seats, and keep safety belts fastened. That also applies to flight attendants. There is no need for alarm; it's just a precaution, that's all.'

'Computed,' the co-pilot said.

'Take us down.'

A dozen aircraft travelling in the wake of BOA 5552 veered away to give the threatened plane a clear path back to JFK. Air Traffic Control Officers frantically endeavoured to keep vertical and horizontal separation outside the FAA stipulated minimums, flight crews obeying their instructions and trusting the air traffic controllers to keep their airliners safe.

Samantha became aware of a loss of weight as the D500 arced downwards. A couple of blasé first class passengers had ignored the captain's instructions and she saw them float into the air, waving their arms and legs ineffectually in an attempt to get their feet back on the floor. A significant handful of others immediately vomited as the aircraft pitched downwards. Pressure built up in her ears and she swallowed repeatedly to neutralize the sensation as the plane dived from twenty-five thousand feet.

Her mind raced. If there were a serious technical problem causing the airliner to go into a crash dive, then there shouldn't have been time for the captain to issue a warning.

She couldn't tell whether the sickening feeling was a result of the rapid descent, or the realization of what must be the truth.

There was a bomb on this flight.

Alex's eyes darted nervously from the barrel of the Sig P226 to the woman's face. She didn't *look* evil. There was no maniacal stare; no twisted smile of madness. She looked… normal.

He suddenly remembered the wrench he held, and surreptitiously slipped it inside his sleeve. It wouldn't be much defence against an automatic handgun, but it was better than nothing. Perhaps more importantly, it acted as a comfort as he rubbed his finger up and down the cold metal.

'It's too late,' he said evenly. 'Nothing can be gained by destroying another aircraft. There's no point in killing several hundred more innocent people.'

'This,' she glanced up at the D500 that towered over them, 'is not the aircraft that is to be destroyed. Once the British aircraft has gone down, war with Israel will commence. It would be impossible for the US or Britain to support Israel if they believe the bombings to be the work of the Zionists.'

She didn't know, he realized. Her image was on the cover of every newspaper in New York, on every TV report, yet she hadn't seen it. The computer-enhanced photos did not do her justice, but the likeness was unmistakable.

'But they know it was you: Mosa Ahmed, a Palestinian. How do you think the rest of the Middle East will react when they hear an Arab blew up an Arab plane?'

'How would they know?'

'You were seen at Barakat International on the day of the crash. It doesn't take a genius to work out what you were doing there. It's over, Mosa. The whole world knows this was a Palestinian plot. It failed.'

Her face remained impassive, her aim at his chest unwavering, but she said nothing.

'Tell me which plane you were going to hit, and we can stop this. There's no point in causing any more deaths.'

She still said nothing.

'Which plane?'

'It is entirely academic, Mr. Jamieson. BOA 5552 *will* be destroyed.' She glanced at her watch. 'Nothing can stop that now.'

Alex felt a wave of regret sweep through him as comprehension dawned. That would be Samantha's flight. He had sent her to her death.

'We've got to stop it.'

'I'm afraid that won't be possible.'

Her stare hardened, and Alex realized that he was about to meet his own fate. He hurled the wrench in her direction, and dropped to the ground, rolling beneath the fuselage.

By a miracle, the wrench actually made contact with the P226, and the shot went wide. It was of little consequence, though. She had another fourteen rounds with which to kill the Englishman.

Alex bolted for the gantries surrounding the tail section. Perhaps the forest of metal would offer some protection, but he knew it was only a matter of time.

Forty-Five

The explosion occurred in the lower section of the fuselage, just aft of the wing struts. Ballooning out in an expanding sphere, the blast wave tore through the airframe, ripping away supporting struts and bulkheads like a hurricane through a paper village. Aluminium skin panels blistered and stretched to the very limit of molecular cohesion, but somehow did not rupture.

Unfortunately, the airliner had been mortally wounded within.

The backbone of the plane was shattered by the blast, carbon fibre violently splintered and severed. Floor beams were contorted, distended outwards, leaving a gaping cavern in the plane's vulnerable underbelly.

With nothing to hold it together internally, the fuselage began to warp and buckle. Hull plates rippled like a ship's sails in a raging gale…

Forty-Six

Samantha gripped the armrests until she thought her fingers would snap. She couldn't have lifted her hands even if she had wanted to, the g-forces being exerted holding her firmly in place as the aircraft attempted to level out. She heard what she thought were the engines screaming at full power, until she realized the sound was coming from the man in the adjacent seat.

From somewhere behind, she heard a muffled thud as the bomb exploded, and at that moment expected the air to be wrenched from her lungs and the aircraft to tear itself apart, ripping her to shreds in the process. She expected to see a wall of fire engulf her, incinerate her clothes, burn away her skin and cook her flesh. She expected to see the finger of death beckon her toward it.

But looking from the window, she could see the horizon was now level, although the choppy Atlantic waves were a lot closer than she would have liked.

She was still alive. She didn't know how. She didn't know why. The important thing was how to stay alive. Samantha was terrified, as was every other soul on the plane, except the flight crew. They were far too busy to be scared as they tried to keep the crippled plane in the air.

Why was the D500 still flying? The low altitude when the device detonated must have been a critical factor, but they would still have sustained substantial damage, though not quite enough to destroy the aircraft.

Then she saw the aisle carpet stretch and begin to tear.

The controller shook his head in confusion. 'Sir,' he beckoned to the watch supervisor.

'What is it?'

'I've just had a report of *gunfire* in building thirty-two.'

'Gunfire?' Eagle repeated. 'Where's building thirty-two?'

'It's the British Occidental maintenance hangar, over there.' He pointed through the control tower's panoramic windows at a large structure to the south.

'That's where she'll be.'

'Who?' asked the supervisor.

'And that's where the AAIB guys are working,' Burnett added.

'What d'ya suppose Mr. Jamieson has gotten himself into?'

Alex wove his way through the steel framework. He didn't know where he was heading; he was just trying to keep some distance between himself and Artemis. Another shot rang out, and he realized that she had circled around and was somewhere ahead of him, but the acoustics of the cathedral-like structure reflected the sound waves around until he had no idea where she was precisely.

He saw a flash of colour ahead. She was coming straight towards him. His heart sank when he saw that behind her was a fire exit. In order to reach it, he would have to go straight past her.

The odds were not in his favour.

His eyes darted wildly around as he searched for an escape route, but there was nowhere to run. Apart from the framework that currently shielded him, and the undercarriage of the airliner, there was nothing but empty space all round. If he were to try to flee, she could cut him down easily. There was only one option.

Alex began to climb the gantry. By doing so he knew he would be trapped, but there was no alternative. It would give him a couple of minutes extra to live.

He was fifteen feet up when he heard Artemis below him. She fired, but the projectile ricocheted off multiple surfaces. The sound of footsteps on metal indicated that she was beginning to climb after him. He comforted himself with the thought that as long as she was climbing, she couldn't take a shot at him. There was little doubt in his mind that all he was doing was buying himself some time. There was a sickening inevitability to the chase. Sooner or later she would catch him. All he could do was try to delay that moment as long as possible. He fought the fear that threatened to overwhelm him. His limbs felt weak, but he kept moving up.

He reached the gantry platform that was level with the horizontal stabilizers, and saw what might be his salvation. It was a simple toolbox, left by a careless mechanic. The framework continued to rise above him, encasing the vertical stabilizer and ending in a second level.

A bullet erupted through the floor he stood on, followed by two more, uncomfortably close to his position. He peeked over the side. She was less than ten feet below, with a clear shot at his head. Alex ducked back just in time to avoid having his head blown off. There was no time for finesse, the instinct for survival taking over. Alex grabbed the tool kit and emptied its contents over the side, in the general area he believed the woman to be. A second later he heard a satisfying scream of pain and rage as several objects hit her, and looked over the side once more.

Artemis dangled from the gantry, her feet kicking wildly as they sought a solid surface to rest upon, and blood poured down her face. But she still defiantly held the gun, and Alex saw the fury in her blood-soaked eyes. He had not stopped her, merely temporarily delayed her. And now he'd made her mad.

He began to climb once more, but there was just the single platform left. After that, there would be nowhere else to run.

The airliner was buffeted by the outside air as it drove its way through the atmosphere, the gaping hole in its underbelly widening all the time. The loss of aerodynamic efficiency around the centre section created a violent turbulence wake, twisting the rear of the fuselage well beyond its design limits, and causing the ugly noises of a slow death within the cabin.

Why was she still alive? As others around her gave in to the terror, allowing despair to overcome them, Samantha went through all the possibilities she could think of. Why hadn't the aircraft been destroyed immediately? The device must have been too small. Why? The explosive device on Flight 4401 was precisely the correct size to destroy the aircraft, she reasoned. Like all professionally trained saboteurs, Artemis had been conservative with her materials. She had obviously calculated that explosive decompression would finish the job of the bomb on 4401. It was reasonable to suppose that the same logic followed here.

She looked down. Strands of fibre within the carpet were snapping. That meant that the floor was collapsing. She visualized the damage in her mind. With the lower main stringer severed, as well as several of the minor stringers, structural integrity would have been compromised. The twisting sensation she was experiencing would be snapping joints where the floor beams met the frame stations. The violent motions of the aircraft would only be exacerbating and accelerating this process. Would the flight crew be aware of the extent of the damage? Maybe. Maybe not. She would have expected to see one of them come back to survey the situation, but they were obviously too busy trying to keep the plane in the air. What she was certain of, though, was that they would be making the best possible speed to get back to JFK before the crippled aircraft came apart altogether.

She knew where the bomb had probably detonated, and could estimate how severe the damage was. These savage manoeuvres would kill this plane for sure.

Samantha unbuckled her seatbelt and stood unsteadily, being lifted and dropped, and swayed from side to side. Flight 5552 had entered a 'phugoid': a sequence of climbs and descents caused by the poor aerodynamics. As the aircraft carved a recurring 'S' shape through the sky, it made movement through the cabin difficult at best. She clung to the seatbacks as she dragged herself toward the cockpit.

'Miss,' a flight attendant said sternly, 'would you *please* return to your seat.'

'Air Accidents Investigation Branch. I need to speak with the flight crew.'

'The pilots are perfectly capable—'

'Shut up!' Samantha cut her off, and propped herself between two seats as she withdrew her AAIB pass, and held it up for the officious woman to see. 'I'm the only person on this flight who is aware of the nature and extent of the damage. Do you really want all these people to die, just because—'

The airliner lurched suddenly to the right, almost pitching her to the floor.

'Just because *you* think you know better than an air accident investigator?'

'I… I can't—'

'Tick-tock. Time's running out.'

'I'll take you to the cockpit,' the woman said uncertainly, and pushed past Samantha, 'but I doubt the captain will agree—'

'He'll agree.'

The flight attendant was much more sure of her footing than Samantha, and arrived at the cockpit door several seconds before the investigator.

'I have a very insistent passenger who wishes to speak to you, Captain,' the flight attendant said over the intercom.

'Not now, damn it!' came the furious reply from the captain.

'You have severe structural damage between frame stations one thirty-five, and one forty-five. You've lost two hydraulic systems, and external damage is affecting our trim,' Samantha said.

There was silence for several seconds, the only sounds the ugly screeching of metal against metal behind her.

'Who the hell are you?' came the captain's voice again.

'Samantha Shore, Air Accidents Investigation Branch.'

The captain thought for a moment before relenting. 'Okay, let her in.'

A few seconds later she heard the latch drawn back and the door opened, the co-pilot nervously looking at her.

Take the jump-seat,' shouted the captain, as the co-pilot returned to his own seat.

Samantha took up her position in the vacant chair reserved for a third pilot, slipping the radio headset on and buckling herself in tightly. Even if they made it to an airport, the landing was likely to be pretty rough. She exchanged a look with the flight attendant, a look which could only be shared by two rival women, before settling down to concentrate on the job at hand.

'AAIB?' the captain said. 'You didn't waste much bloody time, did you? But would you at least allow us to go through the formality of crashing the damned plane before you start work?'

Samantha and the co-pilot both laughed nervously at the levity, her light, feminine tones easing the tension in the cockpit a fraction.

'Hopefully, that won't be necessary. What's our status?'

'Difficult to be sure. We've lost nearly all elevator and rudder control. Diagnostic systems to the tail have been knocked out. Ailerons, flaps, and leading edge slats seem to be working. As you said, we've lost all hydraulic quantity in systems two and three.'

'What about the centre fuel tank?' If that were to rupture and ignite, then it would be all over before they knew it had happened.

'Seems okay. Levels have held steady. How bad do you think the damage to the lower stringer is?'

'On Flight 4401 it was completely severed by the initial blast. We have to assume we've suffered similar damage. What's our airspeed?'

'Varying between two hundred, and two-forty knots.'

'I suggest you take it back to around one-twenty.'

'Negative. Dramar have advised us to make best possible speed to the airport.'

'Captain, the lower section of the fuselage has been severely weakened. These violent manoeuvres will tear the airframe in two. Reducing airspeed will reduce the stresses on the affected areas.'

The D500 reached the apex of the phugoid and began another downward plunge.

'Dramar's technical director reckons we need to put down as soon as possible, and I'm inclined to agree with him.'

'I've studied this aircraft, and in particular the lower main stringer. If you follow Greg Koenig's advice, we'll all die.'

The aircraft lurched to the right again, and all Samantha could see from the cockpit windows was the sea.

Forty-Seven

Alex put a hand over the rim of the top platform and hoisted himself over, immediately rolling to the far side. Again, the floor erupted as bullets blasted through it. They all missed him.

But not by much.

He soon realized, though, that his attacker was simply making sure that he was nowhere near the point where she would be emerging.

The gun was the first thing to appear over the side, swiftly followed by her head and upper body. Artemis vaulted onto the platform, her strength and stamina seeming inhuman to Alex. One half of her face was completely covered in blood, her coveralls saturated and darkened by the viscous liquid. She waved the gun triumphantly in front of her. He had nowhere else to go. She had him.

Alex rose slowly to his feet, clenching his fists tightly in frustration, and surveyed the platform again. However, this time the floor was empty. There was nothing here that could aid him.

The P226 centred on his chest, and he saw the muscles of her index finger tighten.

Alex let his body drop, and a fraction of a second later heard the shot. He didn't know how, but the projectile missed him, passing so close to his ear that he felt the air displaced. The unexpected action had bought him another second, and he used it to launch himself at her in a final desperate bid to survive.

But the distance between them was too great, and she had time to re-aim and fire.

Alex saw the flash from the barrel but heard nothing as the bullet entered his chest. For a moment he thought she had again missed, until a sudden weakness overtook him and he dropped to his hands and knees. As blood poured from the open wound onto the floor of the platform, he knew that it was over. Consciousness would soon desert him, but he lifted his head to give her one final, defiant look of contempt. He wasn't going to let a single bullet defeat him, and was determined to force her to see his eyes as she finished him off.

Through vision that was becoming more blurred by the second, he stared at her, challenging the monster to murder a defenceless man in cold blood. It was one thing to plant a bomb on a plane to kill three hundred faceless strangers, but quite another to look a man in the eye as the trigger was pulled. The look of mocking insolence he wore soon changed to one of bewilderment as he saw a flash of silver, and her head lurched forward.

Artemis dropped to her knees, her hands clasping her skull. A shriek of sudden, intense pain erupted from her lips.

Alex could feel his life ebbing away, and didn't have the strength to crawl to the edge of the platform. He lowered himself gingerly to the floor, and half rolled, half slid to the rim, floundering in his own blood as he did so.

At the base of the gantry he could see the indistinct image of a figure.

Beaumont stared in horror as the bloodied face appeared over the edge. He hadn't had time to climb the framework to help Alex, and had done the only thing he could think of: hurl the wrench he held at the insane woman attacking his friend and mentor.

But he was too late. Alex was dying.

Alex wanted to shout something to him – anything – but he could not summon the energy, and out of the corner of his eye saw that Artemis was once again on her feet, staggering uncertainly in his direction. Somewhere in the distance he heard a screeching sound, and a bright light filled his eyes.

Burnett executed a perfect power slide, the Ford careering sideways through the giant, gaping entrance of the hangar, the headlights on full beam illuminating the dimness within the structure. The tires screamed in protest as he corrected the skid and buried the throttle. The nimble car sped through the expanse of the hangar toward the aircraft at the far end.

Eagle already had the passenger door open, the Glock nestled in his free hand as he used the other to keep the door pushed back against the force of the wind.

Atop the gantry he saw two figures: one lying prostrate and completely vulnerable, the other standing over him with arm outstretched and gun in hand.

Eagle fired a single shot. At this distance and from an unstable moving vehicle there was little chance of hitting her, but the distraction might be enough to spare Alex's life for a few more seconds.

As Burnett swung the car around and brought it to a screeching stop, Eagle allowed the residual momentum to fling him from the vehicle. He rolled several times over the unyielding concrete, but was on his feet again even as he came to a stop, firing three more rounds at the platform. Three shots were returned, strafing the ground around him. Good. As long as the bitch was firing at him, she couldn't hurt Alex.

The downside of this strategy, he realized, was that he was now in the open and exposed.

Samantha felt a violent jolt as another skin section was torn away from the airframe. The pilots struggled to regain control, using the ailerons and asymmetrical power on the engines to get the aircraft level again.

'BOA 5552 heavy, Centre,' came the calm tones of New York Air Traffic Control. 'Communication coming through from Dramar Aerospace. Can you take it? Over.'

'Standby. Reduce three and four. Increase one and two. Hard over!'

The port wing gradually began to rise again, and the horizon came into view from the windows. They were still descending at a frightening rate, but were slowly regaining some control.

'Sorry about that, Centre. Put them through,' the captain replied.

'BOA 5552, this is Claude Brodeur, director of computational dynamics at Skysystems. Do you read me?'

'Claude!' Samantha exclaimed, picturing in her mind the tall black man with his unruly dreadlocks. 'It's Samantha Shore. Remember me?'

'Samantha? Don't tell me you're on that plane?'

'Afraid so. Have you got any good news for us?'

'Maybe. I've been doing some calculations, based on wind velocity, probable damage, stress tolerances of affected—'

'Today, if you please, Mr. Brodeur,' the captain said, inching the nose back to a level position.

'Sorry. The airframe, and in particular the lower main stringer and skin sections aft of frame station one-thirty, have been severely damaged. If too much stress is applied to these sections, that plane will tear itself apart from within. You've got to reduce your airspeed. Are you in a phugoid pattern?'

'Yes, with a heavy pull to the left.'

'Then I'd say you've got some serious external damage. The rudder could also be offset to port. I'll bet you're pulling some pretty wild manoeuvres up there.'

'You could say that.'

'Then let the phugoid take you. Control it, Captain; don't fight it. Keep your airspeed down, but at least ten knots above normal stall speed.'

The captain sighed. '5552 heavy. Your technical director disagrees with that appraisal. He believes we should make best speed back to JFK, and put down as soon as possible.'

'Koenig's an idiot and a crook. Believe me, if you keep tossing that plane around, it'll snap like a dry stick. Samantha, what do you think?'

'I agree. I've been saying that since the explosion happened. Well, Captain?'

The left hand seat was always a heavy burden to carry, but under these circumstances the weight of responsibility was almost intolerable. His hand rested on the throttle levers as he thought through the options. Whom should he believe? Air Traffic Control were not in a position to advise them. British Occidental's technical division back at Heathrow had not been able to offer any useful advice, and were obviously not sufficiently experienced in this kind of emergency. This meant that it came down to Samantha and Brodeur, or Koenig.

The captain's fingers tightened around the throttle levers and dragged them back.

'Reducing airspeed,' he said, and glanced over to the co-pilot. 'But we'll keep at least *fifteen* knots above stall speed – just in case.'

'Acknowledged.'

The nose of the crippled airliner dipped momentarily, before rising again rapidly. A stall warning blasted through the cockpit, and the control columns began to shake wildly as the aircraft pitched upwards in an uncontrolled climb.

Forty-Eight

E agle loosed another volley in Artemis' direction as he made for cover in the shadow of the fuselage. The concrete floor ahead of him exploded in dust as more bullets hit the ground. He could not reach the protection of the underbelly. The FBI agent had no choice but to stand his ground and fight. He fired the Glock twice more in her direction before hearing the sickening click of an empty cartridge.

Artemis also heard it and rose to fire the decisive shot.

Burnett didn't have time to take aim as he leapt from the cover of the car, shooting indiscriminately in the direction of the platform. He succeeded in drawing fire away from Eagle as he fumbled with a fresh clip – but her reactions were faster than his.

With the instinct of a true predator, Artemis shifted her aim and fired a single shot at the new threat, the projectile hitting him in the arm and sending him reeling back.

The gun fell to the floor, three feet from his outstretched hand.

Burnett scrambled forward, desperately trying to reach the weapon, expecting more shots to tear into his body as he did so.

'Hey,' Alex said with all the strength he could muster. 'You haven't forgotten about me, have you?'

Artemis whirled around.

The fresh clip locked into place and Eagle fired three shots in quick succession. One hit the gantry's framework and ricocheted off harmlessly. The second penetrated the platform. The third found its target.

Artemis felt her thigh explode in pain, the bullet ripping through flesh and bone, eventually lodging in the joint between the femur and the pelvis. She screamed with a mixture of pain and anguish, clutching the wound as she fell to the floor.

It was over. She had a single round left. Even if she had a spare clip and was able to kill the two agents, she was now incapacitated. More agents would undoubtedly arrive soon to aid these two. There could be no escape. She had no hope of rescue, and capture was unacceptable.

Artemis half crawled, half dragged herself to the far edge of the platform, near to where Alex lay. Blood dripped from around her fingers and onto the floor, leaving a scarlet trail behind her. The bullet had ruptured a major artery. She made a final, desperate attempt to stand, but the agony was too excruciating to bear, and she almost lost consciousness from the effort. She had no other option now.

Artemis looked to Alex, who drunkenly returned her gaze. He was to be the last person she would ever see, and a part of her wanted to reach out to him; embrace him; and beg for absolution.

They stayed like that for over a minute. For the first time ever, she cherished life. Now that it was about to end, she wanted to live; to breathe; to smell a rose; to hear a melody; to feel the soft caress of a lover. More than anything, she wanted to live. Life, she realized, was something precious and should be treasured, not squandered. She knew that now, at the end.

'Goodbye, Mr. Jamieson, and I am sorry.'

She lifted the gun and placed the barrel in her mouth. The metal was warm and tasted bitter after the rounds that had been expelled.

'Wait,' Alex whispered.

She took one last, lingering look at him, before gently squeezing the trigger.

Eagle saw the flash as he emerged over the side of the platform, saw the back of her head explode in a cloud of blood and bone and cranial tissue, and watched with satisfaction as the body was jolted backwards, toppling over the edge. Seconds later he heard the thud as the corpse hit the ground, sixty feet below.

The bitch was dead. Good. That'd save the American taxpayer the cost of a trial. Burnett was injured, but would live.

Then he looked at Alex, lying in an increasing pool of his own blood and that of his deceased attacker. Was it too late?

He knelt beside the British investigator and cradled his head in his arms. Eagle heard sirens in the distance, and, for the first time in years, prayed. He prayed that they would not be too late. He and Burnett, as FBI special agents, accepted the risks that came with the job. They had both lost colleagues and friends who had died in the line of duty. Those people had also been aware that they may one day be called upon to make the ultimate sacrifice.

This man was an innocent. He had not elected to live a dangerous life. He was just a man doing his job: making the world a safer place for others. He didn't deserve to die like this. Eagle wanted to exchange places, to make the trade with God.

He continued to pray as he held Alex's unconscious head with one hand, while trying to staunch the flow of blood with the other.

The nose continued to rise until the aircraft was at a forty-five degree angle. The captain slammed the throttle levers forward, but Samantha could see the airspeed indicator dropping rapidly: one hundred and eighty knots; one-sixty; one-forty. She glanced at the altimeter. It read three thousand feet. If they went into a stall at this height, there would be no chance of regaining control before the aircraft hit the water.

At one hundred knots, and as a last ditch effort, the co-pilot extended the flaps and leading edge slats to increase the wing profile and generate a little more lift.

They seemed to hang in the air, stationary against the backdrop of the churning autumn sky. The airspeed was down to ninety-three knots, then ninety, then eighty-eight.

All three stared transfixed at the indicator, waiting for the airspeed to continue to bleed away.

But it remained steady for several seconds. Had they done it? No one dared breathe for long moments, expecting the plane to fall from the sky and hit the water in a violent death.

And then the dial moved up one notch. Then another. Then two more. At one hundred knots Samantha saw the clouds begin to creep upwards. The aircraft was righting itself, and eventually returned to the phugoid sequence of climbs and falls. At one hundred and fifty knots the flaps and slats were retracted.

'Well,' the captain said at last, 'I think that could have gone a little better.'

'BOA 5552 heavy, Centre. You guys okay?'

'Still here, Centre. We're going to try that again.'

'Acknowledged, 5552. Good luck.'

'Okay, this time I'll reduce power a little more gradually. When the nose starts to come up, give us ten degrees slats. If it continues, increase angle accordingly and drop the flaps.'

'Roger.'

'Is there anything I can do?' Samantha asked.

'Yes. Keep singing out airspeed and altitude, and keep your fingers crossed.' He keyed the cockpit to cabin intercom, and apologized to the terrified passengers for the "bumpy ride", then began the exercise again.

'Airspeed two-ten. Altitude thirty-four hundred feet.' Samantha didn't know how useful her commentary would be, but at least it kept her mind busy. She couldn't allow herself to dwell on what might go wrong.

The captain gently eased back on the throttles, a fraction of an inch at a time, while the co-pilot manipulated the ailerons on the wings to counteract the yaw to the left.

'Airspeed one-ninety. Altitude thirty-five hundred.'

The artificial horizon indicator moved, mimicking the sky outside, and the first officer extended the slats by ten degrees. The nose settled back to a level position and stayed there for a few seconds, before rising again.

'Airspeed one-sixty. Altitude back to thirty-four hundred.'

'Give me another five degrees of slats,' the captain ordered, and the co-pilot responded immediately.

They continued this juggling act for the next three minutes until they had successfully reached a stable one hundred and twenty knots.

'Airspeed one hundred and twenty-two knots. Altitude three thousand feet.'

'Okay,' the captain said, unable to conceal the relief in his voice. 'Let's try something else. Give us five degrees of flaps, and we'll see what happens.'

The nose of the D500 dropped again slightly.

'Airspeed one-twenty. Altitude twenty-nine hundred. We're descending.'

'Good,' the captain said. 'We have partial control. Have we got JFK's VOR beacon?'

'Confirmed. Frequency 115.9.'

'BOA 5552 heavy, Centre. You are twenty-eight miles out on heading 304 magnetic. Looking good. Recommend landing on runway 13R.'

'5552. Acknowledged, Centre. What length is 13R?'

'Ten thousand feet, but all runways are clear should you need to change.'

'Thank you, Centre. I think we're going to have to put down wherever this plane wants to go.' He knew that their chances of making the airport and landing in one piece were slim, but kept his concerns to himself. His colleagues were nervous enough as it was.

Skin sections continued to be shredded from the airframe as the aircraft was buffeted like a child's toy. The port side of the fuselage had sustained the greatest degree of damage, and the thin aluminium sheets were slowly peeled back like the skin of a banana. As the huge sheets fluttered in the slipstream like the unruly sails of a ship, an enormous amount of drag was created. But when the stresses became too great, the sections would be torn away, causing the aircraft to lurch to the right, and on several occasions the D500 almost spun out of control.

The delicate internal components, not designed to withstand the assault of the slipstream, were twisted and bent. As debris was ripped away, some of it struck these components, including the diagnostic systems to the port wing undercarriage, and the landing gear's locking mechanism.

The port wheel assembly swung down, and hung limply below the aircraft, swinging from left to right in concert with the erratic motion of the plane.

With the diagnostic system in this area disabled, there would be no indication of this new problem on the flight deck.

Forty-Nine

The east coast of the United States was now clearly visible, and Samantha could even make out a few details of the local topography. One way or the other, they would be down within the next five minutes.

'Begin automatic fuel dump,' the captain instructed the co-pilot, who flicked off the safety switch to initiate the process. Thousands of pounds of aviation fuel poured from the wing outlets and into the Atlantic, creating a long, narrow slick which charted the D500's course.

At thirty-five thousand pounds the fuel vents were automatically shut off, which would leave an uncomfortable amount of Jet A on board when they hit, but this was unavoidable. There was no override to the system.

'Pull to the left is worse than ever,' the co-pilot said with exasperation. 'I can barely hold us in a straight line now.'

The Atlantic was just a thousand feet below them, and getting closer all the time. The flight management computer continually buzzed to alert the flight crew of the unusual approach, and occasionally tried to take over control of the aircraft, but each time was given an electronic rebuke as the flight crew reassumed control.

'We're veering left,' the captain said. 'Can't you keep us on course?' There was no antagonism in his voice, just frantic desperation.

'It's no good. Ailerons will only give us a certain amount of control. We'll have to increase power to the port engines.'

'Four miles to threshold,' air traffic control informed them.

'Airspeed one-ten,' Samantha said. 'Altitude now eight hundred feet.'

The captain knew that things were getting worse, but he now had to guess at the next move. 'Increasing power to one and two. Drop flaps by five degrees.'

'Three miles to threshold.'

'Airspeed one twenty-five. Altitude…' She looked at the indicator with dismay. 'Altitude eleven hundred feet. We're climbing!'

'Lowering landing gear.' The captain had no choice but to continue the approach. They could never manoeuvre for a second attempt.

'My board doesn't show anything,' the co-pilot said. 'Is it down?'

'We'll soon find out.'

'Now veering to the right! Jesus, this thing's a bitch to fly.'

'Two miles to threshold.'

The co-pilot twisted the control column away from the extreme left, and the aircraft pivoted on an invisible axis, the wings see-sawing through the sky.

'Airspeed one-forty. Altitude twelve hundred feet.' Samantha could see they were losing control.

'Cutting power to all four.' The captain wrenched the levers back, and shouted over the public address system. 'BRACE! BRACE! BRACE!'

'One mile to threshold.'

The D500 suddenly went quiet as the engines were throttled back. It hung in the air, the nose pitching up as it approached the stall. The Ground Proximity Warning Detector and the Stall Warning burst into life, vying for the pilots' attentions.

Whoop! Whoop! Pull up! Whoop! Whoop! Pull up! Stall! Stall! Stall!

'Firewall 'em!' the captain shouted.

All four engines roared into life once again, but this time it was too late. The time factor just wasn't there for them. The nose dipped and the port wing dropped, despite the frantic efforts of the flight crew to level the aircraft. The plane barely cleared the landing lights and dropped heavily onto the concrete section of the runway, the force of the impact tearing the rear third of the fuselage away from the rest of the D500. The port wing landing gear, which had not been locked into place, collapsed on impact, and the wing tip dropped onto the ground in a shower of sparks. Fragments of flaming metal and composites flew off in all directions as the edge of the wing was ripped apart. The number one engine hit the ground, the impact crushing the nacelle and abruptly halting the spin of the turbines, sending fan blades off in all directions.

'Cutting three and four.' The pilot had no idea that the number one engine had been destroyed, or that his aircraft was now in two pieces.

Samantha clasped her arms around her head and leant forward. All she could hear were the screams and screeches of metal being torn apart and scraping along the ground. She felt herself being spun around. This had to be the end, she thought, and tasted her own tears as she wept, not for herself, but for the crew, for the passengers, and for her parents. They would always wonder if it had been a swift and painless death for her. The loss would hit her father the most, and she wished, in these final moments, that she could tell him that it was all right.

The aircraft continued its uncontrolled charge down the runway, the tail still held on by wiring and cables, thrashing from left to right like the tail of a crazed shark. What remained of the number one engine burst into flames, and was soon sent careering off to the left of the centreline to hit one of the emergency vehicles which were standing by to render assistance. The fire tender exploded upon impact, incinerating the crew, and giving the other appliances a new problem to worry about as the crumpled airliner continued past.

The number four engine also disengaged from the aircraft, rolling and bouncing harmlessly off to the right and embedding itself in the turf adjoining the runway.

The Tin Kicker

The D500 spun through three hundred and sixty degrees four times before it eventually came to rest, flames issuing from the starboard wing where the number four engine had come away, and from the broken stump of the port wing. The airport fire trucks were soon on hand and firing high pressure foam at the source of the inferno as they endeavoured to bring the blaze under control. Flames and black, acrid smoke licked around the fuselage. Terrified passengers scrambled for the exits, but had nowhere to go. The blaze eventually subsided as more and more cannons spewing tons of foam were trained upon it, and a safe escape route emerged at the broken rear of the fuselage. Within two minutes the fires were all but extinguished, and rescue crews were able to move in and help people away from the wreck.

Samantha opened her eyes. Everything was quiet. Deathly quiet. Red warning lights flashed angrily within the cockpit, and a haze of smoke made the images indistinct. It was even snowing outside the shattered windscreen, until she realized that it was foam, and not snow, that was rapidly filling the cockpit. That meant that they must be on fire, and had to evacuate quickly. The two pilots stared straight ahead. Were they alive?

'Did we make it?' she asked.

'We're down,' the captain replied quietly, turning to look at her for the first time. The expression on his face betrayed his thoughts. He obviously hadn't realized how young she was. He shook his head with bemusement, and reached for the cockpit to cabin intercom. 'Evacuate the aircraft. Evacuate.'

She was alive, Samantha thought. She had made it.

Several others hadn't, she would later discover, but the majority of passengers were able to walk away from the crash without serious injury.

The D500 *was* an unsafe aircraft, and she could and would testify to that, having had first-hand experience of the aircraft's fatal flaws. No board of inquiry in the world could ignore the AAIB now. With one of their own investigators on board, the Branch now had an advantage over the CAA. Coupled with this was the information supplied by the FBI, which she still found herself clutching. There would be no more cover-ups, no more bureaucratic attempts to block the withdrawal of the D500 from service.

No more deaths.

Not as long as she had a breath in her lungs, would another one of these death traps fly.

Samantha stumbled over to the emergency hatch and fumbled with the locking mechanism. The pilots joined her and helped to get the buckled and twisted door open. With the three of them pushing and kicking, it finally creaked open, and daylight streamed into the rear of the cockpit. The escape chute had already been deployed, and she was the first to slide down, dazed by the experience but still in control.

She looked at the remains of the D500. It was a mess. The tail section had finally come away from the rest of the fuselage altogether, and rested fifty yards behind the main body. Most of the port wing was missing, and what was left had been blackened by fire. Flame retardant foam clung to everything, and looked a sickly yellow compared to the snow that was now beginning to coat the runway. Samantha shivered, and realized that she was just wearing slacks and a thin blouse. Even her shoes had disappeared, but she was not about to go back and look for them. It wouldn't occur to her until over an hour later that the shaking was a direct effect of shock setting in.

Amazingly, people were walking from the jagged mouth of the tail where the tear had occurred, virtually unscathed – at least physically.

An ambulance crew had reached her, and led the intrepid young investigator away. Just before the ambulance door was closed, her eyes met those of the captain of Flight 5552. The expression of camaraderie he wore was priceless, and she returned it with a simple smile and nod. No words would ever be necessary between these two. They had faced death together, and saved over three hundred lives in the process.

She had faced death – and had survived, she thought as a blanket was wrapped around her.

Fifty

All he was aware of was the sound: a rhythmic beep somewhere off in the distance. He recognized it from some time long ago, when his brother had had the motorcycle accident. It was the sound of an electrocardiogram, discreetly monitoring a heartbeat. Whose? His own, he realized, and faint memories came back to him. The pursuit. The gun. The shot. He'd been shot. He replayed the events in his mind, and recalled the sight of his own blood splashing onto the floor. Images that followed were vague and ghost-like.

Alex opened his eyes slowly, and blinked against the harshness of the light. Everything was blurred into a mass of colours, but he thought he could make out figures around him.

'He's awake,' he heard a male voice say in a whisper. American.

He blinked repeatedly to try to clear his vision, and the two figures eventually became more defined.

'Alex,' Scott Eagle said, 'can you hear me?'

'Yes,' he replied weakly, and cleared his throat to speak more strongly. 'What are you doing here? Come to think of it: where *is* here?'

'Bellevue Hospital in New York. You were shot, but the doctors say you're out of danger now.'

He stayed silent for several moments as all the images came flooding back. The woman had shot him. Artemis. And then she had... He tried to block out the image of her head rupturing as the bullet passed through it. Why had she been there?

Then he remembered, his whole body going stiff.

'The BOA flight. Did it—'

'It landed at JFK,' Leon Baptiste said. 'Eighteen people were killed, but three hundred and thirty survived.'

'Was Samantha—'

'She's fine. She took a flight back to England yesterday.'

Alex relaxed. 'How long have I been here?'

'Two days. Shit has totally hit the fan. Half of Dramar's directors are in custody still. One of them tried to escape to the Caribbean and earned herself a bullet in the head for her trouble.'

Again, he saw the image of Mosa Ahmed, the back of her head exploding in a shower of blood and bone. The most shocking image was of her body collapsing, like a marionette that's strings have just been cut. It had dropped immediately, a lifeless sack of bone and flesh, toppling over the edge. And the sickening thud as it hit the ground sixty feet below.

'It's a real mess, Alex,' Eagle continued. 'But all D500s have been grounded. It seems some details of the investigation were leaked to a TV network. I guess Lewis Kramer got his exclusive.'

Alex wished he had the energy to smile, but could feel the heavy weight dragging at his eyelids. He needed to sleep, just for a little longer.

'We'll leave you to rest,' Baptiste said, gesturing to Eagle that it was time to go.

Alex limply lifted a hand to wave goodbye. Sleep was what he needed. Sleep.

Just for a little longer.

Fifty-One

Khalid moved slowly through the backstreets of Gaza City, relieved to be back in the company of his own people, but ill at ease as Israeli Defence Force soldiers swaggered blatantly through the city.

The Palestinians were licking their wounds and capitulating with little argument. The Quamaris had been enraged by the terrorist attack on one of their own passenger aircraft, threatening to withdraw all support from their cousins in the occupied territories. The death of Mosa Ahmed had done little to appease the people, despite the frantic efforts of the diplomats, and public denials of any responsibility. She had, they said, acted alone and without the sanction of the UNC, but it would be a long time before the Quamaris trusted them again. This had to be a time of consolidation, and despite a few sporadic acts of violence, the country languished in an uneasy ceasefire.

He walked for hours, wearing the loose robes of a native, but missing the expensive suits that had so impressed the young women of Washington.

The Tin Kicker

Khalid finally arrived at the nondescript door, and checked the street before entering. He climbed the stairs to the second floor and found himself in the darkened room that had been so familiar all those years before. The air stank of humanity; a putrid reek of excrement and sweat, rotting flesh and liniment. The shutters on the windows were closed, but sunlight streamed in through the cracks. At the far end of the austere quarters he saw a figure rise unsteadily to his feet.

'Hello old friend,' Samir said with an effort as he struggled across the room, leaning heavily on an improvised walking stick. His face seemed as withered as his frail body, but even in the gloom Khalid could see the eyes were as bright as ever.

'We failed.'

'We did,' Samir admitted. 'But the war is far from over. Mosa was our guiding light for many years, and her teachings will live on.'

'Her death must be avenged. Those responsible—'

'Will pay. But not yet. Her plan was flawed. We must work on a new plan. A free homeland is our goal, and we must not allow ourselves to be distracted by our desire for revenge. But rest assured, my friend, her murderers will pay, and pay heavily.'

Samir was right, of course, but Khalid would not rest until he had achieved *his* goal. Mosa had been his friend, his mentor, and on occasion, his lover.

Those responsible *would* pay.

Epilogue

A wry smile crossed Alex's lips as he read the report. Two days after the dramatic events at JFK, the US President had gone on television condemning the actions of Dramar Aerospace, and promised that legislation would be put in place to prevent such a thing from happening again. All US manufacturers would be placed under closer scrutiny in future, and subject to Federal Aviation Administration inspections without warning.

But the key to the problem, as everyone in the industry was aware of, was self-regulation. Until the FAA were granted the resources to police aircraft manufacture, there was no reason why such a situation could not be repeated. There was also the issue of impartiality. As long as the regulatory body was financed directly by the industry, there was a conflict of interest. This was something else that had not been addressed by the President's speech.

Alex was beginning to wonder what it had all been for. Four hundred and forty-two people had died in three crashes before the CAA had acted.

Initially, all D500s had been grounded, but it had soon been ascertained that the third generation craft were perfectly safe. Alex had to admit that the revision to the main stringers was quite an innovative design. At the centre of the upper and lower main stringers was a titanium girder, surrounded by the J13-25 organic matrix compound.

This was the final diamond in the dust, and everything they had seen had finally made sense.

Tests carried out by DERA had shown the revised stringers to be five times stronger than the systems they had replaced, with only a marginal increase in weight. The remaining aircraft were still grounded, as they underwent major refits.

Dramar Aerospace had received no new orders for D500s, and were being bombarded by legal actions from all sides. It would be interesting to see if the company's new chief executive, Thomas Purcell, could pull off a Houdini act and save the manufacturer. With one hundred and forty thousand jobs on the line, there was little doubt that he would receive all the support he would require from the White House, but it still wasn't going to be easy.

The desk phone rang. 'Jamieson.'

'Alex,' came Stuart Davenport's voice, 'there are a bunch of us heading over to the Southwood Arms for a drink. You want to come? Sam says that if we get her drunk enough she'll sing *Blue Skies* at the karaoke.'

He looked again at the report from Washington, the 4401 file that lay open on his desk, and the mass of papers weighing down his in-tray. 'I guess I'm done here, and I'm not going to pass up on that. I'll meet you there.'

'Bring your wallet, chief. This could be expensive.'

The line went dead.

He stood, picking up his briefcase and raincoat, and walked to the door. As an afterthought he returned to the desk and closed the 4401 file.

That could wait until Monday.

The Tin Kicker

The Tin Kicker

Printed in Great Britain
by Amazon

12016238R00226